CHAPTER 1

Look up. Go on, do it now. Stretch back your neck and stare up, as far as you can. And then a little bit more. That's where you're going to have to look if you want to find Tally Olivia Adams. Up where the sky begins. Up where the only rule is gravity. Up where the world seems small and not so important. Up where the possibilities are endless.

It is a final-days-of-summer kind of afternoon. Fluffy white clouds are scudding across the pale blue sky and the air has a hint of something fresh, something new. A normal day on a normal street in the back garden of a normal house belonging to a completely normal family. Read that last sentence again, out loud to yourself. It's funny how if you say it enough times, the word normal sounds anything but.

So, a normal day. But the girl standing on the roof of the garden shed is not normal in the slightest. She is a warrior, fierce and brave, surveying the land before her. She's a mountain climber, pausing for breath after scaling the heady heights of Everest. She is a trapeze artist, about to step out on to the wire and dazzle the crowds beneath her.

Her right foot rises in the air, shaking slightly as she contemplates the drop. One wrong move and it will all be over.

"Hey! Get down!"

The shout makes Tally wobble and for a split second it seems as if she will tumble to earth. But then her foot makes contact with the roof and she lowers herself to the ridge, sitting with her legs dangling out in front of her.

"You nearly made me fall." Tally glares at Nell accusingly. "Are you trying to kill me?"

Nell puts her hands on her hips. "You seem to be doing a good enough job of that by yourself. What are you doing? You know Mum and Dad said that you aren't allowed to go up there any more. Not after last time."

Tally shrugs. "It's my place. I'm practising the things I learnt in circus school last week. And I can't think anywhere else."

"It's the holidays." Nell taps her foot impatiently. "There isn't anything *to* think about, so just get down."

Tally wonders if her sister has always been this unimaginative or if it's something that happens when you start high school. If that's the case then she's even less keen for this week to be over and September to begin.

"Is it true that people flush your head down the toilet when you're in year seven?" she asks Nell. "Because if it is then I won't be able to drink anything all day in case it makes me need to use the bathroom, which means that I will be seriously dehydrated and my brain won't work very effectively and I'm probably going to fail every single test. And it won't even be my fault because all I'll be trying to do is stay as far away from the school toilets as humanly possible."

Nell snorts. "Only the mouthy kids that don't know when to shut up."

A warm breeze flutters through the garden, picking up the leaves that have fallen on to the lawn. They weren't there last week and their russet-red shine against the long, green grass is a reminder that the summer can't last for ever. Her days at home are numbered.

"What happens if I get lost?" Tally's voice is quiet.

Nell pushes her hair out of her eyes and squints up at the roof.

"Then the two-headed monster that lives in the caretaker's cupboard will find you," she says, as menacingly as she possibly can. "And it will drag you in and keep you hostage amongst the brooms and mops and buckets. And you will have to stay at school for the rest of your life."

Tally doesn't even blink. She isn't afraid of made-up monsters. There are far scarier things roaming the school corridors than two-headed beasts, she's quite sure of that.

"Come on, Tally." Nell is impatient now. "Get down from there. I'm totally not in the mood for Mum and Dad giving me another lecture about how I should be keeping an eye on you. Like you're some kind of baby or something."

"I'm not a baby. And I didn't ask you to come out here." Tally glares down at Nell. "Just go away and pretend that you didn't see me."

"Well, you're lucky it was me that caught you and not them." Nell frowns, imagining the argument that would have followed if her parents had spotted their youngest daughter on top of the shed.

Tally shakes her head. She doesn't feel very lucky to have moaning, nagging, boring Nell ruining her thinking time.

"You'll be grounded for a week if they see you up there," warns Nell. "They won't even let you into the garden if they think they can't trust you."

Tally looks away from her big sister and across the garden fence towards the street. She knows that if she stands up, she can see between the houses and as far as the park. She can see further than Nell can. Up here she is weightless and free. The opposite of grounded.

"Where are they?" she asks Nell. "Mum and Dad."

Nell glances back towards the house, which is almost hidden by the old apple tree, sagging under the weight of all the unpicked fruit. The entire garden has turned into a jungle this summer.

"They're out by the front gate, talking to Mrs Jessop and her gross dog," she tells Tally. "I don't know how she can take it for walks when it looks like that. It's embarrassing."

"It's not Rupert's fault that he's got three legs." Tally is unimpressed with Nell's attitude. "Don't be so horrible. Think about how you'd feel if you had three legs. You wouldn't like it if people thought you looked gross, would you?"

Nell rolls her eyes. "Whatever. But I wouldn't go outside either. I wouldn't force other people to look at my freakiness. Now get down before they come out here and see you."

She waits for a response but Tally isn't listening. Instead, she is clambering to her feet and balancing on the roof, shading her eyes with one hand as she peers into the distance.

"I think there's a fair going up in the park. There's a load of people and caravans and I can see a big truck that looks like it has dodgem cars on the back."

"What?" Nell squints up at Tally. "That can't be right. The fair isn't coming for months yet. And will you please get down before you fall off and I get the blame?"

"I'm not going to fall off. And I *can* see the fair, actually."

"Are you sure?" Nell strains to stand on her tiptoes and look in the direction of the park, but she can't see a thing.

The fair is one of the few things that they both agree is a *good thing*. It doesn't matter that Nell is fourteen and Tally is only eleven – when the fair is in town they are both as excited as each other.

Tally plants her feet more firmly and leans forward, trying to identify the different lorries and vans. "I think I can see the Twirler. And there's something that could be part of the carousel – it looks like one of the horses, anyway!"

There's the sound of scrambling beneath her and suddenly Nell's head pops up from the top of the ladder.

"Where? Are you sure it's actually setting up in our park?" Her voice is eager with an added tinge of apprehension. This wouldn't be the first time that Tally has got things wrong.

"See for yourself." Tally waves her hand towards the distance. "If you don't believe me."

There's a moment of hesitation and then Nell climbs the last few rungs and crawls her way up the roof to where Tally is standing.

"I still can't see anything."

"I can see the haunted house!" Tally looks down at Nell, a huge beaming smile spreading across her face. "I really can!"

It's too much for Nell. She pulls herself to her feet and balances alongside Tally on the ridge of the shed, her hand reaching out and gripping Tally's so tightly that the blood throbs and hums in her fingers.

"You're right! It *is* the fair!"

"I told you." Tally doesn't mind her sister's lack of faith. She knew that she was right all along.

Together, they watch as the lorries are opened and machinery is pulled out and assembled. It's almost magic, the way that the ordinary, clunky bits of metal fit together to create something brilliant.

"I'm sorry that I was being stupid about you starting in year seven," murmurs Nell. "You don't need to worry, Tally. I'll be right there if you need me, and it's not that scary. Nobody is going to flush your head down the toilet, I promise. You'll be fine – school is way less frightening than the haunted house and you can handle that!"

Tally doesn't reply because this is a very ignorant thing for Nell to have said and, sometimes, ignorant comments are best ignored. You can't compare the haunted house to Kingswood Academy. It just doesn't work.

The haunted house is Tally and Nell's thing and they always go together. Tally loves the delicious thrill of the spooky music and weird sound effects and the way that, no matter how many times she's been on the ride, she always jumps in her seat when the sinister, rattling skeleton lurches out at them towards the end. But most of all, she loves the rules that are written down on the board at the entrance.

Do not get out of the carriage.

Keep your hands inside the carriage.

Do not eat or drink on the ride.

Tally doesn't usually like rules, especially if they've come from other people, but these rules are different. They feel helpful and they keep her safe. And anyway, the haunted house is just pretend.

But Kingswood Academy is real. And she knows that while there are plenty of rules, the ones that really matter aren't written down anywhere.

"We have to persuade Mum and Dad to let us go to the fair," says Nell, squeezing Tally's hand. "We have to. Which means that we can't let them find us up here."

And because Tally wants to go to the fair just as much as Nell does, she lets her sister pull her towards the ladder and back to solid ground.

Date: Friday 29th August.

Situation: the summer holidays.

How I feel: relaxed but a bit nervous – the summer can't last for ever, can it?

Anxiety rating: A nice, chilled-out 3 with a hint of 4 creeping in if I think about starting in year seven next week.

Dear Diary,

Tally here. Well, I'm actually Natalia but my friends call me Tally, and so do my family. Let me tell you about my family! I live with my mum, Jennifer, my dad, Kevin, and my annoying big sister, Nell. She thinks she's always right, and even when she is I pretend that she isn't.

Mum's given me this diary so that I can write down how I'm feeling. She says that it might help me to understand how I cope (or don't cope) in different situations, particularly when I get anxious or scared (which happens a lot, by the way).

One thing that you should probably know about me early on is that I'm autistic. I have autism.

Although autism can sometimes hold me up a little in life, my parents say it's a superpower, and I like to believe that. The rest of the world hasn't caught up with us yet, though, and some people seem to think that being autistic is like being a different species. Some people treat me like an alien when all I want is to be treated like any other eleven-year-old. I'll admit that what also sometimes makes people treat me differently is the fact that I wear a tiger mask a lot of the time. I just feel secure and safe in it. When I'm wearing my mask, I don't have to make eye contact (why are people SO obsessed with this anyway?), or pretend to smile at people. I can't catch germs in it and people tend to leave me alone when I'm wearing it. What's not to love? Though, Nell doesn't love it. She finds it excruciatingly embarrassing when I wear it in public. She even tried to hide it once. The mask is Nell's arch enemy. And I like that. *evil laugh*.

There are some things I think people should know about my autism. Let's call them autism pros and cons. I'm going to write them down in my diary as I think of them. (One day I'm going to share these with the world so they can see autism from another perspective.)

Tally's autism facts: Sensory stuff

Pro: I have better memory, sense of smell, eyesight,

sense of touch, hearing and sometimes taste than others might. (I told you that autism is a superpower!) I can hear a piece of music and play it instantly on my keyboard or ukulele, I can mimic voices (which I sometimes get into trouble for), and I can remember where and when we bought every one of my soft toys (and I have over a hundred of them). I usually remember to celebrate all of their birthdays, too, except that time I forgot Billy's (I was devastated).

Con: I can feel even the tiniest of things and it annoys the hell out of me. Seams in socks, a crumb in my shoe, labels in clothes. If we go on holiday and the mattress isn't exactly like my one at home, I can't sleep for feeling the lumps. Mum says I'm just like the Princess in the Princess and the Pea story. Having excellent hearing isn't always so great. It makes it impossible to block out other people's conversations even when I'm all the way upstairs in my bedroom. And when that conversation is Mum and Dad having an argument about me then it's even worse (yet also intriguing I have to admit). But when I let on that I've heard, I get accused of eavesdropping, which is disgraceful really, considering I can't help it.

CHAPTER 2

"It hurts." The words squeeze themselves out through Tally's gritted teeth. "I want to take it off now."

"If you help me, we can get this done really quickly." Mum looks up from her position on the floor. "Then we can treat ourselves to a piece of chocolate as a reward. What do you think?"

Tally's arms stay resolutely folded across her chest. She's not stupid and she knows as well as Mum does that there is nothing quick about this process. The rest of her new school uniform is draped across the end of her bed – they still have to try on her skirt and jumper and the shoes that Mum ended up buying without her because, as Tally overheard her saying to Dad, she didn't have the energy to deal with a shoe shop meltdown as well as everything else.

Not that it would have made any difference if Tally *had* been with her to try on the shoes. They'll still hurt, no matter what. The only shoes that don't make her feet feel trapped and painful are her comfortable old trainers and, according to Nell, Kingswood Academy doesn't include filthy, disgusting trainers in their uniform policy. It was totally Nell's own fault that one of those so-called disgusting trainers ended up bouncing off her head, and Tally still thinks that having her iPad taken away for the evening was an unfair and disproportionate punishment.

"I wonder if you can just move your arms a little bit?"

"I can't. They're stuck."

Mum laughs gently. "Well, fortunately for you, I happen to have some magic unsticking potion right here." She dabs a finger on to Tally's arm. "There! You should be free to move now!"

"Nope." Tally shakes her head. "There's no such thing as anti-sticking potion and my arms are still stuck. There's nothing I can do about it."

"You're doing so well," soothes Mum, but Tally can hear the strain in her voice. "A couple more minutes and we'll be done. I just need to do up the buttons and check that it fits."

Tally can feel the stiff fabric against her skin and resists the urge to roar at Mum. It's scratchy and it's making her feel too hot. She cannot imagine, for even one second, how anyone can expect her to wear something so inflexible and rigid, nor why she would ever need to. She's starting year seven, not going into battle.

Unless there's something that they aren't telling her, which wouldn't be surprising because Tally suspects that there's quite a lot of things that her mum and dad talk about when she isn't around to hear them. Like what they're going to do about her. She feels like she is the Perpetual Problem of Tally.

Outside the bedroom window, the sky is growing dark. Unlike the first day of summer, the last day of the holidays is not crammed with potential. It does not taste of ice creams or smell of cut grass and sunshine. If the first day of summer is all about hope then the last day is filled with gloom. And it knows it. The rain lashes down against the glass and, if she peers hard enough through the eyeholes of the mask that she is wearing, she can see her own reflection gazing back at her, the raindrops on the outside of the window mimicking the tears that are trickling silently down her cheeks.

She sniffs and lifts up her hands to pull the tiger

mask down a bit further. She doesn't want to cry, but it's not like she's chosen the tears.

But moving her arms was a mistake. Mum whips into action, pulling the shirt tight and working the buttons into their holes. The fabric tightens around Tally's neck and for one horrific moment she thinks that she's forgotten how to drag air into her lungs. The chair clatters backwards as she yanks away from Mum's hands.

"Tally!" Mum stands up, her face scrunched and red. "Your shirt!" She unfurls her fingers and there, in her palm, is a pile of buttons. The rest of the shirt lies in a crumpled heap on the floor, next to its equally crumpled owner.

"I told you that it hurt me." Tally's head is pushed between her knees and her voice is muffled. "I told you."

Mum takes a long breath and sinks down next to Tally. Close but not touching. "I know you did and I should have listened," she says quietly. "We're done with trying on uniform for today. It's over."

"I don't want to wear it tomorrow. It's horrible and it hurts me and I won't be able to walk or do lessons or eat any food or even breathe if I'm wearing it." Tally hunches closer to her knees, feeling the cool rubber of the mask pressing against her face.

"I know." Sometimes, Mum hasn't got a solution. Tally understands that. Sometimes, the only thing that Mum can do is to know.

"I can fix the buttons," Mum says now, quietly.

"I don't care about the stupid buttons."

"It'll be easier in the morning."

It won't but sometimes, when Tally is particularly tired, it's simpler to pretend.

"I'm sorry for being such a problem," she whispers, the words so quiet that they barely escape through the mouth of the mask. But Mum hears anyway.

"Oh, Tally," she says. "I'm so sorry I made you feel that way. You are my glorious, fierce, fabulous girl and I love you to the ends of the earth."

Tally looks up at Mum, her eyes shining inside the mask. "Wouldn't you change me if you could?"

Mum smiles and gently shakes her head. "I wouldn't dream of changing a single thing about you. You are absolutely perfect exactly the way you are."

Tally pauses, scrutinizing Mum's face. Checking to make sure that there's not even a flicker of doubt, because sometimes Tally thinks that if she was her mum, she might want to swap her for a different daughter.

"Do you promise?"

"I promise." Mum smiles. "Would you like a hug now?"

Tally nods. Mum shuffles closer and stretches her arm around Tally's shoulders and they sit quietly for a while until the sound of the front door slamming disturbs the peace.

"That'll be Nell," says Mum, pushing herself off the floor and putting the buttons down on the bed. "Shall we go down to the kitchen and get a snack? Maybe some chocolate as it's the last day of the holidays?"

Starting tomorrow, there'll be no more going to the park with Mum or watching films with Nell in the middle of the week. Chocolate might just make that feel a tiny bit better.

But instead, she shakes her head from side to side and growls softly.

"Tigers don't eat chocolate. They are carnivores and so they mostly eat meat. And they hunt their prey, but you can't hunt a bar of chocolate, can you?" There's a pause and it is obvious that inside the mask, there is some serious thinking going on. "Unless, maybe you attached some string to the chocolate and dragged it around the garden and then I could stalk after it and pounce, when the chocolate is least expecting it."

Mum makes a snorting sound that sounds suspiciously like a snigger but that ends up as a cough.

"It sounds like tigers aren't big fans of chocolate. How about a chunk of antelope? I'm fairly sure that tigers like those."

Tally stands up and pulls off the mask.

"I think that actually," she says, stepping over the discarded school shirt, "actually, some chocolate will be absolutely fine."

CHAPTER 3

There are people everywhere. Screeching like a pack of
hyenas. Shouting over each other. Laughing like this is
all just one big joke.

Perhaps it is a joke? But if it is, then Tally cannot
work out the punchline, because there's absolutely
nothing funny about the noise that is flooding across
the concrete yard. It flings itself at her in relentless
waves, pounding against her ears until all she wants to
do is run. She doesn't care where – just anywhere that's
away. Her heart is pounding in her chest and her legs
are fizzing like they always do when she's terrified and
getting ready to run.

School shouldn't be frightening, but Tally knows that
there is absolutely nowhere scarier.

"You have to go into the main hall." Nell's voice

emerges through the thunder. "All the new year sevens have an assembly first thing. Do you know where to go?"

Tally drags her attention back to her sister. Nell is shifting her weight from foot to foot and peering back towards the gate, where loads of kids are pouring into the yard. Tally wonders if Nell's new school shoes are hurting as much as hers are.

"I know where the hall is and I know where my tutor group is because I came on those extra visit days in the summer with Mum," she starts and Nell smiles approvingly. "But there weren't so many people here then."

Nell's smile turns into a frown.

"Is there anyone here you know? I'm going to miss meeting up with Rosa if I don't hurry up."

"Mum told you to take me safely to school." Tally stares at her big sister, her eyes wide with panic. "She said that you had to look after me today and you promised that you would."

Nell sighs. "And I have done. I've let you walk all the way here with me."

"But I'm not safely in school yet, am I?" points out Tally. She tightens the strap on her rucksack and tries to breathe deeply, the way she's supposed to when she can feel everything getting too frightening. "I'm outside. Where anything could happen to me."

But Nell isn't listening. She grabs Tally's hand and points across the yard towards a group of girls that have just arrived.

"Look! There's Layla and Ayesha and that other kid who you used to play with. What's her name again?"

Tally looks. "That's Lucy."

Nell grins. "There you go, then! You've got three friends to go into the hall with. You'll be perfectly safe with them." She gives Tally a little push. "I'll see you later, OK?"

Not that it's a proper question because before Tally can tell Nell that actually, no, it is not in the slightest bit OK, Nell has dashed across the yard and disappeared from sight.

Tally's hands start to flap and she clamps them down by her side before anyone can notice. She does this a lot when she's feeling really stressed or really excited, but she can't do it here. Not in front of all these kids.

Tally looks again at her friends. Nell is right. Layla is her best friend and she's been desperate to see her. She just has to be brave and walk across the yard. Slowly, she moves forward, cringing inside as the noise increases in both volume and pitch.

"Hi." Her voice is so quiet that nobody even hears her. She clears her throat and tries again. "Hi, everyone."

"Tally!" Layla spins round, a huge beam spreading across her face. "I'm so glad you're here! This place is huge!"

"Did you have a good summer?" asks Ayesha. "Did you go on holiday?"

Tally nods, feeling her heart rate start to slow down. Everything is going to be fine. She can do this. She's good at it. She knows how to be around other people – she's been watching and learning since she was really small.

"Of course." She shrugs her rucksack off her shoulders and places it on the floor beside her. "We went to the beach for a week and I made friends with all the stray cats that came into the garden of the place where we were staying. I fed them every day and they got really tame. And when we got home my mum booked me into circus school." She flings her arms wide and grins at her friends. "You are now looking at a certified circus performer! Isn't that wild?"

Lucy laughs and shakes her head. "*You're* wild," she tells Tally. "And you haven't changed a bit since we left primary school!"

Tally looks at her, feeling confused. "It was only six weeks ago. Nobody changes in six weeks."

Lucy tilts her head on one side and gives a little smile. "Some people do. If something really, really massive happens to them."

"What are you talking about?" Ayesha sounds puzzled and Tally is glad that it isn't her who has to ask. "What massive thing?"

Lucy takes a step forward, beckoning the girls to come closer. "If I tell you, you have to all promise to keep it a secret."

"We promise!" chorus Layla and Ayesha. Tally keeps quiet because she doesn't know what the secret is yet and it wouldn't be right to make a promise that she doesn't know that she can keep.

Lucy glances over her shoulder, to check that nobody is listening.

"All right then, as you're all so desperate to find out, I'll tell you. But you're not allowed to say a word to anybody, OK?" She pauses, her eyes sparkling with excitement, and then makes her big reveal. "Luke was messaging me all summer!"

Ayesha and Layla erupt into squeals and giggles as Lucy grins at them all.

"Luke! Are you serious?" shouts Layla, before looking around guiltily. "Sorry! But that's amazing!"

"OMG!" shrieks Ayesha, clapping her hand over her mouth. "He SO fancies you! He's probably going to ask you out, Lucy!"

Tally steps back, her shoulders slumping. This is *not* a massive thing. They're not even talking about anyone important. They're talking about Luke. The same Luke who once kicked a football at her head. The same Luke who used to call her nasty names whenever she walked into the classroom.

"Weirdo Alert," he'd say. Always loud enough for everyone to hear, except the teacher. She really hopes that he's grown out of that kind of behaviour, now that they're all starting year seven.

Layla grabs hold of Lucy's hand and starts jumping up and down. "What will you say to him? I wonder if he'll wait until you're on your own or if he'll do it in front of us? I'll DIE if he asks you in the canteen at lunchtime!"

"Me too!" trills Ayesha. They both twist their heads to look at Tally and she realizes that they're waiting for her to say something.

"Me too," she repeats.

This is awful. She was expecting to have to talk about lots of different things today, but horrible Luke was not one of them. Trying to pretend that she's excited about him sending messages to Lucy is not going to be easy.

"Don't you think so, Tally?" asks Layla, turning to grin at her. The conversation has moved on and she has no idea what they're talking about now. The noise in the yard has got louder and she can smell exhaust fumes from the road. It makes her feel a bit sick.

Tally smiles at her friends and nods enthusiastically.

"Totally!" she says.

It seems to be the correct answer because they all laugh and Layla nudges Tally in the arm with her elbow.

"This is going to be the best year ever!" Lucy beams at her friends. "I can feel it!"

The only thing that Tally can feel is the agony of her new shoes, squishing her toes together. The longer she wears them, the worse they are becoming, which is totally not what Mum said would happen. According to her, Tally would get used to her shoes and she wouldn't even notice them by the time she got to school.

Mum lied.

Tally sits down and pulls off one shoe, breathing out with relief as her toes are released into relative freedom.

There's still the matter of her horrible sock though, so she grabs the top and quickly starts to roll it down her foot.

"Tally!" mutters Layla. "What are you doing?"

Tally glances up. The girls have closed in around her and she can barely even see the sky beyond the three faces that are looming over her, their mouths gaping open and their eyes wide.

"Put your shoe back on."

Tally blinks hard, trying to ignore the knot in her stomach that appears whenever she's told she has to do something. She's at school. She can't make a scene. "I can't. You know that new shoes make my feet hurt. That's why Miss Thompson let me go barefoot in the classroom when we started year six."

"Well, we aren't in year six now." Ayesha glances nervously over one shoulder. "And you're going to get laughed at if you do that kind of thing here."

"What do you mean, *that kind of thing?*" Tally peers up at Ayesha. "My foot hurts so I'm rubbing it better."

"I mean, the kind of thing you were always getting away with in primary school." Ayesha's voice is worried. "You can't do that at Kingswood Academy. You're going to get totally bullied, Tally. The kids here aren't all going to be nice like we are."

Tally opens her mouth as if she's about to say something but then clamps it shut.

Lucy shakes her head. "Don't be embarrassing, that's all we're saying."

Layla crouches down next to her and passes Tally the shoe. "Just try, OK?" she whispers. "And then it'll be fine."

Tally pulls her sock back up and yanks on the shoe before standing up. Layla has been her best friend since they were really small. To begin with, Tally liked her because the name Layla rhymes with Taylor, which is the most brilliant name in the entire universe, but now she likes her best friend for a whole load of reasons. Layla laughs at Tally's jokes and she helps her when things are confusing and she's never made Tally feel bad for being different. She's the only person who knows why Tally is different and it has never mattered to her, not once.

Layla *knows*.

"I wonder which tutor group we'll all be in?" Lucy has moved on from Tally's shoe mistake, which is a relief.

"I hope we're all together!" says Layla.

Tally stares at her, wondering why she'd say

something like that. Of course they'll all be together. They've always been together.

"That'd be great." Lucy shoots a quick look at Tally. "Then we can all look out for each other."

"I'm so excited about having proper art lessons." Layla links her arm through Tally's. "We get to do pottery and make real bowls."

Tally opens her mouth but Ayesha gets there before her.

"I bet I'm going to be rubbish at pottery. Do you remember that plasticine model I made in year four? It was supposed to be a volcano but Mr Hicks thought I'd made a toilet!"

Everyone laughs. Tally joins in even though she knows her way around a good joke and this is definitely not one.

"I've been so scared about today!" proclaims Layla dramatically, squeezing Tally's arm. "I can't believe we're actually starting in year seven!"

"Do you think we're actually going to be OK?" asks Lucy, glancing around the yard. "Some of these kids are huge."

There's a moment of silence and the girls look at each other, their faces crumpled in frowns. Tally is hit with a flash of inspiration. She hadn't intended on showcasing her new talent today but she knows all about the power of distraction and she hates seeing her friends look worried.

"So, shall I demonstrate my circus skills then?" She bends down and undoes the clips on her rucksack, plunging her hand deep inside. "I can't show you my expertise on a trapeze, but I can do this!"

She stands up and waves three items at the girls. "Prepare to be stunned by my incredible, fantastical juggling skills!"

And then, before anyone can say a word, she starts throwing things into the air. An apple. A plum. And lastly, a banana.

"Tally! You can actually juggle!" yelps Layla, before exploding into fits of laughter.

"That is brilliant!" says Lucy, and Tally can hear the admiration in her voice.

"Did you genuinely go to circus school this summer?" asks Ayesha, clapping her hands. "Teach us how to do it!"

"A true magician never shares her secrets!" proclaims Tally, throwing the items skywards. And then she starts singing circus clown music as loudly as she can and kicking out her feet as she continues to juggle.

"Doot-doot-doodle-oodle-oot-doot-doo-doo."

"Tally. Stop it now." Lucy's voice is suddenly urgent and her gaze is not on Tally's impressive juggling skills any more.

"Doot-doot-doodle-oodle-oot-doot-doo-doo!" trills Tally in response, not seeing the three girls take a step back.

"Please, Tally," whispers Ayesha. "Put the fruit down."

"You haven't seen my grand finale yet!" Tally grins, doing her best to ignore her friends' bossiness. "I can juggle and dance at the same time. Look!"

She tosses the fruit as high as she can and leaps backwards. Right into the path of a group of kids who are now standing and staring as if they've never seen anyone like her. Which, to be fair, they probably haven't, because her circus skills *are* pretty impressive.

The juggled objects fall to the ground and the other kids start to laugh. But Lucy, Layla and Ayesha have stopped laughing, even though they were all totally loving her act a moment ago. Instead they are standing very still, their faces frozen in frowns. Tally can't tell if they are angry with her or with these new kids but just as her skin starts to prickle, the bell rings.

Layla springs into action and grabs Tally's arm while Lucy and Ayesha pick up the fruit.

"Let's go," Lucy mutters. "And maybe try to leave the clown behaviour behind, OK?" She hands her the banana and pulls an over-the-top sad face. "Sorry. It doesn't look that good to eat now."

Tally shrugs. She wasn't going to eat it in the first place. It's not entirely Mum's fault for putting it in her lunchbox today – Tally forgot to tell her that she can't eat them any more, not since last weekend when she saw a YouTube video about a spider emerging from a banana when it was opened. She's pretty sure that she'll never eat a banana again for as long as she lives.

The bell rings again and everyone starts heading towards the big main doors. Tally picks up her bag and fastens the straps before heaving it on to her shoulder.

"I'm going to get completely lost," says Layla as they start to walk. "There are so many people here."

"Don't be scared," Tally tells her, throwing the fruit into a bin. There's no way she can eat any of it now, not once it's been on the ground. No amount of washing will get rid of the gross school-germs and she is definitely not prepared to risk getting sick because that might mean going to the hospital. And the loud, too bright hospital with its strong, unpleasant smells is up there with school as one of the most terrifying places on earth. "We're all in the same boat."

Dad told her that this morning. It didn't make Tally feel any better. If anything, it kind of annoyed her because Dad knows full well that there are no boats involved in starting year seven at Kingswood Academy and he also knows that metaphors and idioms seriously irritate her. But the way Dad's voice smiled when he said it makes her think that it was supposed to be reassuring. She remembers the other thing that Dad did and that actually *did* make her feel good, so she stops and pulls Layla towards her, wrapping her arms around her friend in the biggest of hugs, squeezing her as tightly as she possibly can because that is something that always makes Tally feel safe, no matter what.

"Bear-hug," she growls, trying to sound gruff and funny like Dad does.

"Tally!" Layla wriggles away, giggling slightly.

"You're going to be fine, Tally," Ayesha says, linking arms with her. "It's OK to be nervous."

"No, I was just trying to help—" begins Tally but Lucy interrupts her.

"We're going to be right here with you. And if anyone is unkind to you then they're going to have to go through us. Right?"

"Right!" echo the others.

"And if someone is bullying you then you tell us and we'll deal with it," Lucy continues. "My brother has told me all about the things that go on in this place and I'm not going to let anyone treat you badly, Tally. OK?"

Tally's stomach starts to churn. Nell promised her that she'd be fine at Kingswood Academy. She certainly didn't say anything about bullying or people being unkind or *things going on*. She isn't sure what that is supposed to mean but it doesn't sound good.

They reach the steps and the girls close in around her. For a second, Tally imagines that she's a celebrity being flanked by her bodyguards. This is probably how Taylor Swift feels, every single time she steps outside her house.

"Don't worry, OK?" Ayesha's voice sounds quiet and a bit shaky as they climb the first step. "You're bound to get lost and feel a bit scared to begin with but I'm sure all the teachers will be really nice."

Lucy's face is set in a fierce-looking expression. "There's really nothing to be scared about." She slows down as they move upwards.

"We're right here with you. Nobody can hurt you when we're all together." Layla's hand tightens on Tally's arm as they reach the top.

Suddenly Tally is at the front of the group, leading the way as they push through the doors and into the building. And she wonders how they can all be so brave when what she really wants to do, now that she's been told about the scary things that might happen and the possibility of getting lost, is to run in the opposite direction.

There are teachers waiting inside, directing them all towards the hall. Tally huddles closer to her friends as everyone starts to push and shove their way down the corridor. The noise is overwhelming and she squeezes her fists tightly as she stares straight ahead, hoping that if she doesn't look at the crowds then it might be easier.

It isn't any better inside the hall. There are pupils everywhere, all dressed in the same, unfamiliar black uniform that Tally is wearing and all shouting at the top of their lungs. Tally follows Layla and the others as they push their way between bodies and bags and they just manage to find a free patch of floor when there is a loud shrieking noise from the front of the room. It's too much and Tally's hands clamp against her ears, trying to block the hideous sound as her head swivels in the direction of the stage.

"Settle down, please." The microphone squeals again and everyone groans. "Can we sort this out?" The man glances off towards the side of the room where another teacher is fiddling with the sound system. "OK, then. I am Mr Kennedy and some of you might recognize me as the head of year seven. Welcome to your very first day at Kingswood Academy. This is a whole fresh start for every single one of you, and if you give your very best, right from today, then you'll get the best from us. So work hard and get involved in school life and, most of all, take responsibility for yourself." He looks out at the now-silent year sevens. "You have one week to learn the layout of the school and then I expect you all to know exactly where you are going and to turn up to lessons promptly. No giving fake excuses about getting lost in the PE cupboard and taking an hour to navigate your way out, like one inventive year seven attempted last year."

He raises an eyebrow and a laugh ripples around the room.

"Ahem." Mr Kennedy clears his throat and the room goes quiet again. "In just a moment, your tutors are going to call out the names of the people in their tutor group. When you hear your name you will make your way towards that teacher and you will do so *quietly*."

The teachers, who are lining the edge of the room, step forward and the first one starts to shout out names.

Lucy is the first to go. She looks worriedly at the rest of them and gives a little wave before starting to head across the hall, but she hasn't even made it halfway when Ayesha's name is called and Lucy spins round, a huge beam spreading across her face. Ayesha doesn't even glance at Tally and Layla as she races towards Lucy and they have a quick hug before walking to where their tutor is gathering the rest of the group and leading them out of the room.

"Maybe we'll be together too," whispers Layla. "They probably make sure that everyone is with a friend, don't they?"

Tally picks at the skin on her fingers and doesn't answer. She can't. Her head is too busy churning with the words that Mr Kennedy spoke.

You have one week to learn the layout of the school.

She isn't good with new places or directions. There is no way that she can commit the entire building to memory in just five days.

Next to her, Layla suddenly picks up her bag. "That's me," she says to Tally. "Fingers crossed they'll call your name next."

Tally knows that they won't. She already met her tutor last term and he's still standing by the wall, deep in conversation with another teacher. He seemed nice enough when she came to visit in the summer, but that was before she found out that none of her friends would be in the same group as her.

There's no way she could have walked into school this morning if she'd known that she was just going to be abandoned.

Tally watches as Layla walks nervously towards her tutor group and then the teacher lowers her clipboard of names and turns to leave the hall. Layla stares across at her, looking lost.

But she isn't as lost as Tally is going to be, all alone in this place without anyone to help her or a single person who even knows her.

Date: Monday 1st September

Situation: First day at Kingswood Academy

How I feel: Frightened and nervous and like the world is closing in on me.

Anxiety Rating: 9. I would say 10 except I know from experience that it can get worse than this.

Dear Diary,

Well, today was a total and utter nightmare. First of all, it was my first day of secondary school, which is every kid's nightmare but extra terrifying for me: the large, echoey assembly hall, so many new teachers and even more new kids, the millions of new rules to remember, the terror of getting lost.

I was petrified.

My brain was bursting with questions all the way there:

What will the toilets be like?

Will they have good locks on them?

What about those awful noisy Dyson dryers?

What if I get things wrong? Like accidentally talk then get into trouble in front of everybody?

Or what if I don't understand instructions properly?

Or a teacher shouts at somebody else then I embarrass myself by covering my ears?

What if I can't cope with being told what to do and I get scared and then that makes me angry? This would be the worst possible thing that could happen at school.

Tally's autism facts: Demand avoidance

So I have a thing called demand avoidance, which is a trait of my autism. Sometimes it's known as PDA. When I first found out about it, I imagined the letters stood for something funny, like Particularly Damn Awesome or Pretty Dangerously Angry. But actually they just stand for Pathological Demand Avoidance. Which sounds pretty serious.

This is a big part of my autism experience. Demand avoidance makes it sound like I'm avoiding things on purpose, but I have literally no choice in it whatsoever. So I prefer to call it demand anxiety. It's what stops me from having a shower when I know I need one. It's what makes me shout at my dad when he asks me how my day was. When someone asks me a question, it feels like a demand on me. My heart starts racing and I feel as if I've had all my control taken away and I just can't answer. They think I don't want to, but the truth is I CAN'T and I hate that I can't.

Pros: Absolutely none. Sorry but demand avoidance just isn't a positive of autism. It's the bit I feel most guilty about because it's the bit that makes Mum and Dad stressed.

Cons: Sometimes my demand anxiety stops me from doing things that I really love – like, my mum told me if I got dressed now then we could go to Starbucks, but because I wouldn't get dressed, I missed my chance. Mum and Dad can help me by being careful with their tone of voice and by trying not to ask something directly of me, but it's really hard for them to remember, especially when they are busy or stressed.

Anyway, just imagine how school is for me. There are more demands on me in one day at school than anywhere else in my life – be silent, answer this question, stop fiddling, line up here. But I can't act like I do at home. The fear of anyone seeing me like that makes me play the role of the "obedient" kid, but the fear of being exposed is always there. Imagine, every day having a ball of anxiety and fear knotted inside you. Now try learning algebra with all that going on.

CHAPTER 4

It is entirely possible that time has slowed down. The second hand of the clock seems unhurried and lazy, as if it has no idea that it has a job to do. But Tally knows that if she stands here for long enough, it will eventually reach its destination. It has to. That's the rules.

Tick.

Tick.

Tick.

And just when she thought that it would never happen, it's finally there.

"Nell! It's time!" Tally races out of the kitchen and stands at the bottom of the stairs, looking up to where her sister's bedroom door can be seen at the top of the landing. "Let's go!"

The response is underwhelming.

"Nell!" Her feet take the stairs two at a time. There is no time left and this delay is making her uneasy. "Come on!"

Nell's door is closed but Tally doesn't care. The clock in the kitchen is ticking – she can almost hear it from up here and there isn't time for manners or house rules or any of that other stuff. She has to get Nell and get out.

"Hey! You can't just barge into my room. Get lost."

"It's time to go. Hurry up." Tally looks at her sister and frowns. "You haven't even got your shoes on."

Nell shakes her head and looks back at the book in her hand. "I'm not ready yet," she says. "I've just got to finish this chapter."

"But it's been a couple of minutes." Tally is trying to stay calm, she really is. "You said that we could go in a couple of minutes and a couple means two. And it has been two minutes – I know because I watched the clock."

"Of course you did." Nell mutters the words like she doesn't think anyone will be able to hear her. Then she puts her book down and turns to face Tally. "I'll be ready to go in a bit, OK? I promise."

"You're a liar and a cheat and your promises mean nothing to me!" yells Tally, a deep, red colour invading her cheeks. "You said a couple of minutes and it's been a couple of minutes and I want to go *now*!"

She clenches her fists tightly together, trying to stop the terror from escaping. She's put up with school for a whole week and all she wants is for Nell to keep her promise. It's the weekend. It's her time now. That's fair.

"It's just a phrase!" shouts back Nell, standing up. "I didn't literally mean that I would be at the front door in exactly one hundred and twenty seconds. That's ridiculous."

"But that's what you said! You shouldn't say things that you don't mean."

There's the sound of footsteps and Mum appears in the doorway, her arms wrapped around a big cardboard box.

"What's going on?" she asks, looking between her daughters. She sees Tally's fists and Nell's scowl and lowers the box. "Girls? What have I missed?"

"Just Tally being her usual, difficult—" starts Nell but Tally's outrage drowns her out.

"She lied! She said that she'd be ready to go and get ice cream in a couple of minutes but she isn't ready and it's been two minutes and, actually, it was a really long two minutes, but I waited until it was up, every last second. It's not fair and it's all her fault."

Mum's forehead wrinkles up. Tally isn't sure if that means that Mum agrees with her or not, so she keeps going.

"I don't even want her to be my sister any more! She's evil and horrible and completely and utterly stupefying."

Nell snorts. "Oh yeah? I'm stupefying, am I? Please do tell me exactly what you mean by that. I bet you don't even know."

"Nell." Mum's voice holds a warning but nobody is listening.

"I do! I do know what stupefying is. A stupid, lying girl and it's what you are. A stupefying fourteen-year-old." She points at Nell angrily, her finger shaking. Nell will think she's angry but she isn't. She's scared and she's full right up to the brim with feelings. It isn't going to take much more to make her overflow, and she's trying as hard as she can to stop that from happening. Nell getting annoyed with her will definitely be too much.

But instead of Nell's frustrated face, the one she's been making more and more at Tally this summer, where her eyes go very small and her lips go very thin, she does something surprising.

She laughs.

"Are you going to tell her or shall I?" she asks Mum. "Because I think that she should know that stupefying means awesome and brilliant and fantastic." She turns to Tally and gives a curtsy. "You've just given me a wonderful compliment. Thank you!"

And all of Tally's feelings burst out. There is absolutely nothing that she can do about it.

"I don't care!" Tally sweeps out her hand and knocks the lamp off Nell's desk. "You lied and now it's been way more than two minutes and I hate you, I hate you, I hate you!"

Nell starts shouting about her lamp and Mum comes further into the room, putting herself between the two of them. Her mouth is moving and she's saying something to Nell but Tally can't hear her. She closes her eyes, opens her mouth and hums her tune. She's the one who made it up and nobody else knows how it goes. She's the only person who is allowed to sing her tune and sometimes, when everything is going wrong, Tally's tune can make everything safe again.

She isn't sure how long she's been humming, but when she finally opens her eyes again, the world is back to normal. The clocks have stopped their frantic ticking and Nell's lamp is back on the bedside table. Mum is standing in front of her, not so close that she's touching but close enough that Tally can smell her familiar perfume. Nell is next to her.

"Nell has explained that you were right," says Mum quietly. "She did tell you that she'd be ready in a couple of minutes and she shouldn't have said that if she didn't mean it."

"So why did she lie?" Tally wiggles her stiff fingers, suddenly feeling so tired that she could sleep for a week. "I could have waited for three minutes if she'd only said that in the first place."

Mum sighs, just a tiny bit, but Tally misses nothing. She hears all of Mum and Dad's sighing and it usually pushes her straight into a big, hot mood. She hasn't got the energy to do anything right now though. It's always like this after things get too much – a horrid combination of exhaustion and fear and guilt. All mixed together like a nasty soup that makes her stomach swirl and her skin feel shivery.

"Nell wasn't lying to you," says Mum. "It's a figure of speech. It means that the person will be ready really soon."

Tally frowns and looks at Nell. "So why didn't you just say that at the beginning, when you told me that we could get ice cream?"

Nell glances at Mum who gives her a nod. "I didn't think it'd make you upset," she tells Tally. "Sometimes I forget what we can and can't say to you."

"You can say anything to me, silly!" Tally fixes Nell with a hard stare. "As long as it's the actual truth."

There's a moment's pause and Mum gives Nell's arm a squeeze. "Are you ready to go for ice cream now, then?"

Nell nods. "I can finish my homework later. Let's go." She walks across the bedroom, turning when she reaches the door. "Come on, Tally."

But Tally is not moving to follow her sister. Instead, she spins slowly on the carpet, her face blank while she works hard to squash the feeling of panic that Nell's demand has created.

"Not yet." Her eyes scan the room. "I might have some homework to do, too."

Nell is not the boss of her. She doesn't get to decide when Tally goes for ice cream.

Mum puts her hand on Tally's arm. "You've only just started at Kingswood Academy! There's no homework until next week."

"Then I think I might watch one of my programmes first. We can go for ice cream after that."

The room is silent for a moment. Tally turns to leave and then stops. She's tired and a bit miserable and she knows that Mum and Nell are feeling sad too. Ice cream makes things better and she really wants today to be good.

"We can go in one minute," she tells Nell, walking out of the door. "And I do actually mean one minute because I am not a liar."

Her own bedroom is calm and peaceful. The mask is hanging on the post at the end of her bed and she pulls it over her head, the rubbery material feeling cool against her skin. She can still remember the day that Mum gave it to her and the way it felt when she put it on. The way it felt when she looked in the mirror and saw Tiger Girl.

Now she's ready to get ice cream.

"I'm not taking her to the shop looking like that," hisses Nell, when Tally meets them on the landing. "You can't make me, Mum. Not in that ridiculous mask."

Tally ignores her and walks down the stairs. Her trainers are lying on the floor by the front door and she yanks them on firmly so that they'll slide on to her foot. She can do up her laces, no matter what she's heard Mum saying to Dad, but just because she can doesn't mean that she has to.

"Nell! Ice cream time!" she calls, opening the front door.

Her sister plods down the stairs, as if her feet have forgotten that they're taking her to get a delicious treat. Mum follows behind, whispering something that Tally can't hear.

"Let's go!" Tally steps outside and stands on the garden path while Nell gets some money from Mum and finds her own shoes. She's braver than normal when she's wearing her mask and, for a moment, she almost thinks that she could walk to the corner shop on her own.

But then she remembers about the road and the noisy cars, and what if a very loud motorbike were to drive past just when she's about to step off the kerb? Or what if someone decides that they would like to kidnap her? Ever since last year, when she saw a thing on the news about a missing child, she's tried to be extra-careful whenever she's outside the house because being taken away from everything safe would be more terrible than she could even imagine. She pulls the tiger head down a bit more and waits quietly until Nell comes out to join her.

"What flavour are you going to choose?" Tally asks,

the instant that they are outside the gate. "I might get chocolate chip because I like chocolate and it's made from a bean, which is pretty weird, don't you think? Imagine opening a tin of baked beans and they were all made of chocolate! Do you think you can get chocolate baked beans from Heinz?"

"No. And I think that sounds disgusting." Nell nudges Tally. "There's no way someone as fussy as you would eat that!"

"I might. Anyway, I might not get chocolate chip because maybe it's not the right flavour for today. I think I might get strawberry instead."

They reach the crossing and Nell pushes the button. Tally peers through the mask, watching for the road to be clear.

"Strawberry might have bits in it though." Tally bites her lip, suddenly unsure. She doesn't want to choose the wrong thing. Getting ice cream is a treat and it has to be perfect.

A car whizzes past and Tally takes a step back, away from the edge of the pavement. "I don't think I want an ice cream any more," she says, in the quietest of voices.

"Oh, Tally." Suddenly, Nell's hand is holding hers, her fingers linked between Tally's, keeping them from getting all scrunched up. "You can choose vanilla like you always do, OK? You love vanilla."

Nell is right. She always gets vanilla. Vanilla is safe.

"What flavour are you getting?" Tally asks.

Everything hangs on the answer to this question. Tally knows that, even if Nell doesn't. Now that she's thought about it, Tally can't bear it if Nell chooses the wrong flavour and the problem is that Nell always chooses chocolate chip. Every single time.

There's a pause and then Nell squeezes Tally's hand. "I'm having vanilla," she says. "Just like you."

And then the road is clear and it's safe to cross. There is no danger anywhere as Nell heads across the road with Tally's hand still in hers. And inside the mask, Tally starts to wonders if, maybe, Nell does know.

CHAPTER 5

The door of the drama studio swings shut with a bang as Mrs Jarman strides into the room. Everyone instantly stops talking and stands up a little straighter – the teacher's reputation precedes her and nobody wants to start the day with a detention.

"Right then, year seven." Mrs Jarman claps her hands and Tally winces as the sound bounces off the walls of the studio. "Put your bags on the floor and let's get going."

Tally stands still for a moment and watches what everyone else is doing. There is a lot of floor, and Mrs Jarman hasn't made it at all clear about where the bags are supposed to go. The rest of the class are all throwing their bags down by the wall though, so Tally walks across the room and finds a space, hoping that the rest of the lesson is going to be a bit easier.

The door flies open again and two familiar girls scurry through, tripping over themselves in the effort to get inside.

"Sorry we're late, Miss," gasps Ayesha. "We got lost."

Tally waves her hand but neither Ayesha or Lucy see her. They're too busy staring at Mrs Jarman, who appears to be considering her response. Tally holds her breath and crosses her fingers. If they're given a detention they'll be completely miserable.

"It's the first drama lesson," says the teacher eventually. "So I'm prepared to be forgiving. However, this excuse won't wash after today. If you're late again then *your* time is going to be *my* time. Is that understood?"

The two girls nod frantically. Tally is glad that they understand because she does not. How can Mrs Jarman take anyone else's time? It makes absolutely no sense – unless she's some kind of soul-sucking, vampire-demon teacher? Tally makes a silent vow to never, ever be late for a drama lesson. So far this week she's managed to tag on to the end of a group of kids and follow them from one class to another, which is good because she still hasn't got the first idea about how to get anywhere and the thought of getting lost is too awful to contemplate.

She only has a few lessons with Layla and the others and any hopes that she'd had of them being together all day are long gone.

"Now hurry up!" calls the teacher. "We haven't got all day. Let's see if you have the skills to arrange yourselves in some kind of spherical manner."

Tally screws up her eyes, trying desperately to block out the rest of the room so that she can breathe slowly. Mrs Jarman is doing everything completely wrong. She's bossy and she's shouty and she's saying things that don't even make sense. This is supposed to be a drama lesson, not gymnastics, but even if it was gymnastics, Tally knows that she can't possibly arrange herself into anything that looks even a tiny bit spherical. Nobody can do that, except those dancers that Mum took her to see at Covent Garden. And also hedgehogs and armadillos and woodlice. Tally isn't any of those and she doesn't want to make Mrs Jarman cross but she just can't do what is being asked of her.

All around, kids are pushing and barging and bickering as they lower themselves on to the floor. Ayesha and Lucy are on the other side of the room now, too far away to sit with her. Tally watches, hoping for a clue and wishing that Layla had this class with her.

"You there!" The drama teacher is pointing one long, red talon at Tally. If she were an animal, she would be a terrifying raptor. "Come and sit in the circle with everyone else."

If Mum or Dad or Nell spoke to Tally in this tone then Tally's head would start roaring and her stomach would tie itself up into the tightest of knots and she'd have to shout at them for making her feel worried and anxious. But she isn't at home now. She's at school, and when she's here, she has to pretend to be normal. No matter what it takes, because you aren't allowed to be anything else when you're at school.

Tally swallows hard, trying to ignore the feeling building up behind her eyes. Everything in front of her looks cloudy and she stumbles slightly as she moves across the floor, looking for a space where she can hide. She desperately wants to hum her song but she can't risk everyone hearing, so she chews on her lip instead and tries to stay calm.

"Just sit there!" snaps Mrs Jarman, pointing at a gap in the circle.

Tally glances up. A girl who she doesn't know is smiling at her and making room on the floor. Tally sinks on to the ground, her head filling up with fog and her hands shaking. Instantly, an elbow digs her in the ribs.

"Weirdo alert," whispers a voice on the other side of her.

She doesn't have to look up to see who it is.

"Right. Now that we have all finally managed to achieve the first task of sitting down, we're going to start with an ice-breaker game." Mrs Jarman swoops around the circle, fixing them all with her beady eyes. She has quite a large nose and the more Tally stares, the more that Mrs Jarman really does look like a menacing bird of prey.

"We're going to play a game called 'The World's Greatest Sandwich'," continues the teacher.

The floor is hard and uncomfortable. Tally looks around the room but she can't see any chairs anywhere. This is not good. Back in primary school, she was always allowed to sit on a chair because her legs don't like being squished and it's hard to listen when your legs are complaining.

"My name is Jenna and the world's greatest sandwich has chocolate spread."

The game has started.

"My name is Ameet and the world's greatest sandwich has chocolate spread and gherkins!"

The sound of everyone sniggering makes Tally stop thinking about chairs and start listening.

"My name is Ayesha and the world's greatest sandwich has chocolate spread, gherkins and popcorn!"

No. That's not right. Those things don't go together. Ayesha should know better than that.

The next person starts to speak.

"My name is Simon and the world's greatest sandwich has chocolate spread, gherkins, popcorn and mayonnaise!"

Tally's tummy starts to feel funny.

"My name is Aleksandra." The smiling girl sitting on the other side of Tally has a very loud voice. "And the world's greatest sandwich has chocolate spread, gherkins, popcorn, mayonnaise and toenail clippings!"

The room erupts into snorts of laughter, as if nobody else knows that this is wrong. Horrible and wrong, and worse than all of that, a big, fat lie.

But now it's Tally's turn. She waits until everyone has settled down and then looks at Mrs Jarman, who is standing outside the circle, leaning against the wall of the studio.

"My name is Tally Olivia Adams," she says firmly. "And the world's greatest sandwich doesn't have any of those things in it. The world's greatest sandwich is cheese." She glances around the now-silent room. "Just cheese. Not cheese and anything else and definitely not cheese and popcorn or cheese and toenails." She spits the last word out, like the very sound of it makes her feel sick. "I saw it on television and they asked lots and lots of people and they all said that the best sandwich ever is cheese."

There is a pause and then Mrs Jarman flashes Tally a big smile before pushing herself off the wall.

"Excellent!"

She steps back into the circle and turns slowly, looking at each person.

"Never be afraid to speak your mind in drama," she says. "The best drama occurs when we're all prepared to say exactly what we think." She waves her hands in the air. "Don't follow the crowd, year seven! Be brave!"

"Yeah, you're totally brave," hisses Luke, as Mrs Jarman turns away. "I saw the way your lip was wobbling when she told you to sit down. Weirdo."

But Tally doesn't care. Mrs Jarman said that she was excellent. That is not a word that Tally hears very often. She looks at the drama teacher and wonders whether instead of an ordinary old common buzzard, she might just be a magnificent golden eagle.

"OK, I want you all to get into groups and follow the instructions that are inside the envelopes that I'm about to hand out," calls Mrs Jarman.

"This is so boring," moans Luke.

"What was that?" snaps Mrs Jarman and Luke's face drops.

"Nothing, Miss."

The teacher sweeps across the room and everyone freezes.

"I believe that you said that my lesson is boring."

Luke opens his mouth but no sound comes out. Tally wonders if he might have forgotten how to speak and crosses her fingers for good luck.

"Very well then." Mrs Jarman's voice sounds sweet and kind, but it doesn't match the steely look that she is giving Luke, which is a bit confusing. "If any of you have any suggestions for me on how I can improve my teaching, then by all means feel free to pass on your ideas. You can write them on a post-it note and pop them into my Top Tips box."

She points across the room and a nervous giggle spreads around the class. Tally looks, but all that she can see is the bin.

"Are we ready to move on?" The teacher claps her hands again, even louder than the first time. "Good. Now get into groups of four and start behaving like year seven pupils, not silly little primary school kids."

"Aleksandra! Go in a group with me!"

"We've got Ameet so we just need another person. Ayesha – bring Tally over here."

The room is filled with noise. Someone takes hold of Tally's arm and drags her into a corner of the room, where an envelope is already being ripped open and the rules of the task read out by Lucy.

But she isn't really there. Instead, she is making a list in her head of all the suggestions that she can give to Mrs Jarman about how the drama lessons could be better. Because she's asked for ideas and Tally is one hundred percent happy to help.

The first suggestion is so easy that she could tell Mrs Jarman now, but she won't because the rules were made very clear. Write it on a post-it note and pop it into the Top Tips box.

Which she fully intends to do, just as soon as she's figured out where it actually is.

Date: Monday 8th September

Situation: Drama class

Anxiety rating: Started off with a 8 when Mrs Jarman was being very shouty and demanding, but ended up with a 5, which isn't bad. Especially when 8 usually means that I'm going to end up having a meltdown.

Dear Diary,

Hi there. Tally again. I was really bored after school today until I remembered that I needed to make Mrs Jarman's "how to be a better teacher" box, so I got a box from Mum and decorated it with pens and paint and glitter. By the time I'd finished, I was so covered in mess that I kind of looked like a peacock! But it was worth it. Mrs Jarman is going to love it, it's much better than the bin she was pointing to. Come to think of it, why was she pointing at the bin? People are so strange. I thought drama was going to be a terrifying class, but I actually think it's going to work out OK. And now I've survived I just need to make sure that I do whatever it takes to avoid having a meltdown at school.

Tally's autism factsheet: Meltdowns

What are they?

Meltdowns are totally different to being in a bad mood, and they're totally different to Demand Avoidance. Meltdowns are when it's all gone so far that there's no way back and my brain goes into shutdown. They are terrifying and they should be avoided if at all possible.

Isn't that just a tantrum?

Some people think meltdowns can be controlled – like I'm just a child throwing a tantrum – but I don't like the word tantrum as it sounds like it's done on purpose. I think it should be called a stress breakdown. Who wants to do that on purpose? I don't choose to do it, it just happens when I'm at breaking point and no one has helped me and I just can't cope with holding it in any more.

Some people say they don't even feel like it's them when they are having a meltdown. I am usually aware of what's happening and that I shouldn't be doing it, but it is literally impossible for me to control it, which is frightening. Having no control over your own actions while also knowing they are bad ones is terrifying.

How do you feel afterwards?

After a meltdown I feel isolated, guilty and like everyone's against me. And even though I seem calm on the outside, it's still a bit as though there's a war going on in my head. Afterwards I promise myself that next time I'm not going to say things I don't mean and that I will swallow down the whole anger thing. But at the time it's like a devil and angel are fighting on my shoulder and the devil always wins.

What helps you at the time?

What I need at these times is for someone, usually my mum, to come and calm the situation, but she isn't always there, which is hard. So then I usually go up to my room and try to get absorbed in one of my favourite things, like playing my ukulele, to try to refresh my mind.

I don't know exactly who this factsheet is for. Maybe I'll give it to Nell, as she finds it harder to understand me. Or you never know, maybe one day my diaries might get published and I will become famous for helping people to understand autism better than they seem to at the moment. So if you're reading this and you're not me then please pass it on so that everyone can learn. And so that I can get on to Taylor Swift's radar.

CHAPTER 6

The rain has finally stopped and everywhere looks clean and fresh and new, like the world has had a makeover. From the roof of the garden shed, the tiger surveys its territory. The fair is still here, but not for long. Tonight is the very last night and Mum has promised that they can go. But only if absolutely nothing goes wrong today.

The tiger sticks its nose into the air and takes a deep breath. Nothing will go wrong. How could it, on a day as perfect as this?

"Tally! I'm leaving in two minutes and if you aren't by the front door then I'm going without you."

Nell's voice floats on the breeze, like an autumn leaf that has fallen from the tree. Actually, no, that isn't right. Tally is learning about similes in English class and that one doesn't work at all. She needs to try again.

Nell's voice growls angrily, like a raging storm.

Tally smiles to herself inside the mask. Much better. She likes similes because they aren't pretending to be something that they're not, unlike metaphors.

"I'm serious!" Nell's stamping feet match her cross words. "And Mum says that if you want to go to the fair tonight then you'd better not make me late for school."

"That's fine with me!" The tiger raises herself to her full, intimidating height and balances on the roof. "Because I don't want to go to school and I don't want to go to the fair. Not with someone as horrible as you, Nell-nasty-Adams!"

Down below, Nell shrugs. "Your loss. I'm going and everyone says it's brilliant. Apparently the haunted house is the best one yet."

The wind picks up and Tally can sense the fair wafting towards her on the air, inviting her to visit. The sweet smell of candyfloss and the smokiness of the hot dog van. It smells mysterious and hot and dangerous, and she wants to go more than anything.

"I'm ready for school!" she calls, scrambling down off the shed and chasing up the garden after her sister. "But I'm not coming because you told me to, OK? I'm coming because I want to and that's totally different."

"Oh, totally," agrees Nell, pushing open the back door. "You might just think about taking that tiger head off before we go, though. You know – if you *want* to?"

Tally pauses and replays the words in her head, checking to make sure that Nell isn't choosing for her.

"I'll take it off in a minute," she says slowly, kicking off her wellies. "After I've cleaned my teeth."

"You haven't even cleaned your teeth yet?" screeches Mum, entering the kitchen, her eyes darting frantically around the room as if she's lost something important. "You have exactly two minutes to get washed and clean, young lady. Otherwise, no going to the fair for you tonight."

Inside the mask, Tally's eyes go very, very small as she tries to keep herself calm. She'd already decided to clean her teeth – Mum didn't need to shout at her like that.

"I hate you," she whispers, as quietly as she can, not wanting Mum to hear. Those words make Mum sad and Tally doesn't want that, but once the thought has popped into her head she has to let it out, otherwise it'll fester and grow inside her until it's something much worse than words.

"Do what you want, Tally." Nell is standing next to her. "It's your choice. But I'm leaving in one minute."

"I want to go to the fair."

Through the eyeholes of the tiger's head, Tally sees Nell raise her eyebrows.

"So choose that then. But hurry up, OK?"

Tally races towards the kitchen door, tugging off her mask as she goes. She is choosing to clean her teeth and it is her decision to be on time for school and not make Nell late because she really, really doesn't want to miss out on tonight's trip.

"Thank you, Nell," says Mum as Tally leaves the room. "You handled her better than I did."

Tally clamps her hand over her mouth, trying to push the sob back inside. They don't get it. They think she's difficult. They try to understand, she knows that really, but how can they possibly know what it feels like to have to say no when you want to say yes? They have no idea how sad it makes her feel.

It takes approximately forty-three seconds for Tally to slam the toothbrush around her mouth and splash some water on her face. That leaves seventeen seconds to run into her bedroom, grab her rucksack and then hurtle downstairs to the front door where Nell is waiting.

"I'm on time," she pants, reaching for her school shoes. "Stop the clock."

Nell looks at Tally's hair with a critical expression on her face. "Are you seriously going to school looking like that?"

Tally pulls on her shoe and glances down at herself. She has her uniform on the right way round and her school tie is fastened up. She hasn't accidentally forgotten to put on her shirt like last week, even though the collar is still too tight around her neck.

"Yes. What else would I look like?"

Mum bustles into the hallway before Nell can reply, holding out two lunchboxes.

"Here you go, girls. Have a great day, both of you!"

Tally stands up and takes her box quickly, cracking open the lid to peer suspiciously inside. The lunches got confused yesterday and Tally ended up with Nell's disgusting tuna salad instead of her trusted cheese sandwich. She was starving by the time she got home and very, very cross.

"See you later!" Nell calls as she opens the front door. "And don't forget about the fair tonight."

Mum smiles and gives Tally a quick hug. "I won't forget. Don't either of you forget that today needs to be a good day, OK?"

Tally nods. It's definitely a cheese sandwich in

her lunchbox and no sign of any forbidden foods like yoghurts (which are too disgusting unless they're eaten straight out of the fridge when they're completely cold) or raisins (which taste like of out-of-date fruit and get stuck in your teeth). Today is looking like it's definitely going to be a good day.

Outside, the pavements are slick with rain. They walk together until they've crossed the main road and then Nell gets out her phone and starts frantically tapping at the screen. Tally drops behind, jumping over the puddles and wondering if the fairground people will dry the seats on the rides because nobody wants to sit in a wet patch.

Up ahead, Nell finally puts her phone in her pocket and turns back to look at Tally.

"Come on!" she urges. "I need to talk to Rosa about something before tutor group starts. Hurry up."

"Look at this!" Tally points at the pavement and stands still. "Nell! Look!"

Nell huffs and puffs, and normally, Tally would tell her that she sounds like the Big, Bad Wolf about to blow down the Little Pig's house. Right now though, she is too distracted by the sight in front of her.

"Ewww. That's gross." Nell has trudged back down

the road to join her and is now scrunching up her nose as she stares at the pavement. "Let's go."

"It isn't gross. It's a living thing." Tally's voice is quiet as she crouches down and stares at the worm. It's the biggest that she's ever seen and it's lying right here on the path, where anyone could tread on it.

"You need to move, worm."

The worm isn't listening. Or maybe it just doesn't like doing what it's been told to do. Tally can understand how that feels and she doesn't want to make the worm feel bad, but sometimes there just isn't a choice. Not if you want to be safe. Mum and Dad have a list of non-negotiables, and it doesn't matter if Tally screams and shouts and cries, she still has to do those things, like wearing her seatbelt in the car because otherwise she might die, and not hitting anyone even if she's really upset because it's illegal to hit another person, and not going outside the house in the middle of the night, even if it is only into the back garden so that she can lie on the shed roof and gaze at the stars.

"Staying on this pavement is a non-negotiable, little worm," whispers Tally, leaning closer so that the worm can hear her. "You have to move."

"Tally. We are going to be late for school." Nell sounds

snappy. "Get up and start walking or I'm phoning Mum."

"Please just wiggle over to the side," begs Tally. "You're going to get squished if you stay here and squished worms are not happy worms."

"Squished sisters are not happy sisters," mutters Nell. "And that's what you're going to be if you don't move it. Now!"

There is absolutely nothing worse than someone touching you when you don't want them to. Tally knows that. But right now, there's only one option and that means that she doesn't have a choice. Stretching out her finger, she picks up the worm as gently and delicately as she possibly can. Then she stands up and walks across to the grass at the side of the path, putting the worm in the safest place she can find.

"There you go," she tells it. "No stamping feet or speeding cars will squish you over here."

"Finally—" starts Nell but Tally has already moved on ahead of her.

"Come on!" she shouts over her shoulder. "We're going to be late if you don't hurry up."

CHAPTER 7

They see the crowds even before they reach the park. Hordes of people, pushing and shoving to get through the gates and into the fairground. Tally hangs back, clutching tightly to Dad's hand.

"I've changed my mind," she says, squeezing his fingers. "I want to go home."

Dad stops walking and leans down. "OK," he tells her. "But that's a shame because I really wanted to go on the waltzers and you know that Mum and Nell won't go on with me. They hate fast rides. You're the only person who I can ask."

Tally hesitates. It's true, Mum and Nell refuse to go on any ride that's faster than the teacups.

"It's fine, sweetheart." Dad waves his hand in the air to get Mum's attention. "You and I will go home if you aren't in the mood." He gazes across the fence to where the fair is in full swing. "Maybe we can come next time the fair is in town."

Next time. That means waiting, and Tally knows how hard it is to wait for anything.

"Perhaps we can go in for a bit," Tally says slowly. "You know, just so that you can have a look around."

Dad beams down at her. "That would be wonderful!"

"Is everything OK?" Mum and Nell have made their way back down the path to where Tally and Dad are standing. "Do we need to go home?"

Dad shakes his head. "Everything is fine. We're going to pop into the fairground for a few minutes and then we'll head home after that."

"What?" Nell turns her eyes away from the crowds and glares at Dad. "You mean that we can't even go on anything? That's so unfair."

Dad leans across to Nell and whispers something. Normally, this display of bad manners would make Tally feel angry but right now there's too much going on to worry about what Dad might be saying, and anyway, they're walking again and the gates are right ahead and, before she has time to reconsider, they are inside the park and at the fair.

Tally pauses and a boy crashes into her from behind.

"Keep moving!" calls someone else and then she's pushed forward and Dad's hand slips out of her fingers.

The noise is everywhere. Tally spins, trying to catch sight of Dad or Mum or Nell, but all she can see is flashing lights illuminating the faces of the strangers who surround her. She opens her mouth to shout for help but a hand on her shoulder makes the sound freeze in her throat. She knew that coming here was a mistake. There are too many people and now she's going to be kidnapped and Dad will be so, so sorry that he forced her to go to the fair. And he'll hate the fair for the rest of his life because it will always remind him of the day that he lost his little girl and was the worst dad in the entire world.

"Shall we head over to the hill?" The hand on her shoulder tightens. "It's a bit quieter over there and we'll probably be able to see the whole fairground."

Tally spins round and glares at Dad. "You lost me! I thought I'd been abducted or something and everyone was staring at me and laughing and it was horrible. Don't you even care?"

Dad gives Tally a small smile and reaches for her hand. "You let go of my hand about five seconds ago. I could see you the whole time."

Tally shakes her head and frowns but Dad is already following Mum and Nell up the hill, and if she doesn't want to be abandoned again then she has no choice but to let him pull her along.

But she doesn't have to enjoy it. And she doesn't have to be happy. Nobody can make her have a good time, and if she wants to go home then they have to take her because that's one of the important rules and they all know what will happen if they force her to stay.

"Look at that!" Nell's voice is excited but Tally doesn't raise her eyes from the ground. No. She won't look at whatever it is. Not when none of her so-called family even love her enough to be worried when she goes missing and is almost stolen.

"Oh my goodness – that looks terrifying!" says Mum. She's got that right. There are a lot of incredibly terrifying things at this fair and Tally has no idea what they were thinking of, bringing her here. "Do you think you could ride on that, Nell?"

Nell laughs and Tally scuffs her feet in the dirt, wondering what they're talking about.

"Are you kidding? There's no way I'd go on that! Look at how the cages are spinning."

"And the way it swoops around at the same time," agrees Dad. "You'd have to be someone with a head for heights and a need for speed to go on that thing."

He tightens his grip on Tally's hand, so briefly that she thinks she imagined it.

"Well, there's no way I could ever go on it," states Mum. "It makes my stomach turn over just looking at it."

Tally knows exactly what they're doing but she can't resist any longer. Raising her head, she looks at what they're all talking about and there, right in front of her, is a ride that she has never seen before. It's lit up against the night sky and it is the most beautiful thing that she has ever seen.

"Shall we go closer and have a look?" asks Dad.

Tally nods. "But don't let go of my hand this time, OK?"

They walk down the small hill and back into the throng of people. Tally clings on to Dad and they follow Mum and Nell, weaving their way through the crowds towards the incredible ride.

"Can I go on the dodgems?" asks Nell, coming to a halt.

"No." Tally pulls Dad's hand. "We're going over there."

"It isn't up to you," snaps Nell before turning to

Mum. "Please? I can see Rosa and some of the others. I can hang out with them while you take Tally."

Mum frowns and raises her eyebrows at Dad like she's asking him a question. "I suppose so," she says slowly. "As long as you promise not to leave the park and you meet us in – oh, I don't know. How long should we give her?"

Dad looks at Nell. "How long do you need?"

Nell smiles at him. "Maybe two hours?"

Dad laughs and shakes his head. "That's too long. I'll have no money left if I let you girls stay here for two whole hours!"

"How about we meet you by the carousel in one hour – and not a minute longer?" suggests Mum. "Have you got your phone and your allowance?"

Nell nods. "Thank you! You guys are the best!"

She takes off at a run and they watch as she flings her arms around her best friend, the sounds of their squeals carrying through the night air.

"We're the best, apparently," Dad says to Mum. "Fancy that! I'll be reminding her of those words when she's complaining that we never let her do anything."

Mum laughs. "She deserves to have some time off with her friends."

Some time off. Tally knows what that means. Some time away from her. Knowing this makes her want to cry.

Dad lets go of Tally's hand and puts his arm around Mum.

"Shall we go and check out this ride then?" he says. "We've got an hour to kill now."

Mum and Dad start walking and Tally takes a last look at Nell, who is talking and laughing and not even thinking about the fact that she has just gone off and left Tally.

"I guess we aren't going to the haunted house together this year, then," she mutters, throwing Nell a fierce stare. "I suppose I'll just go and *kill some time* while you have fun with your friends."

"Come on, Tally!" calls Dad. "I want to see just how adrenalin-fuelled this ride really is! I'm thinking that I might be brave enough to give it a go."

Tally scurries after them, trying to ignore everything around her. The noise. The crowds. The coldness that is seeping into her bones and making her want to cry.

And then two things happen that make everything else seem instantly unimportant. The ride suddenly looms large ahead of her and she hears someone calling her name.

"Tally! You're here! This is so brilliant – shall we go on together?"

Layla's shiny, happy face appears out of the darkness, and standing behind her are Ayesha and Lucy, cramming candyfloss into their mouths as fast as they can. They wave at Tally and grin.

"It's called the Sky Dancer," yells Lucy, pointing at the ride. "My brother has already been on it and he says it's really scary but excellent!"

The name is perfect.

"If we're going on then we need to queue up," calls Ayesha.

Tally looks. The queue already has quite a few people lined up and more are joining every second. Sky Dancer is clearly the most popular ride at the fair.

"Do you want to go on with your friends?" Dad asks. Tally had forgotten that he and Mum were even there, for a second. "It's OK if that's what you want to do."

Tally smiles, but then her face drops as she remembers. Just because Nell has forgotten about her doesn't mean that she can forget about Dad. She tugs on his hand and pulls him to the side where nobody can hear them.

"You wanted to go on the fastest ride here," she says.

"And that is definitely Sky Dancer."

Dad shakes his head. "I thought I did," he tells her. "But it turns out that what I really want to do is watch my fearless, daring daughter have fun with her friends."

"Nell is over by the dodgem cars," Tally reminds him, scowling. "You can go and watch her if you want to. It's your choice."

Dad's mouth wobbles as if he's trying not to laugh. He bends down and puts his hands on either side of Tally's face, the way he does when he tells her how much he loves her.

"I meant you," he says. "My Tiger Girl."

"Oh." Tally thinks for a moment. "But I'm scared of loads of things, so you shouldn't call me fearless."

Dad lowers his hands and pulls some money out of his pocket. "Fine. I'll call you brave then. Because that's what you are, Tally. You get scared but you still keep on going and that makes me very proud to be your dad." He hands her the money and steps back. "Mum and I will watch you. We'll be right here."

Tally nods and starts to head back to where Layla is lining up with the others. Then she stops and turns back to Dad.

"I'm not actually scared about this ride," she calls. "I

just thought I should tell you, in case you think this is me being brave. I like scary rides, so don't go thinking I'm being courageous or something because I'm actually not."

Dad smiles and gives her a salute, which makes Tally laugh. Sometimes, he can be very silly and she doesn't know what he's talking about, but he doesn't seem to mind if she goes on the ride with Layla and not him, and that makes her incredibly happy because the very last thing she wants to do is make her dad feel sad.

The queue is long but none of the others seem bothered about the wait. Probably because they're too busy talking about horrible Luke and the fact that he messaged Lucy to tell her that he'd be at the fair and that they should meet up.

"It's so romantic!" gushes Ayesha when Lucy tells them how he promised to win her a teddy bear at the tin-can alley.

"It totally is," breathes Layla. "I can't believe he hasn't asked you out yet. Maybe he's waiting to do it tonight."

"It's SO romantic," agrees Tally, beaming as hard as she can and trying to pretend that the person behind her in the queue didn't just ram her with their elbow. "Maybe he'll buy you chocolates and flowers. That's a romantic thing to do."

Ayesha laughs. "You seem to know a lot about it, Tally! Who's been giving you flowers and chocolates, then?"

Tally frowns. "Nobody."

"Oh, come on," giggles Lucy. "It's only us. You can tell us who you fancy!"

"I don't fancy anyone." The noise of the fair suddenly seems to have increased. "So just shut up, Lucy. You shouldn't go around spreading lies, OK?"

"All right, calm down." Lucy holds her hands up in the air. "Jeez – it was only a joke. Some people have no sense of humour."

"Anyway, maybe Luke will turn up tonight with a bunch of red roses," says Ayesha, and Tally is glad that they've stopped saying untruthful things about her. "That he's bought from the garage down the road! How cute would that be?"

Layla starts sniggering. "Can you imagine it? Luke asking you on a date in front of everyone!"

Lucy's cheeks go a bit red. She glances around and shakes her head. "Shhh, you guys. Someone might hear you!"

Tally doesn't think anyone can hear a word they're saying, not over the screams coming from Sky Dancer.

"I think he'll go down on one knee and ask you to marry him," she says. "Right here, in the middle of the fair!"

She doesn't really think that, obviously. But she's running out of things to add to this conversation and she definitely doesn't want the girls to start saying horrible things about her liking any boys, because that's not OK. She needs to keep the focus on Lucy and awful Luke and the only way to do that is to join in.

So she drops to one knee and looks up at Lucy. The other girls gawp at her, their mouths drooping open.

"Do you, Lucy, take me, Luke, to have and to hold, in sickness and in health, for ever and ever? Amen."

Which, actually, is completely disgusting. Tally doesn't want to hold anyone who is being sick, not ever. And particularly not Luke.

Lucy tugs frantically at Tally's arm. "Get up!" she hisses under her breath. "I can't believe you're doing this."

"Ow. That hurt." Tally stands up, rubbing at her arm. "You didn't have to grab me."

"You *were* being a bit embarrassing," Layla tells her. "What if Luke had seen that?"

Tally shrugs. "But he didn't."

The girls start chatting again and Tally stands quietly, flicking the mud off her knee. It was only a joke. Some people have no sense of humour.

Finally, they make it to the front of the queue, and Tally watches carefully as the ride spins round, making sure that she knows exactly what to expect. Each cage is big enough for two people and they swing from side to side until they gain enough momentum to go right over the top in a loop-the-loop. If the sounds coming from the cages are anything to go by, it is absolutely and brilliantly terrifying.

"OK, you two, get into this one." The man running the ride beckons to Tally and she walks forward, Layla beside her. They sit down and the man shows them how to fasten the safety belts, before telling them that they must not, under any circumstances, take them off while the ride is in progress. Tally glances across at where Mum and Dad are standing and they both give her a thumbs-up. Wearing the safety belt is a non-negotiable, and right now, she's very glad that she doesn't have to think about whether she can let herself put it on or not.

And then the wire mesh of the cage is lowered and they move upwards. Beneath them, Lucy and Ayesha are loaded into the next set of seats and they jerk up again as the cages are filled with customers.

"I hope it isn't this jolty for the whole ride," says Layla, clutching the metal bar in front of them. "I don't like it."

Tally says nothing. She is too busy looking out across the fairground. If she squints her eyes she is sure that she can see her street, and the higher that they go, the more her head starts to feel clear and light and empty and quiet.

The cage gets to the top and then slowly starts to descend. They reach the bottom and the fairground man flicks a switch. Taylor Swift's latest song bursts out into the night, the ride picks up speed and they are off, the cages swinging from side to side as they zoom up and then swoosh back down the other side. Tally leans forward and back, making the cage swing wildly on its axis.

"Argghhh!" screams Layla, grabbing Tally's arm. "This is too fast! Don't make it sway so much!"

"Stop screaming!" yells Tally. "You're being too loud!"

Layla nods and clamps her lips shut. Then she closes her eyes and squeezes Tally as hard as she can.

Tally grins. This is why her and Layla are best friends,

because they both love this kind of ride as much as each other.

She swings back and forth, tipping the cage as far as it will possibly go until they are almost upside down. Beside her, Layla groans quietly and Tally opens her mouth and screams as loudly as she can.

"Yes!!!!" Her shouts fly out and echo around the park. "Wooooooooooo!"

This is perfect. Absolutely perfect.

Her stomach flips and turns over as the ride picks up speed and the cages reach their full rotation. She opens her eyes as wide as she possibly can, soaking in every detail as the ground flashes past her head and the dark night sky dances at her feet. It feels like she's tiptoeing between the stars.

It is over too soon. The ride slows and Tally whoops and yells until the very last minute.

"That was brilliant," she says, when they grind to a halt. "Let's do it again!"

Layla opens her eyes and blinks at Tally. "I can't," she mumbles. "That was completely terrifying."

Tally shakes her head, a huge smile spreading across her face. "It wasn't," she assures her friend. "This is the best ride in the world and we've got to have another go, OK?"

Layla sniffs and looks at the man, who is waiting for them to make a decision.

"Do you promise that it's not going to go as fast this time?" she asks Tally. "Because I'm not sure that I want to go on again if it does."

Tally laughs. "I can't promise that! And anyway, I want it to be fast because if it slows down then it won't make my tummy flip in the right way."

Layla nods at the man and grips tightly on to the safety bar as they start to swing upwards. "I am literally the best friend in the universe," she tells Tally. "And you are completely odd for liking this ride."

Tally grins and tilts her head back to look at the sky. It is Layla who's the odd one for panicking, but perhaps she won't tell her that until she's convinced her to go around for a third time.

Dear Diary, Mum and Dad try really hard to help me, but it isn't always easy. So tonight, instead of my diary, I've written a list of dos and don'ts for parenting an autistic child. I'm going to tape it to the fridge and point at it if they're finding it tricky.

DO try to adjust to their needs at times. Pick your battles.

DON'T join in if there is an argument. Calm it down and offer them a way out of it.

DON'T tell them they are different, tell them they are unique.

DO let them know how much you love them. You cannot give your child enough love, but you may have to show it differently.

DO accept their difficulties and find a way to turn them into positives.

DON'T tell them to make eye contact as many kids on the autism spectrum find this hard. Instead, make them relaxed and they are more likely to do it naturally.

DON'T put direct demands on them as they may instinctively avoid them.

DO say exactly what you mean, how you mean it. Never use metaphors or be sarcastic.

Finally, cut the labels out of EVERYTHING they wear.

CHAPTER 8

It's raining again. The kind of rain that isn't content with merely soaking your clothes but won't stop until it has sunk deep into your bones, making them feel creaky and cold. The corridors are rammed with people trying to find a space to sit and chat before the next lesson.

"Tally! Over here!"

Layla is waving and trying to get her attention, but Tally has something else to do. Something far more important than gossiping about the latest *incredible* message that Luke has sent to Lucy, despite the fact that he never turned up at the fair. She ignores Layla and instead carefully picks her way over outstretched legs and abandoned bags, until she reaches the stairs and heads up to the next floor. The only rooms up here are the library and the drama studio and there's nobody about.

Tally stands on her tiptoes and peers through the window to the studio. The room is empty and it looks as if Mrs Jarman is in the staffroom with all the other teachers. She pushes the door open and hurries inside. She doesn't have long until the bell rings.

Mrs Jarman's desk is a complete state. There are books and bits of paper and weird items strewn about. Tally stares at a fake moustache and a bowler hat and wonders if Mrs Jarman wears them at the weekend. There isn't a spare inch of space and the jumbled mess is making her feel uncomfortable, so without stopping to ask herself if it's really OK, Tally starts to tidy up. The books are stacked on one side of the desk and the other things are put in a neat pile next to the chair until finally there is a clear space. Then she reaches into her bag and carefully pulls out the box that she made the other night and which took her ages, arranging it so that it is in the exact middle of the surface.

Then she keeps tidying and organizing the desk. Crumpled-up bits of paper are put in the bin and lever-arch folders are lined up in an orderly manner. And just as she thinks it's all done, she spots the pencils. They are rammed into a pot, but some of them are upside down and when she pulls them out she sees immediately that most of them are blunt, which is ridiculous because there, right next to the pot, is an expensive-looking electric pencil-sharpener. The kind that Tally really, really wishes that she owned.

"I'll only sharpen one," she tells herself, shooting a quick glance at the door. "Just to see if it works."

She inserts the pencil into the mouth of the sharpener and it instantly starts rotating, pulling the pencil slightly from her grip as it shaves off the wood. Tally tugs the pencil back and sees the perfect, pointy end. She smiles and puts it back into the pot. The only problem now is that, in comparison, the other pencils look out of place. Their bluntness is not very pleasing at all.

So she picks up another and then another. The whir of the sharpener is completely addictive and Tally is so engrossed in her task that she doesn't hear the door to the drama studio open, or the footsteps heading across the room. She has no idea that anyone is there at all until Mrs Jarman clears her throat loudly, nearly making Tally scream with fright.

"What do you think you're doing in here?"

Tally spins round, a pencil still in her hand. Mrs Jarman is looking at her with an odd expression on her face, and Tally can't figure out what she's thinking.

She hadn't intended on being here when Mrs Jarman came back and she hasn't prepared anything to say to the teacher, so she's just going to have to improvise, which is not her favourite thing to do when it comes to talking to adults. Although they *are* in the drama studio so perhaps it'll be OK this time, because she is quite good at acting.

"Err – I'm sharpening pencils, Miss," she says, brandishing the evidence. "They were really blunt but now they're sharp."

"I can see that." Mrs Jarman puts her hands on her hips. "But that isn't what I'm asking you. What do you think you're doing, coming in here when it's break-time?"

Tally frowns but then remembers that frowning at adults is generally considered to be a bad thing. She rearranges her face into a smile and beams at the teacher.

"I'm sharpening pencils," she repeats, making her voice a little louder. "And doing some tidying up."

She sweeps her hand in the direction of the desk and steps to the side to let Mrs Jarman see the full glory of her work. The teacher blinks and then narrows her eyes.

"Where are my assessments?" she asks, stepping

forward and picking up the books. "What have you done with my papers?"

Tally smiles even harder.

"It's OK. I put all of the rubbish in the bin. Even those grotty apple cores that were lying about, although I didn't really want to touch them, but it's OK because I pulled my sleeve over my hands and picked them up. Like this."

She yanks her jumper over her hands and shows the teacher, who grimaces.

"You threw away my assessments?"

She turns and walks to the corner of the room where the bin is overflowing. She's muttering under her breath and Tally can't quite make out what she's saying. It's probably something about how very grateful she is, though.

Mrs Jarman pulls the crumpled-up sheets of paper out of the bin and walks back to Tally, a stern look on her face. She opens her mouth to speak but then notices the box on her desk and pauses, her eyes flitting between the box and the girl.

"What. Is. That?"

Tally wonders if Mrs Jarman might perhaps need reading glasses because the name of the box is spelled out in big letters on the side. She thinks about suggesting that the teacher make an appointment for an eye test, but then she remembers how much she hates visiting the optician. The eye-lady always makes her put on some hideous, heavy, metal glasses and then shines a super-bright light into her eyes. It hurts but she never wants to complain because the eye-lady is just doing her job and she'd probably have upset feelings if she knew how much Tally hates going to see her, so she just sits there as still as she possibly can and tries to keep the tears squashed down inside.

Perhaps Mrs Jarman feels like that too, which is why she hasn't had her vision checked. It's probably kinder not to mention her terrible eyesight.

"It's a Top Tips Box, Miss," Tally says, taking pity on her teacher. "You said that we could give you suggestions about how your lessons could be better and put them into your box, but I think someone must have stolen your old one because I've looked really hard and I can't find it anywhere."

She looks at Mrs Jarman, trying to gauge just how delighted she is. The teacher's mouth is slightly open and her eyes are wide.

"Is this a joke?"

Mrs Jarman's voice is quieter than Tally has ever heard it, but even though that should be reassuring, something feels wrong. There is an undercurrent of something dangerous in her tone, something even more powerful than the wind that has started howling outside.

Mrs Jarman obviously doesn't understand the significance of Tally's gift and although Tally's legs have started to fizz and her feet are tapping up and down and she really, really wants to leave, she knows that she has to explain.

"I made you a new box!" Tally wiggles her arms, doing jazz-hands because drama teachers probably like that kind of thing. Plus, her arms want to flap, which is what always happens when she gets nervous. "Ta-dah! And I've put my first Top Tip inside, but you don't have to read it now if you don't want to. I hate it if someone tells me that I have to read something right away – it makes the words go all blurry and impossible to figure out."

There is silence. The only sound in the room is the rain hitting the window and the wind whistling round the building. The sky is cloudy and the day suddenly seems to have got darker. Tally wraps her arms around herself and wonders if she should be saying something more or if Mrs Jarman would maybe prefer it if she showed her some brilliant juggling skills. Juggling is definitely dramatic.

"Are you trying to be funny, is that it?"

Tally stares at the teacher and swallows hard.

"No. But I can try and tell you a joke if that's what you want?"

Mrs Jarman eyes dance, like they're on fire.

"Did someone dare you to do this?" She picks up the Top Tip Box and gives it a shake. "If there is something rude or offensive written inside here then you're going to be in a lot of trouble. It's better that you tell me now, if someone put you up to this."

Tally shakes her head. "Nobody dared me. You told us that we could give you our suggestions, Miss."

Mrs Jarman pauses, looking Tally right in the eye like she's trying to see inside her head. Tally stares back, using the trick that Mum taught her. If she looks at the space between Mrs Jarman's eyes, right at the top of her nose, she'll feel less uncomfortable and Mrs Jarman won't think she's being impolite.

The bell rings and the teacher clicks her tongue against the roof of her mouth.

"You can go now," she says. "But this isn't the end of it, young lady."

Tally nods in agreement and picks up her bag. She knows it isn't the end of it. She's only given Mrs Jarman one suggestion so far – she's got absolutely loads more to go.

CHAPTER 9

The words fizz their way up the stairs and push through the crack between the floor and Tally's bedroom door. She wants to ignore them because the book she's reading is actually really good and she only has a few pages to go before she reaches the end – but the words have other plans. They crackle and buzz above her head, just out of reach, and after a few moments, Tally puts her book down with a sigh and sits up. She'll never be able to focus on the story while they're bothering her and there's no point in trying to pretend that they aren't there. Not while they're suggesting that she might want to listen to what's being said, just in case.

Silently, Tally creeps across the carpet and turns the door handle. Out on the landing, the words are huddling together and arranging themselves into groups.

"You can't be serious?"

Those words are bursting out of Mum's mouth. They sound like twigs – hard but as if they could snap at any second. "What were you thinking?"

"I was thinking that if Mrs Jessop didn't agree to get into the ambulance then we might be dealing with slightly more than a broken hip."

Dad pauses and Tally leans forward. "She was completely refusing to go with the paramedics unless the situation was resolved. I couldn't see any other solution."

Mum groans. "No, you're quite right. It's just a bit sudden, that's all."

"It's not ideal, I know. But it's only temporary."

Tally stands up and walks back to her room, pushing the door closed with her foot. It was a false alarm. Mum and Dad aren't talking about anything important or interesting or to do with her. It's just another one of the boring, nothing kind of conversations that they seem to have all the time. It was sensible of her to check though. Sometimes their conversations are about her and how they can best "manage" her behaviour and she needs to hear those.

At teatime, Dad serves up three big bowls of Granny

Lola's Famous Beef Chilli while Mum hands Tally a plate of rice with some chopped-up ham on the side. Beef chilli smells good but Tally tried it once and the texture of kidney beans was all wrong. She tried to tell Mum but Mum wouldn't listen, which was why Granny Lola's Famous Beef Chilli ended up on the floor. That was ages ago though, back when Mum and Dad were always trying to make Tally do things that she couldn't do.

It's a little bit better now, even if everyone does look at her and see a word instead of a person.

"I saw an ambulance outside earlier," says Nell, scooping up some rice. "Do you know why it was there?"

Dad nods. "It was for poor old Mrs Jessop. She's had a fall and hurt her hip. They've taken her to hospital."

"Can I have a drink of orange juice?" asks Tally. "My mouth is dry."

She doesn't want to think about the scary hospital.

"Can I have a drink of orange juice, *please*," says Mum automatically. "And yes, you can have a drink in a minute. We've got something to talk to you girls about first."

"Is Mrs Jessop going to be OK?" Nell looks worried.

"But I'm thirsty *now*." Tally puts her fork on the table and stares at Mum.

"She's in good hands," Dad tells Nell. "And she's in the right place."

"*Please* can I have a drink of orange juice? *Please*?"

Dad gives Mum a quick look, which Tally can't interpret, but he still doesn't get up to fetch the drink.

"Mrs Jessop is really old, though." Nell is frowning now and Tally wonders why she's still talking about it. "It's not OK for old people to fall over – their bodies take ages to heal."

"I'm still thirsty," repeats Tally.

"I'm sure that Mrs Jessop is going to be fine," says Dad. "But while she's away, we're going to have to be good neighbours and help her out. Step up and do our bit, so to speak. Do the right thing."

Nell looks as confused as Tally feels.

Mum clears her throat. "What your dad is trying to say is that we're going to be having a houseguest. Just for a bit."

This doesn't sound good. Even though Mrs Jessop always waves when she sees them and sometimes brings round a plate of cakes if she's been baking, Tally doesn't know her very well. Not well enough to share a house with, that's for certain.

"I want some orange juice right now because I am

thirsty and I keep telling you that I am but you're not listening and I need a drink but you won't get me one even though I have asked you politely and said *please* twice."

"You can wait until we're finished speaking, Tally." Dad's voice is tight, like a stretched-out elastic band. "We're talking about an old lady who needs some help, not about you and your immediate need for some juice."

His cheeks are going a bit red, like a traffic light.

This face means STOP.

Do What I Tell You.

Do Not Do What You Are Doing.

Tally closes her eyes. She really, really wishes that he hadn't said that.

Mum says something but Tally's voice is louder.

"It's not fair if I have to share my house with an old lady who I don't even know and it's not fair that you won't get me a drink even though I asked nicely which is what you wanted me to do. And you shouldn't tell me to wait for a drink because now I can't and it's all your fault!"

She pauses to take a quick breath and glares at Dad who is sitting quietly in his chair. "And that makes you mean and unkind and I hate you because it's not my fault that Mrs Jessop fell over so why do we have to keep talking about it and pretending that we care when she's not actually in our family?"

Another pause for breath. She's out of her seat now, striding around the kitchen, and the words are pouring from her mouth as if they won't ever stop, and even though everything is a bit blurry-looking she can still see Dad looking sad but that just makes it all worse because it's her who should be upset, not him. It is *her* legs that won't stay still and *her* arms that are flapping, and there's nothing that she can do about it because if she stops stimming then the upset will have absolutely nowhere to go.

So she keeps pacing and shouting until finally her legs run out of steam and her mouth runs out of words and she slumps back into her seat and rests her head on the table in an attempt to make her brain quieten down.

Eventually, a clattering sound makes her look up. Across the table, Nell's bowl is empty and she's wiping her mouth. There isn't a single bit of Granny Lola's Famous Beef Chilli left.

"Mrs Jessop doesn't have any family, for your information," she tells Tally, her voice scornful. "And some of us don't have to *pretend* to care about other people."

Tally doesn't like the colour of Nell's words. She cares about lots of things. In fact, Mum is always telling her that sometimes she cares too much and lets things get to her when she shouldn't. And she knows that maybe she's just said some unkind things but the words that come out of her mouth during these times aren't always words that she means. Not afterwards, anyway. Nell should know that. Also, just because Tally's caring doesn't always look like everyone else's, people think that she's selfish and thoughtless and only-interested-in-herself and that just isn't true.

Mum looks at Dad. "That didn't need to be such a big thing," she tells him. "You could have just explained it more calmly to her."

Dad opens his mouth but when no words come out he shuts it again. Then he shakes his head, pushes his half-eaten meal across the table and closes his eyes, as if he's trying to pretend that he's somewhere else. He does that a lot when Tally gets stressed and she wishes that he didn't. It makes it so much harder when he thinks that she *won't*. He doesn't understand that sometimes, she just *can't*.

Mum stands up and walks across to the sink. "We aren't having Mrs Jessop to stay," she says, keeping her back to the room. "But we do need to look after Rupert, her dog. There's nobody else to take care of him while she's in hospital so Dad said that we'd take him in. Just for a little while, until she's back on her feet." She turns and hands Tally a glass. "Here's your drink."

Tally gives Mum her best smile.

"Where will Rupert sleep?" she asks, taking a sip of her drink. "How long will he stay?"

"Just until Mrs Jessop is better." Mum picks up Dad's bowl and scrapes the food into the bin. His eyes are open now but he doesn't try to stop her and Tally wonders if he secretly hates Granny Lola's Famous Beef Chilli as much as she does. "We'll bring him over here later on this evening and he can sleep in the utility room."

"I'm not going to walk him." Nell pushes back her chair. "I can't be seen out walking a three-legged dog."

Mum sighs. "Nobody is asking you to do anything with the dog, Nell. In fact, I don't want you girls getting too close to him. Apparently he's not that predictable with unfamiliar people, which is why I was slightly surprised that your father offered for us to look after him in the first place."

"I can't do anything right today, obviously," mutters

Dad. "Even trying to help out little old ladies gets me into trouble."

"That's not what I'm saying," snaps Mum. "It's just another complication that we don't exactly need right now."

Tally sits up straighter and beams as widely as she can. "I'll walk him every day! I don't care that he's a complication. Or legless."

Nell makes a snorting noise and Mum hesitates for a brief second before giving Tally a nod. "Let's just see what happens, shall we?"

But Tally is already imagining exactly how it's going to be. She will walk the dog and do all the things that good neighbours have to do while Mrs Jessop is in hospital. She will step up and do her bit (what exactly she's supposed to be stepping on to she isn't entirely sure, but she'll figure it out). She will do the right thing and everyone will be incredibly pleased with her.

Date: Friday 19th September

Situation: We're getting a dog!! (not to keep, just to borrow, but still – it's a dog!)

Anxiety Rating: 2 out of 10. Because dogs make everything better, even Dad getting angry with me and making me feel sad and horrible.

Dear Diary,

I'm so excited about Rupert coming to stay. I LOVE ANIMALS. They are like extra friends that don't judge you. Like, I was watching some dogs in the park yesterday and they just ran up to each other and made friends immediately. No small talk or pretending. I'm jealous of how easy they find it. I've noticed some dogs make themselves look approachable by wagging their tail to show they are friendly – I wish I could do that but I have no tail. The human way of doing this is smiling, so I try and do that when I remember. What else do dogs do to make friends? Oh yes, they sniff each others' rear ends. Maybe I should try that tomorrow. I'll just run around the playground sniffing at all the other kids' behinds. THAT should make me some new friends... Ha ha ha, just kidding!

Animals get misunderstood just like I do. I was

watching *The Cat Goes Or I Do* this morning with these terribly behaved cats. It turns out they're just anxious and misunderstood, and when the owners stop punishing them for their bad behaviour and start treating them differently, with more understanding, and just kindness really, they behave so much better. Teachers should watch more programmes like that. Just saying.

Tally's autism facts: Stimming

Pro: Stimming is a kind of coping mechanism for me. It's when I make movements or sounds, or fiddle. For ages I didn't even know it was called stimming or that a lot of autistic people do it to help themselves feel better. There are good stims that don't do any harm – like beatboxing, which is actually something I need to do because it helps me concentrate. When I'm stressed I do a flappy, clappy thing with my hands – but sometimes I do that when I'm excited too.

Con: The con to stimming is mainly that other people don't usually like me doing it. It irritates or embarrasses them, and they seem to think I'm doing it just to annoy them. Some teachers get so shouty about me humming or fidgeting or whatever, that they make me stressed and want to stim even more – especially because I know I can't. That's when I go to Plan B, which is bad stims. They're more subtle, so other people are less likely to notice them. Biting nails, picking skin, pinching myself, that sort of thing. People don't seem to mind these as much, which is weird because they're much more harmful to me. I get really sore fingers, bruises and other marks all over my skin. I once lost my middle fingernail on my left hand from picking at the skin around my fingers, which led to an infection, which made my nail go black. The doctor said I could have got sepsis which can be fatal. So I reckon that basically means some people might unknowingly cause you to die of a terrible infection rather than let you just do a bit of harmless humming or tapping. In other words, STIMMING SAVES LIVES.

Actually, the more I think about it, the more I reckon that a lot of the cons of autism are not really caused by autism but by how other people react to it. I really do.

CHAPTER 10

"Time to get up, Tally!"

Mum strides into the bedroom and flings back the curtains to reveal yet another bleak, grey day outside.

"Come on, sweetheart. Rise and shine! You don't want to be late for school. Dad's already left for work."

Tally burrows under her duvet and hugs it tighter to her body.

"Close the curtains!" Her shout is smothered by the covers but is still loud enough for Mum to hear. "I'm not ready to wake up yet and it's too bright and you're making it a *bad day*!"

There's a sighing noise and then the sound of the curtains swishing on the rail.

"They're closed," Mum informs her. "It's safe to open your eyes now."

Tally scrunches her eyes tightly closed.

"I can't get out of bed today," she mutters. "You'll have to phone school and tell them that I can't come in."

The mattress dips as Mum sits down. Tally feels Mum's hand on her back, heavy and warm. There's no way she's getting up today, not when it's so cosy and safe in her bed.

"You have to go to school," Mum says calmly. "It's the law. I'll get into trouble if you don't."

Tally shrugs. She's heard this one before and she doesn't even think it's true because that wouldn't be fair. Mum can't force her into school so *she* shouldn't be punished if Tally can't go.

"I'm not well," she says, the duvet muffling her words. "You're not allowed to go to school if you're ill. That's a real rule."

"Tally. There is nothing wrong with you," Mum sighs. "But just in case, I'm going to need you to stick your head out of the covers so that I can check your temperature."

That sounds reasonable enough. Wriggling up the bed, Tally pops her head out of the top and looks at Mum.

"It might be dengue fever," she says, widening her eyes. "I was reading about that yesterday. I definitely can't go into school today if I have that."

Mum tilts her head to one side. "Do you have a rash?" she asks.

Tally sticks her head back under the duvet and has a quick peek at her tummy.

"No," she confirms, pushing herself back up the bed.

"How about your arms and legs? Do they hurt?"

Tally shakes her head and Mum looks at her thoughtfully.

"Hmmm. Well, I know that you haven't been sick because you'd have definitely called for me if you had." She puts the back of her hand against Tally's forehead. "And you don't appear to have a temperature." She stands up. "Thank goodness for that! You haven't got dengue fever after all! Now, do you want to put your school uniform on before you eat your breakfast or afterwards?"

Tally thinks for a second. "Neither."

Mum nods. "OK then. But just so you know, Mrs Jessop's dog is downstairs in the utility room. If you get dressed now then there might be time to say hello to him before you go to school."

She turns and walks out of the room, not even waiting to see what Tally chooses to do.

As quickly as she possibly can, Tally flings off the duvet and pulls on her uniform. Then she runs into the bathroom and splashes a tiny bit of water on her face because Mum has been going on about her making more of an effort now that she's in year seven. Her hairbrush is on the shelf where it always is, almost as untouched as the day it was bought. Tally hates that hairbrush more than anything else. The sensation of the bristles on her head feel like someone is stabbing her with one thousand needles and, on the very rare occasion that Mum insists her hair is brushed, the tears start falling from the very first stroke.

There is no good reason that Tally can think of that would ever justify inflicting that kind of pain and misery on herself. She overheard Nell telling Mum that she looks a state and that it's embarrassing to walk to school with her when she looks like she's got a bird's nest on top of her head, but Tally knows that's just Nell being unkind, and anyway, who is even bothered about what another person's hair looks like? Not her, that's for sure.

Drying her hands on a towel, Tally races out of the bathroom and down the stairs. Mum is in the kitchen buttering toast and Tally's mouth waters at the smell.

"Would you like peanut butter or honey?" Mum asks, as Tally sinks into her chair.

Tally thinks for a moment. Peanut butter is nice, but Mum bought a different brand last week and it had lumpy bits in it, which made Tally feel sick and resulted in the new jar being flung across the kitchen and against the wall. She can still see a few stains on the white paint if she looks closely enough. The jar in Mum's hand is the right brand but she feels a bit suspicious about peanut butter now. There's a chance that it's been ruined for her for ever.

"Honey, please." Tally looks up at Mum. "Can I see the dog now?"

Mum smiles at her. "As soon as you've eaten your breakfast."

She puts the food down on the table and Tally reaches her hand towards the plate before pausing.

"I want to see the dog now." Her voice is quiet. She doesn't really want to be saying the words but she doesn't have a choice. Not really. Mum said that she could see Rupert if she got dressed and she has done that. It's not OK for Mum to just keep making up the rules as she goes along.

"And you can. As soon as you've eaten your toast."

Mum turns away and Tally knows that the conversation is supposed to be over.

"I. Want. To. See. The. Dog. Now." The words spit from between her lips, each one louder than the last. "You have to listen to me."

"I bet I can finish making the packed lunches before you've eaten all that toast up!" Mum's voice is jolly, like this is a game, and for a second, Tally considers taking the easy way out because she's still quite tired. But then Nell stomps into the kitchen and the moment is lost.

"Have you seen my PE kit?" she asks Mum. "I put it in the laundry basket last night."

"I want to see the dog." Tally whispers.

"Have you tried looking in the laundry basket then? Seeing as that's where you last saw it?" Mum cuts some cheese and places it on a slice of bread.

Nell groans. "Muuum! I need it for today! Are you saying that you didn't do any washing last night?"

"I'm going to see the dog now and you can't stop me!" Tally pushes her chair back and starts to stand up, but Mum stops her mid-rise.

"That's quite enough, the pair of you!" She isn't shouting but her voice is hard and Tally sinks back into her seat, her tummy starting to swirl.

Mum makes a neat cut down the middle of the sandwich before looking up at both girls.

"You can see the dog when you've eaten your toast, Tally. That's the rule. And Nell, that's exactly what I'm saying! In between trying to finish my latest painting and shopping for food and cooking supper for everyone and helping with homework, I did not actually get the time to check the contents of the laundry basket." She pauses to catch her breath. "And, as you are fourteen years old and entirely capable of operating a washing machine, I would have thought that you could have done it yourself."

Nell's cheeks flush red. "I'm sorry," she murmurs. "I didn't mean to sound ungrateful. I just really need it for today."

Mum wraps the sandwich in paper and puts it into Tally's lunchbox. "You're forgiven," she tells Nell. "But after school today, you and I are having a lesson on how to do your own laundry."

Nell nods and walks across the room, pulling Mum into a quick hug. "I really am sorry, " she repeats. "I know that you do everything for us and it isn't exactly easy."

Tally rocks back in her seat, pushing the front legs

off the ground. She watches as Mum and Nell hug and then Mum makes another sandwich for Nell while telling her to get her PE kit out of the laundry basket and spray some deodorant on it to mask any sweaty smells, which for some unknown reason makes them both laugh.

It is so easy for Nell. She does something wrong and then she says sorry and it's all OK again. Tally *can* say sorry, but sometimes it just doesn't sound right and so she tries to *show* that she's sorry rather than just say a word.

The toast is going cold on the plate in front of her and it doesn't look very appealing any more. But Mum made it for her and she'll be sad and upset if it doesn't get eaten. Slowly, taking the tiniest of bites, Tally forces herself to eat. Each mouthful lands heavily in her swirling tummy, eddying and spinning around like Nell's PE kit should have been doing in the washing machine, but Tally keeps going.

"It wouldn't have killed you to say sorry too," Nell hisses, as she sits down at the table.

Tally looks at the congealed honey as it solidifies on the toast and tries not to feel sick. She *is* saying sorry. It's not her fault that Nell can't see that.

Finally, breakfast is over and the table is cleared.

"You can go and say hello to Rupert now," says Mum. "He's in the utility room and I've dug out your old stair-gate from the garage, so he can't get near you. Just don't go too close – he's very unpredictable."

The utility room is next to the kitchen, with a back door that leads into the garden. As Nell and Tally approach, they can hear a panting sound and then a padding of paws as Rupert plods across the floor to greet them.

"Hello, Rupert," says Tally softly, walking straight up to the gate. "Did you have a good sleep last night?"

"Don't go any closer," warns Nell, hanging back. "Remember what Mum said."

"I bet it was strange sleeping at our house, wasn't it?" continues Tally, ignoring her sister. "I was going to sleep at my friend Layla's house once, but then I changed my mind because I wouldn't be in my bed and I like sleeping in my bed best of all. It smells right."

"Talking of smell, this dog pongs!" complains Nell, waving her hand under her nose. "Why did we have to get stuck with a gross three-legged dog, that's what I want to know? Rosa's family just got the cutest little spaniel and it's adorable. Not like this lanky animal."

"Don't listen to her," Tally tells Rupert. "I never do."

She leans closer and puts her hand on the stair-gate. "I bet you don't like being imprisoned behind here, do you, boy? I bet you'd like to run free!"

"Tally! Don't you even think about—" begins Nell, but before she can finish, Rupert suddenly throws himself at the gate. Nell grabs hold of Tally and pulls her out of reach as the dog smacks his head into the metal bars, growling loudly.

"Mum!"

Mum's footsteps pound out of the kitchen.

"Come away, girls," she calls. "What on earth happened?"

"That awful dog tried to attack us!" cries Nell, still clinging on to Tally. "Look! He's trying to get out and bite us!"

Mum mutters something rude under her breath and ushers them away from the door. "Are you both OK?" she asks, sweeping her gaze across her daughters. "Did he hurt you?"

Tally shakes her head and opens her mouth to speak but Nell beats her to it.

"I could feel his hot, fetid breath on my arm," she shudders. "I swear, he's got rabies or something. I'm sure I saw foam coming out of his mouth."

Mum frowns. "I'm sure he hasn't got rabies, Nell. But all the same, I'm not having a dangerous dog in the house. You girls go to school and I'll phone Dad. It was his brilliant suggestion to bring Rupert here, so he can deal with this. That dog can find another place to live."

CHAPTER 11

It's cold outside. Nell strides ahead as usual, tapping at her phone while Tally lingers behind, wishing that she'd put her gloves on. Mum was in a proper state about the dog and she didn't give Tally enough time to get ready before she was pushing them out of the door, muttering that her day was busy enough as it was, without having to deal with difficult men and difficult dogs and difficult children. Tally isn't sure what Nell did this morning but she's obviously done something wrong, which isn't that surprising because she's been getting more and more moody lately.

Probably because she's a teenager.

Nell is waiting when Tally finally reaches the pedestrian crossing.

"Is it possible for you to walk any slower?" she asks.

"I'm pretty sure I just saw a snail overtake you."

The green man starts flashing and Nell marches across the road. Tally dashes after her but once they have reached the safety of the pavement, she pauses.

"I think that I could be a little bit slower, " she says, lifting one foot off the ground, as if she's moonwalking. "If I walk like this."

She takes an exaggerated step, making her foot hover in the air for as long as she can hold her balance. "I could probably enter a slow race, don't you think, Nell? They're an actual thing, you know? The winner is the very last person to reach the finish line but you can't ever stand still – you have to keep moving all the time." She places her foot down and lifts up the other, very carefully and deliberately. "I could totally beat a snail in the slow race, couldn't I, Nell? Let's find one and then I'll show you."

Nell makes a groaning sound.

"I'm serious, Tally. We're going to be late for registration and then we'll both be in trouble, and you don't want to get a detention, do you?"

This gets Tally's attention. The thing that she is most afraid of is getting a detention. She shakes her head and slams her foot on to the ground. "Let's go. How much time have we got?"

Nell looks at her phone. "Eight minutes. And then we're literally doomed. We're going to have to run."

Tally tightens the straps on her rucksack. "OK. Just don't go too fast because you know that I'm a bit slow at running."

Nell nods and takes off, her long legs striding down the pavement. Tally takes a deep breath, shakes out her arms and then, just as she's about to launch forward, glances down at the ground.

"Stop!"

The shout is loud and Nell screeches to a halt, swivelling to face her sister.

"What's wrong?" she calls, jogging back to where Tally is standing, one foot trembling in mid-air. "Why aren't you moving?"

Tally points and Nell looks down in disbelief.

"You're having a laugh, aren't you?"

"No." Tally frowns. "There's nothing to laugh at. Look. It's the worm. It's come back and I nearly trampled on it."

"I wish you had trampled on it," snaps Nell, her face unkind. "Then it wouldn't keep being such a problem."

Tally stares at her in disbelief. "How can you be so

horrible? You are a very unkind girl, Nell Adams. First you were nasty to poor Rupert and Mum is going to send him away when he didn't even do anything, and now you don't care if this little, defenceless worm gets trodden on and killed."

"It's a worm!" howls Nell. "Why would I care about a horrible worm?"

"You're a horrible worm!" shouts Tally. "And I hate you!"

Nell's face goes tight. "Oh, here we go. Tally doesn't get what she wants and so she throws a temper tantrum. Well, guess what? I'm sick of it."

Nell has just said a forbidden word. Tally doesn't have tantrums. Tantrums are something that spoilt children do to get their own way; something that you have a choice about. Tally would never, not in a million years, *choose* to be so scared and anxious that she can't control what she says or what she does. It's not like any of this makes her feel good about herself – it's the exact opposite and Nell should know that.

Nell takes a step forward and leans into Tally's face. "I've had enough of you always getting to behave like a little brat, whenever you feel like it. We all tiptoe around, terrified about upsetting you in case you have a meltdown because apparently you're *different* and you find things difficult and we all have to understand when you say things that hurt us or when you kick off and ruin yet another family day out or mealtime."

Tally steps back, not liking Nell's breath on her skin. It smells like Weetabix and Tally thinks that, probably, Nell did not clean her teeth this morning after she'd eaten her breakfast, and it is behaviour like this that makes Mum mutter about *difficult children*. Nell will be sorry when they next go to the dentist and she has to have all her teeth pulled out, which is one of Tally's greatest fears and the only reason that she puts a gross, bristly toothbrush anywhere near her mouth.

She starts humming to herself, trying to block out Nell's spiteful words, because if she lets them in then they're going to have to come back out again and they aren't going to do that quietly. She can't risk losing control out here, where anyone could see her.

"You think that just because you're different you can do whatever you want." Nell hasn't finished yet. "Well, I've got news for you, little sister. I'm done. Mum and Dad can punish me however they like, but I am done with being your babysitter. You're not the only one who's important around here, OK? So get over yourself and stop making life so difficult for everyone."

A car speeds past, the tyres making a squelching noise against the road. Up ahead, a mum pushes a pram towards the park and Tally can hear the baby crying. Maybe it doesn't like being strapped into the seat. Maybe it doesn't even want to go to the park, but nobody thought to ask it because it's just a baby and nobody seems to care what babies think.

"I'm going to school now," warns Nell. "You can come with me or you can stay here and get a detention."

Tally understands how choices work, and this one just isn't fair. If she goes with Nell then the worm will die, but if she saves the worm then she'll be late for school. When Mum asks her to choose there is always an option that sounds good, but the choices that Nell have given her are both bad and that's not how it works.

"I don't want to get into trouble," she whispers.

Nell nods approvingly. "Good. If we really run then we might just make it on time. Let's go."

"Being squished to death would be really, truly horrible though." Tally stares at the ground and bites her lip.

"I'm counting to three and then I'm going, with or without you." Nell glares at Tally. "One."

Tally jiggles from foot to foot.

"Two."

There is a crack in the pavement that she didn't notice before. If the worm falls down there then it will be lost for ever and it'll never get back to its worm family and that might make it sad. Although if it has a despicable, appalling, uncaring, wormy big sister, then maybe it wouldn't mind too much.

"Two and a half." Nell's voice is rock-hard underneath, with a smattering of worry on top. "I'm really serious, Tally. I'll leave you on your own and you know how scared you get when there's nobody to look after you."

It's true. Tally hates being outside alone. There are just too many dangers. Fast cars and scary strangers and what if someone drops a bomb right where she's walking or a tree gets blown down in the wind and hits her on the head? She heard about that on the news last week when there was a storm. Someone went out to walk their dog and a tree branch fell on top of them and they had to be airlifted to hospital. At least the dog was OK, thank goodness.

"Two and three quarters," snaps Nell. "Last chance. It's me or the stupid worm."

Tally crouches down and looks at the worm. It looks

kind. It doesn't look like it's ever done anything to hurt anyone in its entire life, and yes, it is a *tiny* bit not very clever because it keeps coming back out here on to the pavement where anything can happen, but sometimes it can be hard to remember what you're supposed to be saying or how you're supposed to be behaving and you just have to do the thing that pops into your head.

Besides, Nell has asked her to choose between her and the worm and that choice is easy. The worm hasn't just said a whole load of nasty things to her.

"Three! I'm going." Nell turns around and starts walking away. "And don't you dare tell Mum and Dad about this because they'll just blame me."

"They should blame you," murmurs Tally, as Nell storms off in the direction of school. "Because you are a hateful person and if I get squashed or exploded then it'll be all your fault."

Then, with her heart beating fast in her chest, she picks up the worm and transports it to the safety of the grass verge.

"Please stay there," she instructs it as she lowers it to the ground. "I know it's hard but you have got to follow the rules, OK? No more wiggling on to the pavement. I do not want to see you out here again, is that understood?"

And then, even though she hates running and normally will think of a thousand excuses to get out of any kind of exercise, she sprints down the road as fast as she possibly can, determined to get to school before the bell rings.

CHAPTER 12

Tally is watching the clouds zip across the sky. It's the only good thing about her maths class — her seat is right next to the window and she can spend the entire lesson imagining that she's out there, feeling the wind on her face, instead of in here where the air is hot and stuffy and stale.

The bell rings and her whole body goes rigid. She's been at Kingswood Academy for a few weeks now, but she's not sure that she'll ever get used to the shrill, piercing sound of the school bell, and no matter how many times she tries to remind herself that it's coming, it always startles her.

"Weirdo Adams is scared of the bell! Look — she nearly wet herself that time!" Luke's voice trickles into her ears from the desk behind and Tally can hear the sniggers of the people around him.

Tally doesn't turn around but her cheeks are flaming a bright, hot red. He does this every single lesson and each time it seems like he's getting louder and louder.

"Don't forget to hand in your homework as you leave," calls Mrs Sheridan. "Anyone who hasn't done it can expect a lunchtime detention – you know the rules, people!"

Tally reaches into her bag and pulls out the sheet of maths questions that they were given last week. She finished it last night, even though she didn't want to do it and Mum ended up sitting with her for ages, trying to get her to pick up the pen. It was Mum's fault that it took so long. If she hadn't told Tally to do her homework before supper then it wouldn't have been a problem. Mum must have been tired because she wouldn't normally make such a silly mistake.

Outside, the corridor is busy. Tally looks at her timetable and sees that her next lesson is PE. She knows how to get to the games department on her own, which is a relief because, after Luke's humiliating comment, she doesn't particularly want to have to tag along with anyone else from her maths class today.

Everyone seems to be going in the opposite direction

to the way that she needs to go, and Tally flattens her body against the wall, watching as kids pour by her. They remind her of shoals of fish, all following the leader without wondering where they might be heading or what they might be expected to do when they get there. A group of girls push past her, giggling and shouting over each other. They make it look so easy. Maybe life *is* simple if you're the same as everyone else. Maybe they don't have to plan everything in advance and figure out what they might say in reply to a hundred questions or what their face is supposed to look like when they feel excited or happy or surprised or scared.

Maybe they never feel scared.

The crowd starts to thin out and Tally sees Layla walking down the corridor towards her. She raises her hand to wave and call out like she usually would, but then lowers it quickly, pressing herself back into the lockers and trying to blend in. Layla is deep in conversation with another girl. Tally recognizes her from their PE class but she doesn't know her. She didn't think that Layla knew her either.

The girls walk past and Tally peels herself away from the lockers and follows them. She can't hear what they're talking about, but the sound of Layla's laughter floats back down the corridor. Tally grits her teeth and tries to focus on the posters that are taped to the walls, but she can't stop the thoughts from flooding into her head.

Layla has a new friend. She might like her more than she likes Tally and who could blame her, because it's probably safe to assume that nobody calls this girl Weirdo Adams. Tally knows exactly what's going to happen next – she can see it all now, like it's a movie in her head. Layla and the new girl are going to start spending more and more time together and at first, Layla will try to include Tally and say that they can all hang out together with Lucy and Ayesha as one big group. Only that will be a lie because what will really be happening is that Layla and this girl will be doing stuff on their own and becoming best friends and Tally will be left out because five people is an odd number and it can never work – everybody knows that.

If Layla doesn't want to be Tally's best friend then Tally doesn't want anything to do with her either. She isn't going to beg her to be friends. Not when Layla is obviously a traitor and a betrayer and doesn't even care about Tally in the first place. Not if she's happy to hang out with a cuckoo-girl, who is clearly just waiting for the opportunity to push Tally out of the friendship nest and move in to claim Layla for herself.

"Tally! There you are! I was looking for you." Layla has stopped at the entrance to the changing rooms and is peering back up the corridor, a smile on her face. "We've got hockey now – I can't wait!"

The other girl has disappeared through the door without a word. Tally looks warily at Layla.

"Will you be my partner if we have to go in pairs?"

Layla laughs. "Of course! We always go together, don't we?"

"Who was that girl you were talking to?" Tally can hear that her voice sounds hard and she doesn't mean to be unkind to Layla, but she has to know.

Layla looks puzzled for a second but before she can reply, footsteps pound down the corridor and Miss Perkins strides around the corner.

"Girls! This is not the time for idle chit-chat. Get in there and get changed. Move it!"

Of all the teachers at Kingswood Academy, Tally is most afraid of this one. Miss Perkins is young and trendy and she absolutely loves the sporty kids. If you can kick a football or run super-fast then it doesn't matter if you are the meanest kid alive – Miss Perkins will love you. Which means that she does not love Tally, not one little bit. Miss Perkins does not believe that anyone who dislikes sport is worth knowing, and you could put her in a room with Albert Einstein or Michelangelo or Amadeus Mozart or even Taylor Swift and if they couldn't shoot a basketball hoop then she would scowl at them and probably say that they were a waste of space. And then she'd make them sit on the benches with the other dorky kids and untangle the skipping ropes, while the popular kids got to play games.

The girls' changing rooms are possibly one of Tally's very worst places in the entire world, but unless she wants a detention then there is no choice but to do as she's been told. Taking a deep breath and trying to pull in as much clean air as possible, she avoids Miss Perkins' hard stare and follows Layla through the door.

Inside, it is just the same as always. Girls are packed in around the edge of the room, in various states of undress as if they don't care who sees them in their underwear. Bags are thrown on the floor, and when Tally finally has to release the air in her lungs and breathe in again, the air smells mouldy and wet and sweet all at the same time.

It is too bright and too noisy and too dirty.

It is completely too much.

Layla pushes her way through the room to the corner, where there is just enough space for the two of them to sit down if they squish into a gap between two other girls. Tally scowls when she sees that one of them is the girl who Layla was talking to on the way to class. She's already out of her uniform, and as Tally sits down she reaches across to grab her bag, the skin on her leg brushing against Tally's arm. Tally flinches, hoping that the girl won't notice. She's already feeling stressed out and the last thing she wants is for anyone to touch her when she isn't expecting it.

"I haven't got a disease, you know!"

She has clearly failed to be discreet.

"What are you on about?" calls a girl on the other side of the room is looking over at them. "What disease?"

"I said, *I haven't got a disease*." The girl next to Tally raises her voice. "My leg just bumped against her arm and she started rubbing it, like I've got germs or something."

"Well, that's a bit rude," says the second girl, and when Tally looks up, there seem to be hundreds of pairs of eyes boring into her.

"Oh, it's her," says someone else. "I wouldn't pay any

attention to what she says, Jasmine. She's in my maths class – she's always saying weird stuff!"

"I didn't say—" Tally stutters, but they've all raised their eyebrows at each other and turned away.

"Just leave it," whispers Layla. "They'll have forgotten about it by the end of the lesson."

The door opens and Miss Perkins strides in.

"Hurry up, girls!" She glances around the room, her eyes narrowing when she sees Tally still sitting on the bench, fully dressed. "Today we will be starting a new rule. If you aren't all outside in three minutes then every single one of you will be in lunchtime detention."

The reaction is instant.

"That's not fair!" calls someone. "Some of us have been ready for ages."

"We shouldn't be punished because of the people who are too slow," adds another. "It should be them that gets the detention, not us."

Miss Perkins shakes her head. "It's called teamwork, girls. You are only as efficient as the slowest member of the group. I expect to see all of you outside in three minutes and the clock is starting now."

She stalks out and the changing room erupts in a flurry of activity.

"Aleksandra! Can you pass my trainers?"

"Has anyone seen my PE top? It was here a moment ago, I know it was!"

"How much time have we got left? Hurry up, everyone!"

Tally sits still as all around her, girls throw their clothes on the floor and yank PE kits over their heads. School shoes are kicked under the benches and bags lie open, their contents spilling across the floor. It's like watching a film that has been sped up and she leans her head against the wall and closes her eyes, letting the noise wash over her in waves and trying not to feel like she's drowning.

What did that girl mean about her saying weird stuff? She always makes sure that she only says what everyone else is saying but nobody calls *them* weird.

"Come on, Tally!" hisses Layla, standing up to pull on her shorts. "You heard Miss Perkins – we all have to be outside together, on time."

Tally blinks and the room comes back into focus. The very last thing that she wants to do is to follow Miss Perkins' instructions, but she knows that she has to. Opening her PE bag, she pulls out her shorts and then she stands up and puts them on underneath her skirt.

Once the shorts are on, she takes off her skirt and jumper and tie and starts to unbutton the shirt. The top button is always really stiff and her fingers scrabble to push it through the hole, but she gets there eventually although it takes precious moments of time. Then once the buttons are all undone, she huddles forward towards her knees and pulls her PE top over her head. There might be some girls in year seven who don't seem to care if anyone sees them getting changed but Tally is not one of them.

"Come on!" yells Jasmine. "We've got less than one minute!"

Tally pushes her arms out of her sleeves and looks up. Most of the girls are already racing out of the door and the ones who are left all seem to be glaring at her.

"If you make us late then we'll all get in trouble." Jasmine stands up and puts her hands on her hips. "Please hurry up!"

"She won't be late," says Layla, coming to the rescue. "Look! She's only got to put her trainers on. You all go out and we'll be right behind you."

Jasmine stares down at Tally and then glances across the room. Tally sees the look that flashes over her face as she makes eye contact with the remaining girls. She knows what that means. They think that she's going to let them down. They think that it will be all her fault if they get detentions.

"I'm coming!" As quickly as she can, Tally yanks on one trainer and then the other before springing up and giving a quick twirl. "Look – I'm ready! Let's go and play hockey! I can't wait!"

Jasmine turns back and rewards Tally with a smile. It's a very tiny smile but it's still a *good thing*. Maybe it means that she isn't planning on stealing Tally's best friend, after all.

"Come on then!"

Layla pushes past Tally and heads towards the changing room door, following everyone else outside.

"Hurry up, Tally!" she calls. "We've got about twenty seconds left."

Tally takes one step forward and then stops abruptly. There is something inside her trainer and there's no way that she can walk with it stabbing into her foot.

"Tally!" The cry comes from outside. "We've got ten seconds!"

She takes another step. It hurts. It hurts really, really badly.

"Come on!" Layla's voice sounds frustrated and

maybe even a little bit cross and Tally's heart starts to speed up.

Another step. Then another. Her body feels like it's on fire. Something is poking into the delicate skin on the sole of her foot and it feels like a needle or a pin or a very, very sharp splinter.

Tally wants to cry but there isn't enough time to let the tears flow and then hide them again so they are just going to have to stay where they are, brimming against the backs of her eyes and making it hard to see properly.

"I can't let everyone get a detention," she whispers to herself as she hobbles across the tiled floor. "I just can't."

She pushes open the door and daylight hits her eyes, making her blink. In front of her, the rest of the girls are lining up in teams. Miss Perkins is handing out hockey sticks and she doesn't notice that Tally is a few seconds over the deadline.

"Over here," hisses Layla, giving Tally a small wave. "Stand behind me."

"We're going to start off by running two laps of the field!" yells Miss Perkins. "You will carry your hockey stick and anyone who doesn't make it round in less than eight minutes will be spending their lunchtime tidying the PE cupboard."

Tally has seen inside the PE cupboard and it's a complete state. And she still remembers what Mr Kennedy said on their first day, about a year seven getting lost in there for one whole hour. She knows that he was joking – she's not stupid – but still, she hasn't been able to forget about it. Some nights, the PE cupboard haunts her dreams.

Miss Perkins blows her whistle and the girls at the front of the line start running. Tally inches forward, taking the hockey stick when it is handed to her, and then she runs too. Every single step feels like agony and the feeling in her foot gets worse and worse until she can't think about anything except the pain.

But she does not stop and she does not cry. Not once. Because the girls were pleased with her for getting changed on time and it made them forget that they think she's weird. If she keeps running then she's exactly like they are, and people like it when you behave like they do.

Even if it hurts more than you can tell them.

CHAPTER 13

Mum is shouting at Dad as Tally and Nell walk back into the house. Tally hadn't known if Nell would even be waiting for her after this morning's fight, but Nell has obviously forgotten about the worm and how angry she was because she didn't say a word about it all the way home. Tally hasn't forgotten though.

"I'm not happy about this!" yells Mum, as they push through the door. "Surely there's someone else who can have him until she's out of the hospital?"

Dad walks into the hall, looking tired.

"There's nobody else," he calls over his shoulder. "Hello, you two. Have you had a good day?"

Nell grunts something unintelligible in response and hangs up her coat before heading into the kitchen. Tally stands still and stares at Dad. What sort of a question is that?

"Have I had a good day?" she repeats, dropping her bag on to the floor. "How can you even ask me that when you know that I've had to go to school?"

Dad smiles gently. "It *is* possible to have a good day at school, " he tells her. "I've been reliably informed that it can happen, every now and again!"

Tally closes her eyes briefly and when she opens them again, they are blazing with fury.

"You don't know anything!" she snarls at Dad. "You haven't got a clue what it's like for me. And you don't even care! You just want to make stupid jokes and pretend that everything is fine when it isn't!"

"Hey, hey – what's going on?" Mum comes into the hall, wiping her hands on a towel. "What's the problem?" She's got paint on her nose and, usually, this would make Tally laugh, but she hasn't got any laughter inside her, not today. Not after everything.

Tally points at Dad. "*He* is the problem."

Dad makes a noise in his throat. "Now hang on just one minute. All I did was ask if you'd had a good day. I hardly think that makes me—"

"You don't even know what happened to me today!" screeches Tally, kicking off her shoes and throwing herself on to the ground.

"Oh, here we go – another tantrum," mutters Dad. He says it quietly but Tally hears him, just like she always hears everything that anyone ever says about her, because she isn't deaf and she has ears.

"I'm not having a tantrum, you horrible man! Why can't you understand me? I'm not being naughty or like a baby and you should know that by now!" she yells. "And I wasn't having a tantrum this morning either, for your information. I was just trying to save a worm and Nell, your daughter, who I completely hate, didn't care and ran away and left me all on my own!"

"Nell left you alone?" Mum's face goes hard. "I'll deal with that in a minute. Is that what's got you so upset or is there something else?"

"It's everything!" screams Tally. "And I am not *upset*! I am *hurt* and that's different but nobody even knows. And if Nell gets hurt then she gets all the sympathy and people are sorry for her and she gets to lie down on the sofa with a blanket and be looked after but when I get hurt then everyone just says, 'Oh, it's only Tally having a TANTRUM and she's a bit upset,' but I'm not upset."

She stops and heaves in a huge breath. "I. Am. Hurt."

"And we want to help you," says Dad, leaning against

the wall. "But you have to stop shouting at us."

Tally's brain floods with worry. He's telling her what she has to do and now she can't do it, which means that she might be shouting for the rest of the night.

"I don't have to do anything you say!" she wails, picking up her shoe and flinging it down the hallway. "I can say whatever I want, even if you all think that I'm *weird* – because I have a voice and I'm allowed to use it!"

"Nobody said that you were weird or that you aren't allowed to use your voice." Dad looks confused. "I think we're all painfully aware that you have a voice right now. The people in the next street are probably in no doubt that you have a voice that is in full working order."

"I'm sorry that you were hurt," says Mum, shaking her head at Dad as she crouches down next to Tally. "It sounds like you've had a tricky day. Would you like to lie on the sofa with a blanket?"

Tally pulls her knees closer to her chin and wraps her arms around her legs.

"No."

Mum tries again. "How about a nice hot drink and a biscuit, then? That might help."

Tally shakes her head.

"Just leave her," murmurs Dad. "Remember what the doctor told us? She said that sometimes Tally might just need a bit of space."

Mum hesitates and then stands up. "I'm going to go and clear up the kitchen," she says. "I've left my paints everywhere and it's a real mess. You know where I am if you want me, sweetheart."

Tally lowers her face into her knees and waits until she hears the kitchen door closing. Then, as quietly as she can, she tiptoes upstairs and into her bedroom. The tiger mask is hanging from the end of her bed and she pulls it on, inhaling the familiar smell.

And then she walks across the room and looks in the mirror, staring at the strong, powerful creature in front of her. At the brave, magnificent Tiger Girl who doesn't feel pain and doesn't get hurt and doesn't worry about what other people think of her. If only she could be this girl all of the time then nobody would ever say unkind things or give each other *the look* that everybody always gives when she's around. The look that means she's done something wrong again, even if she doesn't know what it is or how not to do it next time.

She stares and stares at her reflection until the Tiger Girl goes blurry and then she walks downstairs and along the hallway until she reaches the door to the utility room. Rupert is lying down behind the stair-gate. He looks different, and the muzzle that is fitted snugly over his face wasn't there this morning.

"Don't be scared," Tally whispers. "Can you see me?"

She used to ask this question all the time when she was younger. Every time she put on the mask. And she was never quite sure what she wanted the answer to be. Whether it was better to be hidden or to be seen. Whether it was better to be Tiger Girl or Tally.

Rupert peers at her from above the muzzle and then slowly lumbers into a standing position, keeping his distance from the tiger that is filling the doorway. They stare at each other for a while, both hidden behind their masks.

"He's going to have to stay for a bit longer." Dad comes up behind Tally. "So we got him that muzzle, just to make sure that he's safe. Mum isn't very happy about it, as you can probably tell."

"He isn't dangerous," Tally says, resting her hands on the top of the gate.

"No," agrees Dad. "Not any more. But he's still quite unpredictable, so don't go in there with him, please. Do you want that drink now?"

Tally nods. She doesn't want a drink but she's got an important conversation to have with Rupert and she doesn't need Dad to hear her.

"My foot really hurt today," she says, as Dad disappears into the kitchen. "And nobody was even a tiny bit bothered. But you understand, don't you? Because you've only got three legs and that must have hurt quite a lot."

Her eyes prickle and she scrunches her eyes up hard because tigers don't cry, not even when they're thinking about how terrible it is that Rupert has lost a leg and they can't bear to think about how sad he must feel about it.

"They don't get it," she says softly. "They all think you're angry and dangerous. But I know that you're not. You're just scared, aren't you, boy?"

Rupert takes a tentative step forward, hopping on his one back leg.

"You're going to have to wear the muzzle for a little while," Tally tells him. "I hope it isn't too uncomfortable. I'll make them see that you aren't a bad dog though. I promise."

Rupert growls, a quiet rumbling noise that comes from deep within his chest. Inside the tiger mask, Tally smiles and blinks away the tears. They are going to understand each other perfectly.

Date: Tuesday 30th September

Situation: A terrible PE lesson and then a meltdown at home.

Anxiety Rating: 9

Dear Diary,

I'm supposed to be in bed but there's no way that I can go to sleep right now. Not with everything churning around in my head.

I've had another utterly terrible day. It was bad enough having what felt like a drawing pin (and turned out to be an apple pip) in my trainer, gouging into my foot, as I was forced to do laps round a field, but also my potential "best friend" low-key abandoned me.

To add to that, I was also having the odd flash of terrorizing thought that the worm I rescued this morning had innocently slithered back on to the pavement and got squished by a careless person. The thought makes me feel physically sick.

Sometimes, just sometimes, I wish I was like anybody else: someone who doesn't care if there's something in their shoe, gets over it when they lose their best friend and can easily brush away the worm thoughts (if they would even have them in first place, which they probably wouldn't). What I'm saying is I'm just like one mouldy blueberry in a packet. I'm not sure I'm wanted by the others as I make the whole packet look bad. I never fit in with anything or anyone. I feel like a key that doesn't fit properly in the lock.

Anyway, you're probably wondering what the whole deal with Layla is. To be honest, I am too. I don't want to be the kind of friend who doesn't let her friends hang out with other kids and gets jealous if they do, but I just feel she has forgotten about me. What if she has? What if she's bored of me? My friendships mean everything to me and the thought of having to do all that awful socializing to make new ones fills me with dread. I'm never going to sleep tonight.

Tally's autism facts: Sleep

Sleep can be an issue for a lot of autistic people. I hate going to sleep. It feels like the minute I go to sleep the exciting side of the world wakes up and I miss out on that. Even miniscule things like knowing that Mum and Dad are downstairs watching TV makes me feel as if my part of the world has to stop but the rest has kept on going. It makes me feel pretty lonely sometimes and then I start worrying about things.

Sometimes, to help me sleep, I start arranging my soft toys in order of their birthdays and I say goodnight to all of them in alphabetical order. I call these my special tasks – things I have to do in order for everything to be OK. Then I might realize that I've left three of them downstairs. I really won't want to get out of my warm cosy bed but try as I might to ignore the discomfort of leaving three of my toys out, I won't be able to. So I'll drag myself out of bed and go and fetch them. Then I will have to rearrange the whole line to fit them in properly. And then I have to start the saying goodnight ritual all over again from the beginning.

CHAPTER 14

"I don't know why you can't walk to school on your own," grumbles Nell as they walk down the street. "I had to do it when I started in year seven."

Tally isn't listening. She can hear Nell bleating away like a lamb but she isn't letting the words go in through her ears. She's always been able to do this, for as long as she can remember. Not listen if she doesn't want to. It's quite a useful skill to have.

She stares down at the pavement, jumping over the cracks and keeping an eye out for worms. She doesn't expect to see any today – the rain has stopped and all the worms are safely inside their earth tunnels, but she looks, just to be on the safe side. Besides, looking at the ground is more interesting than looking at nasty Nell.

"You need to develop some independence. You're not

going to have me looking out for you for the rest of your life." Nell stabs at the button on the pedestrian crossing with her bright-blue fingernail. "It's ridiculous, the way everyone treats you like you're made of glass."

Tally looks up.

"It would be terrible to be made of glass," she says, as the green man starts flashing. "Imagine if someone bumped into you or you fell over. You'd break bits off yourself and they'd never go back on."

"A bit like that horrible dog with its three legs," mutters Nell. "No wonder you like him so much – you're both broken."

Time and Tally both stand still in shock because Nell has gone way too far this time. There are lots of things that Tally is worried about, but this is her biggest fear of all and it's a fear that just won't go away, no matter how hard she tries. Whether she's up on the roof of the garden shed or lying in bed at night. Whenever someone gives *the look*. When things go wrong and she knows that it's all her fault. The voice in Tally's head, whispering that she is broken, has never sounded like Nell before today, but she knows that it will now, for ever and ever.

"That's not true." Tally stands in the middle of the

road. "I'm not broken and neither is Rupert. I'm not, Nell! Take it back!"

"Don't just stand there!" Nell grabs Tally's arm and hauls her across the road. "You're going to get run over!"

"Get off me!" yells Tally, wrenching her arm away. "You've been in a bad mood for days, ever since Mum found out that you abandoned me to walk to school on my own, but you shouldn't take it out on me because it's not my fault and I'm not broken!"

Nell's mouth drops open.

"Mum didn't *find out*, Tally. You told her!"

"It's the same thing." Tally glares at her sister. "And you deserved to have your iPad taken away because I could have been taken hostage and then you'd have been an only child. And how would you have felt then?"

"Relieved." Nell yanks her gloves out of her pocket and pulls them on. "Now hurry up, because I am not going to be late for registration today."

Tally plants her feet slightly apart. "I'm not going anywhere until you take it back."

Nell huffs, making clouds of breath in the cold air. "Fine. Whatever. I take it back, OK? Are you happy now?"

Tally shakes her head. "I am absolutely not happy,"

she informs Nell. "Because I have a spiteful, unpleasant, malevolent big sister who thinks it's OK to say whatever she wants to me. And you hurt my feelings."

Nell shrugs. "I'm sorry I hurt your feeling with my – what was it? Malevolence?"

"My *feelings*," Tally reminds her. "Plural. I have lots of feelings and you have hurt pretty much all of them."

They walk in silence up the road, Tally dragging her feet as slowly as she dares. She doesn't want to be late either but she can't let Nell think that she's won. Up ahead, two older girls are leaning against the wall by the school gate. They stare at Nell and Tally as they get closer and the sound of their feet tapping against the bricks makes Tally slow down even more. They straighten up as Nell draws level with them and Tally sees one girl glance at the other before they both step into Nell's path and start to speak. She's too far behind to hear their words but the wind carries the sound of their screeching laughter towards her and she watches as they knock Nell's bag from her shoulder before turning away and sauntering casually in the direction of the school.

Nell stands still for a moment and then picks up her bag before glancing back over her shoulder.

"Can you try to look normal, just for a change?" she asks, narrowing her eyes as Tally walks towards her. "Would it really be so difficult for you?"

Tally peers down at her body, feeling puzzled. There doesn't seem to be anything unusual about her clothes or her coat. There's a bit of mud on her shoes from when she went out in the garden this morning and clambered up on to the shed, but other than that she looks perfectly ordinary.

A group of kids approach and Tally steps to the side, letting them go past. One of the boys has a rucksack with a picture of a zombie on the front, blood dripping from its mouth and hands outstretched. Tally looks away. She hates zombies. Up until last year she had a Peppa Pig rucksack, but she isn't daft enough to think that she could bring it with her to Kingswood Academy. Her head would definitely get flushed down the toilet if she showed up wearing that. Nell said so.

"Just stop making that face!" hisses Nell, taking a step closer. "People are going to stare at you."

"What face?" Tally frowns. She isn't doing anything. "This is just my face."

"No, it isn't." Nell is getting really cross now. "You're pulling odd expressions and it makes you look ridiculous.

Just be normal, please."

A girl zooms past on her bike, nearly knocking Tally off the pavement. She tightens her grip on the boring-but-normal red rucksack that is the exact same one that Layla and Lucy both have, and turns to look at Nell.

"This is *my face*," she says, giving Nell one more chance. Nobody should ever say that she isn't a forgiving kind of girl. "I was born with this face and I can't make it look any different."

"Why can't you be ordinary?" pleads Nell. "For just one day."

"Maybe you'd prefer it if I looked like this?" asks Tally, making her voice sweet. She holds her hands up in front of her and when she releases them, her mouth is stretched into the widest grin imaginable. "Ta-dah! This is my *happy face*! Is that any better?"

"Tally. Just stop it." Nell glances about nervously. "Go into school."

Tally whips her hands up again, holding them in front of her for the tiniest of moments before flinging them out and revealing her new expression.

"Or how about this one? I call it *sad face*. This is the face that you have to show if you are ever unhappy or hurt. If you don't show this face then how can anyone possibly know that you're feeling bad? If you're feeling sad inside but you don't put this face on then it's your own silly fault if the whole world thinks that you're fine."

"I don't know what you're playing at, Tally – but it isn't funny, OK?" Nell glares at her. "I'm going into school now and you can pull whatever face you want."

Tally stands and watches Nell storm off before making her own way towards the main entrance. On the outside, her face is calm and still, but inside she is shaking because Nell didn't have to be so unkind. Which must mean that she wanted to be horrible to Tally for no reason at all.

The first lesson is drama and Tally is still feeling miserable when she walks into the studio. And then she sees Ayesha and Lucy deep in conversation with awful Luke and the morning becomes officially terrible.

Any hopes that Tally may have had about Luke becoming nicer over the summer are long gone. He has changed, that's for sure, but not in a good way. He's had his haircut, and he's obviously started wearing deodorant because Tally can smell him from across the other side of the room. He's got taller and the way that he moves is different too. He doesn't really walk any more – it's more like he struts around the school. He reminds Tally of a chicken.

A chicken who all of the girls seem to think is absolutely fascinating, for some completely bizarre reason.

"Right then, year seven! Let's get started!"

Mrs Jarman swoops in through the door, her eyes roaming the room. They pause on Tally for a second and shine with a brief smile before flicking across to the desk, which Tally is slightly disappointed to see is back to being a complete state, despite her attempts at tidying it up the other week. The Top Tips Box is still there though – she can see it underneath a pile of paper and books. What she can't tell is if Mrs Jarman has read her first Top Tip or not. She hopes she has because it was a really important one.

Top Tip #1: Do not shout or make unexpected loud noises or say things in an angry tone of voice because it makes it difficult for me to understand you if my head is worrying about feeling scared or embarrassed.

"Put your bags by the wall and find a space," yells the teacher, over the chattering of the class. Then she claps her hands loudly.

Tally can't help it. The sound echoes around the room, bouncing off the sides of the studio and right inside her head. Before she can stop herself, her hands are clamped to her ears and she has turned to face the wall, blocking out the noise around her. That answers the question of whether Mrs Jarman has read her Top Tip or not.

"Don't freak out the weirdo!" calls Luke, loud enough for her to hear. Tally squeezes her eyes shut as the laughter floods in from around the room.

"That's quite enough!" snaps Mrs Jarman, and then she says something that Tally can't hear. The laughter continues for a second longer and then it stops and the room is silent.

Tally opens her eyes and lowers her hands, turning slowly away from the wall. In front of her, Mrs Jarman's mouth is moving but the sound coming from her lips is barely audible. Tally takes a step forward, trying to get close enough to hear what she's saying. The rest of the class look at each other in confusion before copying Tally, everyone tiptoeing across the room in silence, their eyes fixed on the teacher.

"That is better," whispers Mrs Jarman, as they creep

towards her. "I'm sorry that my voice was so loud a moment ago. This is a place of expression and creativity. We do not need to shout and scream to make ourselves heard in the drama studio – sometimes, the strongest voices are those who are speaking the quietest, which is something that I have to remind myself about at times too."

"That's stupid," says Luke, in what he obviously thinks is a hushed tone.

It isn't hushed enough for Mrs Jarman's eagle senses though.

"I have a two-strike rule, young man," she murmurs, giving him a hard look. "And quite stunningly, you have managed to use up both of your strikes in the first two minutes of this lesson."

"What did I do?" protests Luke, standing up as tall as he can. "I haven't done anything!"

"Absolutely," agrees Mrs Jarman, taking a step forward. "With your disrespect to both your classmates and to me, you are currently contributing absolutely nothing to this class. So, please." She gestures towards the door. "Remove yourself and trot along to Heads of House. You can tell them that you have been instructed to leave my drama studio until you have something of merit to bring to the group. There will be no more rudeness and no more unkindness and definitely no more shouting in this room."

Luke stares at her in shock and Tally feels a bubble of happiness exploding inside her body.

"I didn't mean anything—" he starts, but Mrs Jarman is not listening.

"Yes, you did," she tells him. "And now you must deal with the consequences."

She waves at the door and the class watch as Luke picks up his bag and scurries out of the drama studio, his strutting forgotten in his embarrassment. Then she turns to look at the rest of them.

"If we can't make each other understand what we're trying to say without shouting or sounding angry, then we probably aren't saying it in the quite the right way. Someone told me that, recently." Her eyes flicker again to Tally.

"Now, I would like you to get into pairs. We're going to start with a warm-up exercise that's called 'Sounds Good', and it's rather appropriate for today's lesson because it's all about the *way* we express ourselves, rather than the actual words that we say."

Tally stands still as all around, people find partners

and make their way to a space. Ayesha and Lucy have gone together, and she doesn't know anybody else so she has nobody to pair up with, but she doesn't mind. All she can think about is that Mrs Jarman has obviously read her Top Tip and this makes her happier than she ever thought she could possibly be at school.

CHAPTER 15

"Are you sure that you don't want to take one of your cuddly toys?" asks Mum, for the millionth time.

Tally rolls her eyes and folds up her pyjamas. "I've already told you," she says, shoving them into the bag. "Nobody is going to be taking a toy with them. I'll look like a baby."

Mum seems unconvinced. "You could stuff it down at the bottom of your sleeping bag," she suggests. "Nobody would even know it was there, then."

Tally hesitates for a second. That's not a terrible idea. She could take Billy – he deserves a treat after she forgot all about his birthday last month. It might be quite nice to know that he was there with her.

"No." She shakes her head firmly. "I'm not taking a toy to Layla's sleepover. I'm eleven years old now, Mum

– you've got to stop treating me like I'm still little."

Mum zips up the bag and gives Tally a smile.

"I know that, sweetheart. You're getting so grown-up now that you're in secondary school. Dad and I are really proud of you – and here you are, going on your very first sleepover!" She ruffles Tally's hair and pulls her in for a hug.

"Mum! You're so embarrassing!" Tally twists away but inside she's smiling too.

"Right then, I think that's everything." Mum picks up the bag and turns towards the door. "If you're absolutely sure about not taking something to cuddle?"

Tally glances at her bed, where the duvet is almost hidden by the army of soft toys that are lying on top.

"I'm sure," she says, taking a deep breath. "I'm not a little girl any more."

Mum drives the short distance to Layla's house, and the whole way, Tally can barely keep still. The excitement is making her legs jiggle and her hands flap and Mum keeps giving her worried little glances which makes Tally tell her off because the driver should always keep her eyes on the road when she's driving the car, unless she wants to cause an accident.

The moment that the car stops, Tally launches

herself out of the door.

"Have you got all your stuff?" calls Mum, opening the boot. "If you've forgotten anything then I can always drive back. It isn't far, so don't worry about phoning me if you need anything, OK?"

Tally wonders if Mum is going to be OK while she's at the sleepover.

Together, they carry the sleeping bag and rucksack up the path and Mum knocks on the door.

"Tally! You're here!"

Layla grabs Tally's arm and drags her inside the house. Ayesha and Lucy are standing at the bottom of the stairs and Tally wonders if they've been here for long.

"I'm so glad that you actually came this time! Mum thought you'd cancel again but I told her that you promised you'd come!"

"Hello, Tally." Layla's mum is standing in the hall, making a frowning face at her daughter. "It's great that you're here."

"Hello," says Tally, suddenly feeling awkward. "It's great that you're here too."

There's a pause and Tally replays the greeting in her head, realizing too late that she's got it wrong. What was she thinking, saying that to Layla's Mum? Of course she'd be here – it's *her* house. Tally clenches her fists, digging the nails into the palms of her hands and hearing her voice saying the same pointless thing over and over again. She wanted today to be perfect but she's already ruined it.

"Thanks so much for having her. She's been really looking forward to it." Mum has stepped inside. "And of course, if there's any issues then just—"

"It'll all be fine, Jennifer," interrupts Mrs Richardson, which is quite rude of her but after messing up with saying hello, Tally thinks that she probably shouldn't address the issue of Layla's mum's bad manners right now. "You go and have a fabulous evening with Kevin and relax for once." She turns to look at the girls. "They're all going to have a marvellous time!"

"Let's take your stuff up to my room!" says Layla, pulling Tally towards the stairs. "We aren't eating tea until later so we've got tons of time!"

Tally allows herself to be dragged along, throwing a quick look back over her shoulder at Mum.

"I'll see you tomorrow," calls Mum. And then, just before Tally turns away, she silently mouths *I love you* and blows a kiss. Nobody else appears to notice, which is a relief, because the last thing that Tally needs is

Mum getting all silly and soppy about her staying over at someone else's house.

Layla's room looks like there has been some kind of explosion. Clothes are flung everywhere and the surfaces are dripping in make-up and hair things and jewellery. The smell of perfume lies heavy in the air, and when Tally walks inside it feels like she's drowning in a sea of pink.

"Put your things over there!" says Layla, finally letting go of Tally's arm. "And then we can give you a makeover!"

Tally looks at where her friend is pointing. There is a small patch of carpet that hasn't already been claimed by Ayesha and Lucy, so she pulls out her sleeping bag and squeezes it into the space.

"Now sit here and then we can begin!" Lucy flings out her arms, gesturing towards Layla's dressing table. Tally isn't entirely sure that she really wants to sit down, but she sinks obediently on to the stool because she has done enough research on sleepovers to know that a makeover is definitely a normal thing to do. And it is very important that she is normal for the next eighteen hours and thirty minutes.

"I'm going to make you look beautiful," promises

Layla, standing next to Tally. She looks at their reflections in the mirror and tips her head to one side, looking thoughtful. "I think you would look great with a smoky eye and some really sharp definition on your cheeks. What do you think, Ayesha?"

Ayesha comes up on Tally's other side and puts her hands on her hips.

"Maybe," she says slowly, peering at Tally's face. "But only if you balance it with a pale lip. And obviously, you're going to need to use some white liner on her lids to make the eyeshadow really pop. Also, I'm wondering about some eyelash extensions, because hers are quite short. What do you think, Tally?"

Tally thinks that it is entirely possible that they are speaking some kind of alien language, but she doesn't want to be rude.

"That all sounds great!" she says, beaming as widely as she can. "Especially that bit about popping! And making one eye look smoky – are you going to make me look like a panda?"

Ayesha and Layla start giggling. Tally feels the rush of happiness that she always gets when she makes her friends laugh. She can do this. She really can.

Over by the window, Lucy is messing about with her

phone and suddenly the room is filled with the sound of Taylor Swift's voice. It feels like a good omen so Tally relaxes back into the chair while Layla sorts the make-up and Ayesha sits on the carpet and starts lining up bottles of nail varnish, reading the names of each one out loud.

"We've got Blue Moon," she says. "And I love this colour – it's called Sparkle Tips!"

"I got that last Christmas," says Layla, squirting something on to her hand. "It's lush, isn't it?"

"I think Tally would look good in this yellow one," says Ayesha, holding up a bottle of something that reminds Tally of a banana. "It's called Vomit Comet – how brilliant is that!"

"I don't want anything called vomit on my fingernails," says Tally, but she says it very quietly and nobody can hear her over the noise of Taylor Swift.

"Now, you need to stay really still," says Layla, turning to face Tally. She dabs a sponge into the squirty stuff that is now on the back of her hand. "This is just to give you a blemish-free base, but you don't want it to go in your eye because it really stings. Believe me, I know!"

Tally scrunches her eyes closed in panic and Layla tuts. "No! You can't do that! You'll get wrinkle lines –

we're trying to make you look gorgeous, not like an old lady."

The sponge makes contact and Tally flinches. It's unexpectedly cold, and as Layla moves it around her face, Tally's skin starts to feel tight and hard and uncomfortable. She counts in her head, returning to zero every time she reaches ten, just like Mum taught her.

It isn't really enough to make the situation any better though.

Finally, Layla steps away and Tally opens her eyes.

"Are we done now?" she asks. "Is it time for tea?"

Layla laughs and Tally hears a snorting sound from over by the window.

"We haven't even begun properly yet," says Layla. "That was the boring bit – now the fun can really start!"

Tally opens her mouth to tell Layla that she can't stay in this chair for one minute longer but then she closes it again. What is she going to use as an excuse? She can't say that she needs to go to the bathroom because that would be way too embarrassing. And if she tells them that she doesn't like makeovers then they'll wish that they hadn't invited her and she'll ruin everything. The only thing she can do is to make her body as rigid and still as possible so that she doesn't start stimming – the girls might be her friends but she's pretty certain that they won't cope with the real Tally showing up at this sleepover.

The phone switches to another song and Taylor Swift's voice is replaced by a man who is shouting very loudly about something that his girlfriend has done to upset him and how she's going to be sorry that she ever crossed him.

"Oh, I love this one!" squeals Ayesha. "Turn it up!"

Lucy raises the volume and then Tally watches as she advances towards her, brandishing an item that makes Tally's stomach flip over in fear.

"I'm in charge of your hair today," Lucy tells Tally, waving the hairbrush in the air. Her voice sounds fake, just like the perfect people on television – the ones who are always bossing imperfect people about and telling them that they have to do a better job of being a human. "And I have got to say, I've been wanting to get my hands on your head for a long time now, my darling!"

Ayesha laughs and shuffles forward until she is kneeling next to Tally's legs.

"Give me your hand," she orders. "I'm going to give you one of my fabulous manicures!"

Tally can't take her eyes off Lucy and the hairbrush,

so, without really paying attention, she lets Ayesha tug at her arm until her hand is dangling over the side of the chair.

"Isn't this great!" says Layla, picking up something that looks like a pencil. "It's so much fun having you here with us, Tally! This is going to be the best sleepover ever!"

She grins and Tally smiles back. The smile that she has practised in the mirror – the smile that says she is having a brilliant time and that there is nowhere else she'd rather be.

And then they attack her.

It isn't the tiny needles stabbing her in the head that push her too far. Nor is it the sharp stick that is rammed into her fingernails, making unbidden tears spring into her eyes. It isn't even the smell of Layla's breath, hot and heavy as she leans forward and pokes Tally's face over and over again. None of these things push Tally over, although they make her feel like she is clinging on to the side of a cliff while her friends all peel her fingers off the edge, one at a time.

But she doesn't let them see it. The pain as Lucy tugs the brush through her tangled hair that hasn't seen a hairbrush for weeks. The torture as Ayesha pushes back the skin on her cuticles. The agony as Layla applies the liner, occasionally slipping and prodding her in the eye.

She doesn't let them see how much they are hurting her because the whole time they are chatting about nothing and singing along to the music and giggling about what she's going to say when she sees what she looks like, and she knows that *they* think they're being kind. She knows that they have chosen her for the makeover because it's supposed to be a nice thing to have done. She knows that there is nothing more normal than hanging out with your friends on a Saturday afternoon, even if it makes her feel like she's being torn to pieces.

It is only when they are done and Layla instructs her to open her eyes that she finally tumbles over the edge of the cliff.

"What do you think?" squeals Ayesha, jumping up and down. "Do you like your new look?"

Tally blinks, the bright lights around the mirror making it difficult to focus. Then her reflection swims into view and she leans forward, unable to believe what she is seeing.

"I told you we'd make you look gorgeous!" boasts

Layla, grinning. "You look like a completely different person."

It's true. Tally's hair is no longer scrunched back into a scrappy ponytail. Instead, it lies flat against her head and it seems to be shining and glossy. And her face is almost unrecognizable. Her eyes look huge – they remind her of a fly, big and bug-like. Apparently a smoky eye does not make a person look like a panda.

"Ladies, we have outdone ourselves," states Lucy in her television voice. "Her transformation is complete! She is a caterpillar no longer – she's a beautiful butterfly!"

"Do you love it?" asks Ayesha again, peering at Tally. "Because we can show you how to do it yourself and then you can come to school looking a bit more—"

"Ayesha!" snaps Layla, cutting her off. "Just shut up, OK?"

In the mirror, Tally sees Ayesha's face go bright red. "Sorry," she mumbles. "I didn't mean to say that."

"Looking a bit more *what*?" asks Tally, lowering her eyes away from her reflection. "What were you going to say?"

Layla glares at Ayesha as loud music fills the room. The dressing table is covered with make-up and one of the bottles has leaked all over the wooden surface. It's messy and chaotic and Tally has had enough.

"What were you going to say?" she repeats, pushing the chair back and standing up. "You can show me how to do the make-up myself so that I can come to school looking more *what*?" She marches across the room and turns off the music. "Tell me."

"Looking a bit more normal," says Lucy, shrugging her shoulders. "It's not a big deal, Tally. We just thought that you might want to look a bit more like us, you know – to fit in."

Tally stares at the three girls in front of her.

"I didn't know that I looked *different* to you," she whispers.

"If you don't like it then we can wash it off," says Layla worriedly. "It was just a bit of fun, Tally." She looks helplessly at the others. "We didn't mean to upset you."

From somewhere very deep inside of her, Tally finds a final surge of strength. She closes her eyes for a second and when she opens them she is ready to hurl herself back up on to the clifftop.

"I'm not upset!" she says, as brightly as she can. "Well, maybe I am a bit upset that you made me look like a boring, ordinary girl and not a panda, but never mind – you can do that next time!"

"Yeah!" Layla looks relieved. "We could have an animal-themed sleepover and get face paints. I'd be a zebra! What about you, Lucy?"

"Oh yeah, that sounds totally amazing," sniffs Lucy, rolling her eyes. "If we were, like, six years old, maybe."

Layla walks up to Tally and puts her hand on her arm. "Do you want to wash it off?" she asks quietly. "Because that's OK."

Tally wants to wash it off more than she wants anything else in the entire universe right now. The make-up is making her skin feel prickly and it smells strange and she can't bear to look at herself in the mirror because she doesn't look like her and she hates butterflies actually, with their fakery and deception and pretending to be something that they're not. What's so wrong with just being a caterpillar?

But she looks *normal*, apparently. She looks like Layla and Ayesha and Lucy.

"I don't want to wash it off," she lies. It is a white lie and that is OK if it helps to make her friends feel happy again and stops the sleepover from going wrong.

But Lucy is still scowling and Ayesha is busying herself with tidying up the nail varnish bottles and not looking at Tally. She obviously hasn't said enough to make everything right. She needs to try harder.

"I love it," she says, making an effort not to sound like a robot. "My transformation is complete. I love my new look. Thank you for turning me into a butterfly."

"Girls! It's time to eat!"

Layla's Mum's voice floats up the stairs, breaking the awkwardness.

"Oh good, I'm starving!" says Layla, turning for the door. "We're having pizza and chips – I hope you're all hungry!"

"Pizza is my absolute favourite!" Ayesha drops the bottles and spins round. "Especially with pepperoni!"

"No way – ham and pineapple is the best!" says Lucy, the frown dropping from her face. "It's the combination of fruit and meat that makes it perfect."

"Well, nobody needs to worry because Mum bought three pizzas and we've got pepperoni, vegetable supreme and ham and pineapple." Layla opens the bedroom door and beckons them all to go through. "So everyone should be happy!"

Tally hates pizza. She hates the spicy pepperoni that makes her tongue feel as if it's being invaded by an army of red ants. She hates ham and pineapple together because they are totally different food groups and they shouldn't be mixed up. And she just hates vegetables, full stop.

"Pizza is my absolute favourite!" she says, turning slightly so that she can walk out of the room without looking in the mirror. "I'm starving!"

CHAPTER 16

It's cold on top of the garden shed but Tally doesn't care. Slowly, making sure that her footing is secure, she lies back against the roof and stares up at the stars. Mum and Dad think that she's in bed but there's no way that she could sleep, not after everything that has happened this evening.

The sky is dark but it isn't black like everyone always thinks. It's a dark, indigo blue, and Tally stares into the distance until the stars become blurry and the sky seems like it's pushing down on top of her like a very heavy blanket.

The sleepover might just about have been saved if she'd had her special weighted blanket with her and not the slippery, shiny sleeping bag that Mum made her take. She'd struggled her way through supper, picking bits of pineapple off her slice of pizza and hiding them under a pile of chips so that she could just eat the ham and the cheesy base. Then she went upstairs and sat on Layla's bed and watched a film that Lucy said would be great but that clearly stated at the start that it was only suitable for viewers who were aged over eighteen. When Tally questioned whether they should choose something else, everyone had laughed. And then Lucy asked her if she was scared and so she had to pretend that it was all fine, even though the part where the clown peered out from the drainage hole and gave a creepy smile made her head swirl in a horrible way.

She'd even kept going when the film finally ended and they went to the bathroom to clean their teeth and Layla's big brother was lying in wait for them behind the bathroom door. He jumped out as they walked in and Lucy and Layla screamed so loudly that Tally's ears were ringing for ages afterwards. Ayesha started crying, which made Tally feel strange and a bit embarrassed and awkward. She wanted to cry too but there was no way that she could ever do that in front of her friends and so she pushed the feeling deep down and tried to think about happy things like Rupert and the top of the garden shed.

When they'd eventually calmed down and Layla's Mum had stormed upstairs and shouted at her brother and then told them all off for watching an unsuitable film (which was completely unfair because Tally didn't even want to watch it in the first place), they settled into their sleeping bags and Tally saw that they all had something in their hands. The other girls were snuggling up with their favourite soft toys – Lucy had her teddy bear and Ayesha had a battered old penguin that she said she was given when she had to go to hospital and Layla had a whole load of them on her bed. Not as many as Tally has on her bed at home, but still, quite a lot.

And that was when it all went wrong. So wrong that Tally couldn't stop it. She had told Mum that she didn't need to bring a cuddly toy because she was sure that it would be breaking one of the rules of the sleepover, but they all had something to cuddle and she had nobody and that wasn't OK.

Layla had turned off the light and the rest of them started talking. About horrible Luke and who might fancy Layla and whether Ayesha was brave enough to ask out some boy in their drama class. But Tally couldn't listen to a single thing they said. All she could think about was the fact that Billy was lying on her bed at home and she was lying on the floor of Layla's bedroom and the distance between them was further than she could bear to contemplate. She had wriggled uncomfortably, feeling her feet getting tangled up and hot at the end of the sleeping bag. And the pillow smelt funny and the girls' voices were high-pitched and shrill, but even so she could still hear the sounds coming from the television downstairs and there was no way that she could go to sleep with all that noise going on.

She'd whispered it too quietly the first time and nobody had heard her. They were too busy giggling about whether it was more romantic to go to McDonald's or Burger King on a first date. So she said it a bit louder but they still weren't listening, which meant that the third time it came out a bit like a shout and that made everyone stop talking straight away.

Layla had tried to persuade her to stay. She told Tally that the sleepover would be ruined if she wasn't there with them. All Tally could hear was the sound of Lucy's words from earlier, telling her that they wanted to make her look *normal*. Then Layla started to cry, saying that her Mum would be really mad at her if Tally went home and would blame her because of the scary film, but the only noise in Tally's head was Ayesha's voice, squealing about her *new look*. Tally didn't want a new look. She liked her old look.

Layla was right. Her mum was cross. She tried to get Tally to stay too, but Tally just kept on trying to stuff her sleeping bag back inside the ridiculously tiny sack that it was supposed to go into, and when that failed, she picked it up in one hand and her rucksack in the other and marched downstairs, the sleeping bag trailing behind her. By the time Mum arrived she was sitting outside on the front doorstep, with Layla's mum fussing around her and Layla's dad muttering about how all the heating was going straight out of the open door.

But now she's home, and the instant that she heard Mum and Dad's bedroom door close, she grabbed Billy and headed out to the garden. Her face has been washed clean by Mum, although all the tears that she cried in the car did most of the job for her. She looks like her and she feels like her, and up here on the garden shed, she can breathe properly for the first time all day.

Date: Sunday 12th October
Situation: Sleepover from hell
Anxiety Rating: 10. Absolutely 10.

Hi, Tally again with yet another nightmare story. I think this one's the worst – last night I had one of the worst nights of my life EVER. Even sitting up on top of the garden shed didn't make me feel happy like it usually does. Instead I just felt like I was missing out on everything. I bet Layla and everyone had the time of their lives without me.

I keep trying to forget about it, but then I have a flashback of everyone crowding round me like a swarm of angry wasps, grinning in my face, pulling at my hair and smothering my face in thick make-up. The thought makes me so stressed I have to pace round and round my bedroom to try and calm myself down. Why do I get so anxious and stressed about stuff that other people wouldn't care about? I know it's just how I am. I just have a different way of seeing and feeling the world. I'm like a fly: I view the world through many lenses, and if someone approaches me without caution I take off and, just like with flies, people don't always feel empathy for me. Which is ironic when people like to think I'M the one without empathy.

Tally's autism facts: Anxiety

Pro: I'm hyper sensitive to my surroundings and that makes me want to protect myself from danger, because I can sense it more than other people might. This means I'll probably live longer. I find this quite funny because some people seem desperate to prevent autism like it's a disease, but actually I think we are outperforming the neurotypicals. That's probably why they are always trying to "cure" us! Dad says this would be a great film plot. Neurotypical people are people who think and behave in the way that the world thinks is normal, by the way. Sometimes they even think that their way of being is the only right way, which is ridiculous when you think about it. I do a lot of thinking, as you can probably tell. And anyway, most autistic people I know wouldn't want to *not* be autistic. It's part of what makes us who we are, even if it is really, really hard sometimes.

Con of anxiety: ANXIETY ... duh.

Ugh, fine I'll explain. Well, with anxiety you always think immediately of the worst-case scenario. And everything's an emergency. For example, my mum was out shopping and told me that she was going to be an hour but she was seven whole minutes over an hour. SEVEN! I was convinced she'd been kidnapped and I cried for ages. So what I'm trying to say is that I overthink a lot of things. It feels like being trapped in a crazy persuasive brain that makes me believe incorrect and extreme thoughts.

CHAPTER 17

The day after the sleepover is a bad day. If Mum would just let her stay in bed all day then it might have been saved, but instead, she insists that they all go out for a nice family walk to the park. Mum isn't calling it a *nice family walk* by the time they get home, though. Instead she is pressing her lips together and walking as if she's in the army, her arms held tightly against her sides and her legs marching up and down like she's taking part in an exercise class. Tally, on the other hand, is quite tired, but that might be because she always feels exhausted after a huge meltdown.

"Nice job," mutters Nell, trudging along beside her. "That's yet another family outing that you've managed to ruin."

"It's not my fault." Tally shrugs. "Mum should have

packed Billy in my bag yesterday. The sleepover would have been fine if I'd had him with me."

"I told you to take him!" Ahead of them, Mum stops and spins round, her face twisted and red. "We had a whole conversation about you taking him with you and you decided that you wouldn't."

Tally stares at her. "But I didn't *know*," she tells her. "You're the mum. It's your job to know."

Mum shakes her head and opens her mouth as if she's about to start shouting.

"Can we just get home?" asks Nell quickly. "This has been embarrassing enough already."

Mum blinks very fast and nods at Nell.

"Sorry, sweetheart," she murmurs. "None of this is your fault."

Which Tally knows is code for *this is all Tally's fault.* This knowledge makes her head roar and her stomach churn and her legs fizz.

And it's impossible to keep the fizzing and churning and roaring inside.

It has to come out, one way or another.

The bad day just got a lot worse.

The next day isn't turning out to be any better. Tally

doesn't see Layla or the others all morning. They don't have the same maths class as her, but when she looks in the usual places at break-time they are nowhere to be found. She eats her packet of crisps alone, wondering if she's forgotten that they were going to meet somewhere different today.

By the time the bell rings for lunch, she's feeling scared. She hates the school canteen, with all its noise and smells, and the only way that she can possibly go in there is if Layla is with her. There's only one option and that is to track them down, as quickly as possible.

Walking along the emptying corridors, Tally peers into each classroom. The French rooms are silent, as are the English rooms. She turns the corner and heads towards the history block, and that's when she hears it. A giggle and the screech of a table being pushed across the floor. It's very faint but Tally knows instantly who the laughter belongs to. Picking up speed, she strides the last few steps and pushes open the door to the classroom, a big grin on her face.

"Hey! How come you're all in—" The words die on her lips. Layla is sitting on a table next to Ayesha and Jasmine, the girl from PE. Lucy is at the front of the room next to the teacher's desk and next to her is Luke, his hands frozen in position inside the open drawer.

"Oh my word," gasps Lucy, the first to recover. "You nearly gave me a heart attack, Tally! I thought you were Mr King."

"What are you doing?" asks Tally, staring at Layla. "Why weren't you waiting for me at break-time?"

"Can you get rid of her, please?" snaps Luke. "We haven't got long and we don't need her messing this up."

Tally turns her attention towards him. He's pulled a sheet of yellow paper out of the drawer and is bent over the desk, scanning the page as if it contains something very important.

"You should go, Tally," mutters Layla, looking down at her shoes.

Tally nods in agreement. "You should come too. It's lunchtime. We have to go to the canteen to eat our sandwiches."

"Is she for real?" Luke glances up and scowls at Tally. "Just get out, Weirdo Adams."

Tally glares back at him and then takes a step towards Layla. "Are you coming?" she asks. "There won't be any seats left if we don't hurry up."

Layla's eyes flicker towards Jasmine and Ayesha. "I'm

going to stay here," she says quietly. "But it's probably a good idea if you go, Tally."

"Yeah – off you toddle." Luke waves his hand dismissively in the air. "Go and find some other weird kids like you – I'm sure they'd be happy to let you hang about with them."

"You shouldn't call me *weird*," snaps Tally, standing her ground. "Should he?"

She turns and looks at each of her friends, but none of them will look back at her. Lucy is staring at Luke with a strange expression on her face while Ayesha gazes out of the window. Layla opens her mouth as if she's about to speak, but then Jasmine puts her hand on Layla's arm and shakes her head slightly, and Tally sees something that she never thought she would ever see. Her best friend, rolling her eyes and giving *the look*.

It feels like she's been punched in the face.

"Nobody cares, Weirdo," says Luke as he stuffs the sheet of yellow paper into his bag. "Now do us all a favour and disappear."

The room is silent as Tally turns and stumbles to the door. She doesn't know how she opens it because her eyes are too blurry to even see the handle, but somehow she manages to make it outside, down the corridor and into the girls' toilets where there is an empty cubicle at the end of the row.

Going inside, she turns and locks the door and then leans back against it, closing her eyes so that she doesn't have to look at the disgusting toilet. Her hands clamp over her ears, blocking out the sounds of the chatter and the shouting and the constant whirring of the hand dryer. And she stays there when other girls bang on the door and make it rattle against her body. She doesn't move when they shout rude things that she can still hear, even with her hands clasped to the sides of her head, right up until the bell rings and the sound of stamping feet tells her that everyone has gone. Tally's tummy is rumbling as she quietly unlocks the toilet door. Her lunch box is still filled with the sandwiches that Mum made for her this morning but she can't eat anything now. She'll have to throw it all away.

The first lesson of the afternoon is drama. Tally heads towards the stairs, losing herself in the mass of people who are surging in from all directions. The noise is overwhelming and she feels like she's being surrounded on every side by bodies and voices and opinions and emotions and life. Without Layla to distract her, it is almost more than she can bear.

The door to the drama studio is open and Tally tags on to the end of the line of people who are walking inside. She can see Lucy and Ayesha ahead of her, deep in conversation with Luke, and she hangs back, unsure about the reception that she'll get if she tries to join them. They didn't exactly say anything mean to her at lunchtime – it was Luke who did that, which is hardly a surprise – but when she looks over at them her heart starts to beat a little faster and her head fills with a buzzing sensation that makes her feel worried and anxious.

"I hope you're all ready for an exciting lesson today," says Mrs Jarman, strolling through the door. Her voice is quiet and there is none of the loud clapping that Tally hates so much. "I thought we would start with a quick game of two truths and a lie to get us all warmed up! Everyone come and sit in a circle on the floor, please."

Tally puts her bag down and reluctantly joins the rest of the class. The buzzing is getting louder and she closes her eyes, trying to ignore everything except the feeling of her own breath and the sound of her mum's voice in her head.

Breathe slowly in. Breathe slowly out. Count to five and press the pads of your fingers against the pad of your thumb. Breathe in again. Feel the pressure. Press harder. Breathe out. Repeat. Repeat. Repeat.

"I'll start," says Mrs Jarman. "So – my first statement is that I holiday every year in South America. My second is that I have five children and a dog. And my third statement is that I am constantly learning new things from my pupils. So – which one is the lie?"

"That is so easy, Miss," says one of the boys. "We're supposed to learn from you, not the other way round! The third statement is the lie."

Mrs Jarman grins. "I wouldn't be much of a teacher if I didn't listen to you lot now and again. Even if what I'm learning is that young people today have no idea about what constitutes a fashion crime." She stares intently at the boy. "You are aware that your trousers are a good three inches above your shoes, aren't you?"

He grins back at her. "It's called *style*, Miss. We could give you some lessons if you like?"

Mrs Jarman shakes her head. "No, thank you. I think I'll cope without that particular privilege. OK – which of the two remaining statements is the lie?"

"The first one," calls Ayesha. "Nobody can afford to go to South America every year – that kind of holiday costs so much money!"

"So does that mean that you've got five kids then,

Miss?" shouts someone else. Tally shudders. It's bad enough having to share a house with Nell. The idea of four brothers and sisters is absolutely terrible.

Mrs Jarman shakes her head. "Nope. I don't have any children and nor do I have a dog. Which is why I can afford to go on holiday and it is also why I am the winner of that round! So – who wants to go next?"

All around the circle, hands are thrust into the air. Mrs Jarman scans the class and then points at Luke. "Off you go, then. Two truths and a lie."

Luke grins at Lucy and runs his hands through his hair.

"OK. First of all, I'm unbeatable at playing Fortnite, and if any of you losers want to take me on then be warned – you're going down!"

Laughter ripples around the circle like a Mexican wave, only stopping when it reaches Tally.

"Well, that's a lie for starters because I completely annihilated you when we played last night," interrupts Ameet, causing another laugh.

"My second statement is that Portharbour Football Club have asked me to try out for their junior league," Luke continues, looking smugly at Ameet who murmurs something under his breath. "And the third statement is that I think *every single person* in this room is normal and great!"

As he says this, his eyes catch on to Tally and his mouth turns up at the corners, reminding her of a face that Nell sometimes makes and that Mum says is called *smarmy*.

The buzzing intensifies, like one thousand angry wasps have invaded her head.

"I very much hope that I am not going to have cause to remove you from the room again, young man," says Mrs Jarman, giving Luke an intent stare.

He looks back at her and raises his shoulders, his face looking puzzled. "No, Miss. I just did what you said to do. I've told you two truths and a lie."

"Hmm." Mrs Jarman looks unconvinced and Tally crosses her fingers, hoping that she'll just send Luke out now. "Well, let's give you the benefit of the doubt, shall we? Who can guess Luke's lie?"

The room goes quiet. Everybody knows which one is the lie, but nobody wants to get in trouble by saying it. Everybody except Mrs Jarman saw the look that he gave Tally, which is always what happens because kids like Luke are masters of avoiding the teacher's gaze. Tally knows that.

"Come on," prompts the drama teacher. "Someone has to guess."

"I still think he lied about Fortnite," mutters Ameet. "I've got a way better rank than him."

Luke grins and shakes his head. "Wrong!"

"In that case, you lied about thinking everyone is this room is normal," says Aleksandra, rolling her eyes. "Which is a pretty nasty lie."

"I agree," says Lucy, quietly. "It's just mean and stupid."

"Is that the lie?" asks Mrs Jarman quietly, although the warning in her voice is loud and clear.

Luke gives his best surprised look. "No, Miss! The lie is that I haven't been asked to try out for Portharbour Football Club. I've been asked to try out for Rovers – and of course I think that everyone in the room is normal." He grins and looks straight at Tally. "Why wouldn't I think that?"

"I think that perhaps you and I need to have a little chat," starts Mrs Jarman, but before she can say anything else there is a knock at the door and another teacher walks inside.

"Can I just have a quick word?" he asks, beckoning to Mrs Jarman. "The Head needs some information on data from last year and apparently he needs it yesterday."

Mrs Jarman nods. "You can all read through scene one of our new play," she tells them. "We'll be working on it next lesson. Aleksandra – can you hand out the books, please?"

And then she retreats to her desk with the other teacher and starts to talk animatedly about something, her hands flying all over the place like Tally's hands do when she's particularly excited about something.

The words on the pages of the script don't make any sense, even when Tally reads them through for the third time. So she gives up and instead pulls a piece of paper out of her notebook, writing down a new Top Tip for Mrs Jarman and sneaking it into the box at the end of the lesson. Nobody notices her, which isn't a surprise because what she's already learnt about year seven is that the only time anyone actually sees her is when Luke says something cruel.

The rest of the time she is invisible.

CHAPTER 18

The first lesson of the day is history. As Tally turns the corner she sees the girls gathered in a group ahead of her. She can hear them whispering and phrases like "what if she tells?" and "can't keep a secret" float down the corridor. Then Layla sees her coming and flashes her a quick smile.

"Are you OK?" she asks, as Tally gets closer. "Did you go to the canteen yesterday lunchtime? I looked for you when we got down there but I couldn't see you anywhere."

Tally shakes her head. "No. I ended up doing something else."

"Why didn't you come and sit with us in drama?" asks Ayesha. "We were saving you a space."

Lucy puts her arm around Tally's shoulders and pulls her into the group.

"We have to look out for each other, remember?" she says. "Have each other's backs. We can't let anything get in the way of us being friends."

Perhaps Tally has got it wrong. Maybe they weren't all trying to avoid her. Maybe she misunderstood the situation yesterday when it seemed like they just wanted her to go. These girls have been her friends for ever, after all, and Lucy is right – they all made a promise to be there for each other.

The voice is in her head before she can stop it. Nell's voice, the one that tells her that she's broken, is now reminding her that her so-called friends weren't really there for her when Luke was calling her a weirdo. They should have stopped him but none of them said a single word. She blinks hard and tries to focus, pushing Nell away. They are her friends. There's no way that they'd just abandon her. Tally must have made a mistake – it wouldn't exactly be the first time.

"I'm sorry," Tally says, giving them all her best smile. "I should have come and sat with you but I had a headache and I just needed to be on my own for a bit."

It's not a lie, not really. The buzzing sensation isn't exactly the same as a headache but it still makes Tally feel like her brain is about to explode. That's why she put the second tip in Mrs Jarman's Top Tip box.

Top Tip #2: Every school should have a quiet place where kids can go when they need to be on their own.

"Well, let's sit together now," says Layla, linking arms with Tally. "I hope Mr King isn't going to show us yet another PowerPoint presentation today!"

But when they get inside and sit down at their desks, Mr King is not standing at the front, ready to talk them through five hundred slides on Medieval Britain. Instead, he is rooting through his desk drawer with a frown on his face. He straightens up as the last pupil enters the room and turns to the face the class, looking puzzled

"Has anyone seen a piece of paper with lots of questions on it?" he asks them. "I could have sworn that I left in in my drawer but it's nowhere to be found."

Everyone shakes their head.

"Was it important?" asks a girl at the front of the room and Mr King nods.

"It had the questions for the quiz I was telling you about last lesson," he explains. "The one that helps me to predict your history grade for this term."

"Does that mean that we won't have to take a test, sir?" calls Ameet. "Maybe we should all tell you what grade we think we deserve and you could put that in our reports?"

"I definitely deserve an A star!" shouts Jasmine. "My mum said that she'd give me ten pounds for every grade above a B that I get on my report."

Mr King frowns as other voices call out, contributing their own thoughts about the grade that they should be getting.

"I'm not sure that I've seen any work worthy of an A star from this class," he tells them, once the noise has died down. "And as for getting money for good grades, well…" He looks at Jasmine. "I rather think that education itself should be the reward."

This earns him a big laugh from the back row. Tally isn't listening though. Instead she is remembering what happened yesterday lunchtime in this very room. The way that Luke told her to go and find some other weird kids to hang out with, as if her own group of friends weren't right there in front of her.

"Well, it's a mystery to me because I'm sure it was there yesterday morning," continues Mr King. "And it's a complete pain because now I'm going to have to print out another copy which means that we can't do the test until next lesson."

He frowns and then starts writing on the whiteboard. Tally glances around. Across the aisle, Luke is staring at her and as her eyes swing past him, he mouths a word at her. Silently but somehow still managing to get the attention of the people around him so that they all see her face as he narrows his eyes and calls her the word that she hates most in the world.

"Did you see the test, Luke?" Her voice rings out clearly in the quiet room. "When you were looking in Mr King's desk drawer?"

Several things happen at once.

Layla groans quietly and shifts in her seat, moving closer to Jasmine and away from Tally. Luke's face flushes a furious red and he half rises in his seat, looming menacingly across the aisle. The kids on the back row start to make jeering sounds that to Tally's ears sound like people at a football match. And at the front of the room, Mr King spins round and fixes them all with a fierce look.

"That's quite enough!" he bellows, making Tally squirm in her seat. "The next person to utter a single sound is going to be in detention for the rest of the term!"

The room falls into silence, but it isn't a still or peaceful silence. Instead, there is a fizz of energy crackling in the air and Tally wonders if there is about to be a storm.

"Would you like to repeat that last sentence?" Mr King is staring right at her. Tally clamps her mouth shut. He literally just said that the next person to make a sound would get detention and if this is a trick then she isn't going to fall for it.

"Did you say that Luke was looking in my desk drawer?" asks the teacher. "Is that what I heard you say?"

Tally nods because he didn't say anything about the next person who moves their head getting a detention.

"This is complete and utter—" starts Luke.

"I'll stop you there," interrupts Mr King, holding his hand up. "Before you get yourself into even more trouble." He turns back to Tally. "And did you see Luke taking the test paper?"

Tally hesitates and Mr King nods at her. "Hold on one second."

He beckons to Luke to join him by the door and the rest of the class start to murmur quietly.

"Just shut up," Lucy hisses to Tally, turning round from the row in front. "I don't know why you said that but you need to shut up, OK, if you ever want to be friends with us again."

"Tally – will you join us?" calls Mr King. "And the rest of you, turn to page fifty-six. And if I hear one peep out of you then you can expect to be doing history homework in every spare moment of every day for the rest of the year."

He leads Tally and Luke out into the corridor, much to the disappointment of the rest of the class.

"I don't know what she's on about," explodes Luke, the second that the door closes behind them. "She hates me and she's always trying to get me in trouble."

"Is that true?" asks Mr King, looking at Tally.

Tally pauses. "I'm not always trying to get him in trouble," she says slowly. "But I do hate him a bit because he says very unkind things about me and I don't like it."

"But did you see Luke taking the test out of my desk?" Mr King's face is serious. "This is really important, Tally. You need to tell the truth."

Tally looks down at the ground and scuffs her shoe on the floor. Mr King is being very demanding right now and suddenly she doesn't think that she can say anything, not while he's scowling like that. But then she remembers how Layla told her to shut up. There's actually been a bit too much shutting up around here already. If they hadn't all shut up when Luke called her a weirdo then none of this would have happened. Sometimes you have to answer a question, even if you think it's almost impossible to make the words come out of your mouth.

"If the test was on a piece of yellow paper then yes, he was looking at it yesterday, during lunchtime," she says, still looking at her feet. She's not doing anything wrong. She's doing exactly what Mr King is asking her to do. She's just telling the truth.

"Are you seriously going to accuse me just because Weirdo Adams thinks she saw me doing something?" wails Luke.

"Be quiet!" snaps Mr King but Tally has had enough.

"It's in his bag!" she says, raising her head and looking right at Luke. "He picked it up and stuffed it inside his bag, right before he told me to do everyone a favour and disappear."

Luke's face has gone pale and he's stopped shouting. "I bet it's still in there," she adds, trying to be helpful. Mr King turns towards Luke and reaches out his arm.

"We can do this one of two ways," he tells him. "You

can either consent to a bag search here or come with me to the Head's office and we can take it from there. Your choice."

Tally smiles. She doesn't mean to but she just can't help it. Mr King clearly doesn't understand the rules of choosing any better than Nell does. Both of the options are always supposed to be good but Luke's choices are both terrible and she is glad because he is a terrible person and terrible people don't often get caught, in Tally's experience.

Luke scowls and thrusts his bag at Mr King.

"I'd prefer for you to remove the test for me," says the teacher. "If you would." He turns to face Tally. "You can go back into class," he tells her. "And I think Luke would appreciate it if you didn't speak about what has just happened with anyone else, for the time being."

Tally nods and opens the classroom door, stepping inside and then closing it quietly behind her. Then she turns to face the room and the twenty-five pairs of eyes who are staring back at her accusingly. There was no need for Mr King to tell her not to talk about it. They already know and from the looks on their faces, they are not impressed.

CHAPTER 19

"I'm not going and that's the end of it."

Tally folds her arms across her body and glares at Mum.

Mum looks right back at her.

"It would be really helpful if you could put your shoes on, please. You can choose your trainers or your boots, it's up to you."

They've been standing in the kitchen for the last ten minutes and their conversation is going round and round in circles, neither of them prepared to give up.

"We're going to be late," says Dad for the third time, popping his head around the side of the kitchen door. "Shall I just ring the restaurant and cancel the booking?"

"No!" exclaims Mum. "It's your birthday and for once we're going to go out and celebrate." She turns and smiles at her daughter, but Tally can see that the smile is stretched and thin. "Are you going to wear your trainers or your boots?"

Tally knows the rules. Mum offers her a choice and she chooses one of the options. It's the deal. It's what is expected of her.

Which means that being given a choice is not really a choice at all.

"I don't want to wear anything on my feet," she says, sitting down heavily on one of the kitchen chairs. "They're hurting me really badly and if I put shoes on then it's just going to make it worse." She looks up at Mum. "I think that I might have athlete's foot. I probably need to rest."

"How are *you* supposed to have athlete's foot?" sneers Nell, pushing past Dad and coming into the room. "You don't do any exercise."

Tally sighs sadly. For someone who is supposed to be a clever fourteen-year-old, Nell can be surprisingly dense sometimes.

"I think you'll find that I ran very quickly to school on that day that you *abandoned* me," she reminds her sister. "I probably got it then, which makes it all your fault, so nobody should blame me if I'm in too much pain to go to the restaurant."

"Nobody is blaming anyone for anything," says Mum, picking up her bag. "And athlete's foot isn't caused by exercising."

"Ha! I told you I could have it," gloats Tally, smirking at Nell.

"It's actually a type of fungus," continues Mum. "Is that what you've got, Tally?"

Tally pauses. She knows all about fungus from science lessons at school. Mushrooms are fungus and so are gross, disgusting germs. She shakes her head quickly. No way does she want that on her foot.

"Are we all going out for this meal, then?" asks Nell, pulling her phone out of her back pocket. "Or is it just going to be me and Dad, like every other time that Tally ruins our plans?"

"I don't ruin anything!" shouts Tally, pushing back her chair and standing up. "It's not my fault that – that – that…"

She stops because she doesn't know what else to say. There are a thousand different reasons why she can't leave the house this evening, but right now, she can't remember any of them. She does know that Dad has been looking forward to this meal for ages. She also knows that last year they only got as far as the front path before she had a meltdown and Mum had to stay at home with her while Dad and Nell went off without them.

"I'm going to my room," she mutters, stomping past Nell and through the kitchen door. However, once she's out in the hallway and out of sight, she pauses like she always does. This is how she gets to hear what they really think about her – the stuff that they're too afraid to say to her face in case it makes her angry.

"I'm sorry, love," Mum says to Dad. Her voice sounds grey and flat. "If it's any consolation, she's made you a wonderful birthday card. She spent hours on it yesterday, trying to get it just right. I'm hoping that she'll give it to you later."

"She didn't need to do that," replies Dad, but his voice sounds smiley and warm and Tally creeps a bit closer so that she can hear every word. "Just going out for a meal together would be enough of a treat."

"I don't know why we have to take her with us." Nell's sulky tone slinks and squirms through the doorway. "Can't we just go without her and have a nice, normal meal like everyone else does?"

"No." Dad is firm, which surprises Tally because she

often suspects he secretly wishes she'd just go away. "We're a family and we don't leave people out. If Tally won't go to the restaurant then we'll just stay here. I don't mind what we do as long as we're all together."

Outside in the hall, Tally stands very still. Dad doesn't understand. It's not that she *won't* go out – it's that she *can't* go out and that is absolutely not the same thing. This week at school has been truly horrible and nobody will speak to her. And even though it's now the start of the half term holiday and she doesn't have to go to school for nine whole days, nothing is OK. Tally doesn't think that she's ever felt so lonely, and the last thing that she feels capable of doing right now is leaving the warm, safe house and heading out into the dark evening.

Nell makes a huffing sound. "But she's so difficult," she moans. "Nobody else has a sister who behaves like she does. It's just not fair."

The sound of high heels taps across the floor as Mum walks over to Nell.

"You do know why she behaves like she does though, don't you? It's not that she wants to spoil things for everyone. I bet she's upstairs right now feeling awful."

"I just wish that she wasn't such hard work," grumbles Nell. "I'm so fed up with having to put up with all her issues. Don't you wish that she could be normal, now and then?"

"What's *normal*?" asks Dad before Mum can speak. "I'm not sure that I know anyone who thinks they're normal, Nell. And I know that it isn't always easy but I wouldn't change anything about this family. I love you and I love Tally, just the way that you are."

The clock in the hall makes a ticking sound as the minute hand lurches towards seven o'clock. Tally bites her lip and stares at the half-closed kitchen door before making a decision. Then she spins round and dashes up the stairs to her bedroom to find the things that she needs.

The clock is about to chime the hour when she hurtles back downstairs.

"Are you ready to go?" she asks, skidding to a halt on the kitchen floor. "You need to hurry up or we're going to be late!"

Through the eyeholes of the tiger mask, she can see Mum's eyes widen in surprise. Across the room, Nell shakes her head in disgust.

"I'm not going out with her looking like—" she starts, but Dad leaps into action before she can finish.

"Right then, let's get going!" he calls, rubbing

his hands together and looking pleased. "I've heard wonderful things about this restaurant – apparently their seafood pasta is to die for!"

Tally frowns but decides to ignore this lie. She hates it when Dad says things that aren't true. He isn't going to actually die for the pasta, no matter how good it is, so why say something so ridiculous?

"You are a fabulous girl," Mum whispers as they put on their coats. "And you've just made Dad very happy!"

Tally smiles. Tiger Girl can do the things that Tally cannot. Tiger Girl is brave and adventurous and makes people feel good. If only Tiger Girl could go to school instead of her, then Tally knows that everyone would love her. Nobody would tell Tiger Girl to disappear and they wouldn't whisper horrid words like *snitch* when she walked down the corridor. Best of all, Luke would be terrified of Tiger Girl and he would tremble in fear whenever she stalked into the classroom.

Outside, the night air is cold and Tally is pleased that the mask is covering her ears. They walk down the road and she doesn't mind so much about the cars that are racing past, their bright headlights dazzling her every time they go by. Nell walks next to her but she isn't in a chatting mood, and after a few attempts to start a conversation, Tally stops bothering and instead stares through the eyeholes at the pavement, keeping a close lookout for any worms that may have got lost after the last downpour.

Eventually they reach the high street with its lit-up shop fronts and people pouring into the doors of the many pubs and restaurants that line the main road.

"It's just down there." Dad points further down. "And we're nicely in time for our reservation. Good job, everyone!"

Tally strides ahead, brave behind her mask. And then everything goes wrong.

She hears them before she sees them, their laughter rippling up the high street in waves. She turns her head and there they all are. Layla and Ayesha and Lucy and Jasmine, standing outside McDonalds. They're huddled over a paper bag, and next to them are Luke and Ameet, leaning over and shoving their hands inside before emerging with fists full of fries.

Tally's hands leap to her face and she wrenches off the tiger mask, her heart pounding in her chest.

A handful of fries land on the ground, right at her feet and when Tally looks up, Luke is staring at her. He gazes at her for a moment, his eyes flickering down to the mask in her hands, which Tally quickly thrusts behind her back. Then he turns and whispers something that makes them all turn to look in her direction.

"Aren't those your friends?" asks Nell, coming up beside her.

But Tally hasn't got any words and she can't move. She can't do anything except stare back at the group.

Nell turns around and beckons at Mum and Dad to speed up. "Let's go," she tells them. "Now." Then she pulls gently at Tally's arm. "Just keep walking."

"Off we go, then," murmurs Mum, putting her hand on Tally's shoulder. "We don't want to miss our reservation."

Tally allows them to propel her forwards but she isn't listening to a word they say as they walk down the rest of the high street. Instead, she is replaying what just happened, over and over again on loop. Luke saw her, she knows that much. They all did. But did he see Tiger Girl? And if he did, is he going to tell everyone?

They approach the restaurant and Tally's feet slow down. She's already scared and worried – there's no way that she can go inside if everyone can see her. The tiger mask is still scrunched up in her hands and she glances quickly back up the street, checking that they haven't been followed. But the pavement is empty and there's no reason for Luke or Layla or any of them to come somewhere like this.

"Did they see me?" she whispers. "Did they see the mask?"

Nell bends her head next to Tally. "No," she says firmly. "Definitely not. I was right there and you took it off before anyone noticed."

Tally isn't convinced but she slides the mask back over her head, inhaling the rubbery smell and allowing the cool sensation to comfort her. Surely if Luke *had* seen the mask then he'd have shouted something unkind at her? But then again, they *were* all whispering and staring at her.

Tally's stomach swirls like a washing machine and she clenches her fists as tightly as she can. She can't lose control right now, not when they're supposed to be celebrating Dad's birthday.

Inside the restaurant, they are shown to a table that is right in the middle of the small, cosy space. Mum frowns and asks the waiter if there is any chance of them being seated in the corner but he just shrugs and gestures with his hands to the packed room.

"It'll be fine," Dad tells her. "Just relax, Jennifer."

As soon as they sit down, Nell pulls out her phone.

"Not at the table," Mum says automatically. "You know the rules." She pushes a menu across the table. "Why don't you take a look at the main courses? What about you, Tally? What are you going to eat?"

"I want toast," says Tally, her mind still whirling from the encounter outside.

Mum laughs. "You can have that anytime at home. Why don't you look at the menu and choose something different? There's a really nice burger on here that I think you might like."

"I'm definitely having the pasta," says Dad, smiling at Mum. "Thank you everyone – this is a brilliant way to celebrate my birthday!"

"Are you all ready to order?" enquires the waiter, arriving at the side of the table. "We have Beef Bourguignon as the special, and the soup of the day is Stilton and broccoli." He glances at Tally and pauses before looking at Mum. "And also, I'm afraid we have a No Head-Covering rule inside the restaurant unless it is for religious reasons."

"God," mutters Nell. "This is so embarrassing."

"I'm sure that your rule doesn't apply to children though, does it?" asks Dad, giving the waiter a friendly smile. "It isn't hurting anyone!"

The waiter makes a small noise under his breath. "It's policy," he informs Dad.

Tally looks around the room. At the table next to them is a family of five. One of the teenage boys is wearing headphones and the mum has a pair of sunglasses on, even though it's half past seven in the evening and has been raining for most of the day.

"They've got stuff on their heads," she says, pointing across at them.

"Tally – don't be rude," whispers Mum.

"But they have!"

"You still shouldn't talk about other people. Or point at them." Mum sounds like she's either about to get very cross, or start crying. Tally hopes that she doesn't choose the crying because that would be seriously embarrassing.

"I'll sort this out." Dad stands up and beckons to the waiter. "Can I have a quick word in private, please?"

They walk towards the entrance, Dad talking non-stop. The waiter listens and frowns and then they both turn to look back at their table. Dad points at Tally and she wants to shout at him that if he'd been listening to Mum then he'd know that pointing at other people is rude but then she remembers that it *is* his birthday and that, as she didn't get him a present and ended up binning the birthday card because she couldn't get her drawing quite right, then maybe she can let it go this one time. Even if she is still feeling horrified after seeing Luke and the others.

"You could just take the stupid mask off," mutters Nell, tearing bits of bread roll and ramming them into her mouth. "Don't you think it's already caused enough trouble for one day?"

"That's enough, Nell," says Mum, giving Tally's hand a squeeze. "Dad is sorting it out and then we're all going to have a lovely meal."

Dad and the waiter return to the table and Dad smiles at Mum.

"Everything is fine," he tells her. "Now. Shall we order?"

Mum and Dad order their food and after Nell has spent a few minutes deliberating between the chicken salad and the risotto, the waiter finally turns to Tally.

"And what would you like?" he asks. His voice isn't very friendly.

"I want toast," she says. "Please."

The waiter pushes his lips together. "We don't have toast on the menu," he tells her.

"Why don't you choose the burger?" suggests Mum. "I'm sure that we could ask for it to be served without the relish or the gherkins?"

"Certainly, Madam," says the waiter.

"But I want toast," repeats Tally. "I don't want a burger."

"And as I said, we don't offer toast." The waiter gives Tally a hard look. "We can adapt any item on the menu but you cannot order a meal that we don't actually offer."

"Look, Tally, how about you—" begins Dad but Tally doesn't let him finish.

"I want a piece of toast!" she shouts. "Plain, white toast with nothing on it. That's the easiest thing in the entire world to cook, even I can make it at home – so why can't I have it here?"

There is a sniffing sound from the next table and when Tally glances over, she sees the entire family of five staring at her. It reminds her of the way that her so-called friends were staring at her outside McDonalds.

"It's rude to stare!" she yells. "Didn't anyone ever teach you that?"

"That child needs to be taught some manners," tuts the mother, and the people at the table behind her nod in agreement.

"Give her two days living in my house and she wouldn't be behaving like that out in public," mutters another woman. "I blame the parents. They're incapable of disciplining their children these days."

"It's too much screen time," agrees the first woman. "You just have to lay down clear rules and boundaries right from the get-go, that's what I always say."

"I just want a piece of toast!" howls Tally, not caring that Nell's face is flushing a deep red and that Dad is resting his head in his hands. "It's not that hard!"

"May I politely suggest that another establishment may be better suited to your needs?" says the waiter in a chilly voice. "Maybe somewhere a little less upmarket and with a clientele who may not mind this kind of commotion."

"And may I politely suggest that you and your establishment can go and take a running jump off—"

But Tally doesn't get to hear the rest of what Dad thinks because Mum is bundling her and Nell out of the restaurant and on to the street, their coats draped over her arm and her mouth quivering in rage.

Dad emerges after them and they stand on the street, Mum murmuring quiet words into Nell's ear while rubbing Tally on the back. Tally isn't really sure why she's doing that but it seems to be making Mum feel a bit better, so she doesn't move away, even when it starts to get a bit annoying.

"Well, who's up for some birthday toast at home?" asks Dad eventually. "I think there's a jar of chocolate spread lurking in the back of the cupboard. We can go all-out on the indulgence and open that!"

They start to walk up the road and then Tally stops outside an open door, scanning the area quickly to make sure that the others have gone.

"I'm really starving, " she says. "Can't we go in there?"

"They don't serve toast either," says Dad, attempting a laugh. "I don't think that establishment is any better suited to our needs than the last one, in all honesty."

The smell wafting on to the street makes Tally's tummy do little flips of hunger. She looks at the rest of her family and shakes her head.

"But I don't want toast now," she tells them. "I really, really want a burger."

"Are you kidding me?" mutters Nell. "You can't cause all that trouble and then change your mind like that."

Tally frowns. "What trouble? And I didn't change my mind. I just want something different now."

"Your middle name is Trouble," mutters Nell,

scowling.

"It is not." Tally rounds on her. "It's Olivia, actually. But you're too ignorant to know that."

"OK, OK, that's enough of that," says Dad. "We need to make a decision here."

He looks at Mum who shrugs her shoulders. "It's up to you," she tells him. "It's still your birthday."

"In that case," says Dad, taking Tally in one hand and Nell in the other and leading them inside McDonalds. "In that case, I would love to celebrate my birthday with a huge burger and a packet of fries! It sounds a whole lot nicer than anything that was on the overpriced, pretentious menu at that last place!"

"Happy birthday, Daddy," whispers Tally as they join the queue. "I hope you've had a good day."

"It's pretty great right now," Dad whispers back. "And that's what really counts."

Date: Friday 17th October
Situation: A family meal to celebrate Dad's birthday
Anxiety Rating: 8 to start with, which went down to 3 once I had my tiger mask on.

Dear Diary,

Tonight I was totally and utterly stuck. I knew I was being difficult and I felt like such a struggle to be with. It was as if an icy hand had me gripped by the throat making me behave that way. Let me explain.

Tally's autism facts: Getting stuck
Con: Everyone gets bad moods but mine can be triggered by just about anything, and when it happens it's really hard for me to move out of it. It seems like I just FEEL everything more than anyone else does: the more I go over it, the more I get stuck in it.

When I'm stuck in a bad thought or feeling, its like the whole world is depressed and grey and I'm almost trapped in a body that's not my own, and that feels uncomfortable, which just makes me want to cry. It can put me in a bad mood when people give off negative body language. And definitely when people ask me to do something. And, of course, a difficult day at school will always do it. So imagine how stuck I was feeling after the last few days at school. It's like that "stuck in the mud" tag-game that we used to play at primary school where you can only be free if someone crawls between your legs. Only I haven't got anyone to free me.

When I get hangry, thangry or tangry, things get even worse*, but I'm not always good at knowing what my own body needs and giving it to myself, e.g. food, drink, sleep, as those things feel like demands on me.

Things that help when I'm stuck:

1) I have something called a squishy. It's a bit like a stress ball made of foam. It helps my anxiety because It feels good, smells good and has just the right amount of squish in it. I take ages choosing just the right squishy in shops. Nell gets embarrassed 'cos I have to open all the packets and try them out first.

2) Getting really absorbed in something, like playing piano, watching Taylor Swift on YouTube, and writing like I'm doing now. Sometimes when I do this stuff, I realize that the mood disappeared without me even noticing it.

*Hungry + angry = hangry   Thirsty + angry = thangry   Tired + angry = tangry that the mood disappeared without me even noticing it.

3) Animals. Animals make everything OK.

4) People who ignore my bad mood and don't take it personally can help lift me out of it quickly by being calm. You can never be too calm when I feel like this. Its like I'm stuck in a pit and a calm person saying kind and soothing things is throwing in a rope to help me out. Often though, people get angry with me and then it's like they jump in the pit with me then and hold me down in it, making me stay there even longer. When you're both in the pit, the only way out is together, talking about how you can move on and get out of it.

5) Sometimes my friends can make me laugh, which jolts me out of it, but it has to be natural. I hate it when people try too hard with a non-funny joke and I have to pretend to laugh. That's a Dad thing, by the way! But at least he tries, which is more than I can say for my so-called friends right now.

Pros: A bit of a pro of these moods is that I'm getting quite good at helping when my friends get down –

knowing what helps me, I'm sometimes able to suggest this to my friends. I actually think when you're autistic, you sometimes understand feelings better, instead of worse as some people think. Maybe because you are stuck with so many of them that you just HAVE to learn about how to make them feel better.

CHAPTER 20

"It's just me, Rupert. So don't be scared, OK?"

Tally checks quickly over her shoulder but there's nobody around. Dad has gone to work and Mum is in the kitchen, setting up her easel so that she can work on her latest painting. She hasn't seen Nell this morning, which is just as well because her sister has been in a foul mood for the whole of the half-term holiday. It has been one of the most boring weeks that Tally can remember, but she doesn't really mind. After the stresses of school, it's been quite nice to just lounge around in her pyjamas all day and not have to go anywhere. She'd happily stay at home for another week but school starts today. At least things might be better after so much time away.

As quietly as she possibly can, Tally tiptoes down the hall and up to the door of the utility room. Rupert is lying on his bed, gazing up at her with a doleful expression in his eyes. He's still wearing the muzzle – Mum insists that he has to keep it on during the day, which Tally thinks is completely cruel, even though Mum keeps trying to tell her that it doesn't hurt him and that he can still eat and drink with it on. Dad takes him for a walk every morning and evening, and Tally has heard him agreeing with Mum that Rupert seems to be getting more boisterous and uncontrollable than he was before. They've both agreed that if the muzzle doesn't calm him down then he'll have to go to a dog shelter, if Mrs Jessop doesn't get better soon.

"You have to promise not to get stressed out if I sit down," whispers Tally, lowering herself slowly on to the floor beside the gate. "I'm not even in the same room as you and I won't try to touch you, OK? It's all right – you don't have to do anything except be here with me."

Across the room, Rupert's eyes are trained on Tally and, as she takes a ball out of her pocket, he shifts his position so that he can watch everything that she's doing.

"This is one of my favourite squishies," she explains, squeezing it in her hand. "It's really soft and when I'm feeling worried I like to give it a good squidge."

Rupert makes a low, grumbling noise in his throat

and Tally nods.

"Exactly. I know that you're worried about being here, but it's OK, Rupert, it really is. You just have to stop being so nervous and scared because people get annoyed when you jump up and make lots of loud noises." She gives him a hard look. "I don't like it when you do those things, OK?"

The dog's eyes flicker as she passes the ball from hand to hand. A door slams upstairs and Tally knows that she hasn't got long until Nell storms down the stairs, demanding that they leave for school. So without giving herself time to really think about what she's doing, she leans forward and rolls her favourite squishy through the bars of the gate and across the floor, right up to Rupert's front paws.

He looks down at it and then his gaze goes back to Tally.

"You can borrow it," she tells him, "while I'm at school. But please don't chew it up or slobber all over it because that's not very considerate and I won't let you play with my things ever again if you don't treat them with respect."

Rupert tentatively stretches out a paw and bats it against the ball. Tally laughs and stands up as she hears

Nell calling her name.

"I'll come and see you when I get home," she promises. "Have a good day."

The bell is ringing as Nell and Tally walk in through the school gates. Nell dashes off without a word and Tally sighs, wondering what she's supposed to have done wrong this time. Then she sees Layla and the others up ahead and all thoughts of moody big sisters are pushed out of her mind. There's been a whole week in between last week's awfulness and today. Surely they'll all be back to normal by now?

"Layla! Hey! Hang on!" Shouldering her rucksack, Tally runs across the yard and up the main steps, catching up with them at the door. "Wait for me!" she pants, pushing past a couple of bigger kids. "Layla!"

"Did you hear something?" asks Lucy, pausing by the wall and glancing around. Her eyes skim over Tally as if she isn't there.

"No," answers Ayesha, wrinkling her nose. "I didn't hear a thing."

"Layla?" Tally waves her hand at her best friend, but Layla isn't looking at her. Instead, she's staring down the corridor and when Tally follows her gaze, she sees an unwelcome sight. Jasmine and Luke are walking straight towards them.

"Hi!" Layla leaps forward and pulls Jasmine into a big hug. The kind of hug she only ever used to give Tally. "How was your half-term?"

"Boring," moans Jasmine. "My mum made me look after my brother and wouldn't even give us the money for a McDonalds. She says that it's a waste of money – like she knows anything!"

"Good job that we all went together then, hey?" Ayesha grins at her. "How fun was that?"

"The most fun!" Jasmine flicks back her hair. "I wish I'd been allowed to hang out with you guys all week too!"

Tally opens her mouth to join in but then closes it again with a snap, remembering the scene outside McDonalds on the way to Dad's birthday meal at the restaurant. She spent most of half term going over and over whether Luke saw her in her mask, but now, with everyone right here in front of her, she wonders for the first time why they were all out in town together without her.

"We should do it again this Friday," says Lucy. "Maybe we can bring along a few other people too!"

"The more the merrier," adds Luke. "Everyone is welcome – other than *snitches*, obviously."

He turns to stare at Tally but she isn't interested in anything that he has to say.

"Why didn't you invite me?" she asks, looking at Layla. "I would have come to McDonalds with you."

It's not exactly the truth. Even if Mum and Dad had let her go out on her own, which is extremely unlikely, there's no way she'd have been happy to hang around town without any adults. Anything could happen.

But it would have been nice to be asked.

"Did you not just hear what I said?" asks Luke, making a snorting noise. "Everyone is welcome except snitches." His mouth spreads into a big, fake smile. "Which means that everyone is welcome except *you*. And anyway, you had plans with your parents that night, didn't you? Jeez – they must have a horrible life, being your family. I bet they constantly wish that they were somewhere else."

"I would have come to McDonalds," Tally repeats, registering the insult but not taking her eyes off Layla, who is now rummaging around in her bag as if she's lost something. "Did you forget to ask me?"

"Nobody forgot to ask you, Tally," says Lucy, sighing as if she's incredibly bored. "We didn't want you there – not after what you did to Luke in history. Obviously."

Tally frowns. "But I didn't do anything to Luke! He's the one who stole the test paper, not me. It wasn't *me* that put it in his bag."

"But you told Mr King that it was me, didn't you!" explodes Luke, his face going red. "He wouldn't have known if you hadn't ratted on me."

Tally shakes her head, trying to ignore the audience who are gathering around their group.

"He asked if anyone had seen it," she says. "I only told the truth."

Luke's eyes go very small. "You were trying to get me in trouble."

"I was just being honest," protests Tally. "Layla – tell him."

"You hate me and you wanted Mr King to put me in detention." Luke steps forward but Tally doesn't move, not even when she can feel his breath on her face.

Someone laughs nearby and Layla glances around, looking nervous.

"Let's just go. I told you, she can't help it. It's not her fault."

"That's not true though, is it?" Luke gives a small laugh but Tally knows that he doesn't really think any of this is funny. "It wasn't a mistake. She knew exactly what she was doing, so stop trying to make excuses for her, Layla. I don't know how you've put up with her for so long, to be honest."

"You shouldn't have called me *weirdo*," Tally whispers, clenching her fists. "It's your own fault that I told Mr King."

"So you *were* trying to punish me!" shouts Luke, his voice triumphant. "I knew it." He turns to the others and raises his eyebrows. "You heard her. She was mad at me so she snitched."

"That's unforgiveable," mutters Jasmine. "You didn't have to go that far, Tally."

"That's not what I said." Tally's eyes dart around the hall. "I didn't mean to—"

"Did you know that Mr King sent an email to Luke's dad?" asks Lucy, putting her hand on her hip. "He told him that Luke was caught with a stolen test paper in his bag and Luke's dad went ballistic!"

"Shut up, Lucy," mutters Luke, picking his bag up off the floor. "It's none of her business what my dad did."

There's an awkward pause for a moment and everyone suddenly seems to be looking everywhere but at Tally or Luke. The unfairness hits Tally like a thunderbolt out of the sky, so sudden and shocking that it makes her wobble on her feet.

"I don't care about Luke or his mum and dad," she says loudly. "Now can we stop talking about it? Unless we're going to talk about what a horrible life they must have, putting up with such a foul boy for a son. I'd run away if I was them."

The silence that follows is not awkward. It's loud with apprehension and anticipation. Tally stares as a previously unseen look plasters itself across Luke's face. It isn't anger or disgust or menace or cruelty or any of the other expressions that she has come to associate with him. Instead, his eyes look like there are flames dancing inside them and his mouth drops open in complete and utter disbelief.

The bell rings again and the gathering crowd reluctantly start to move, but the small group in front of the awards cabinet stays frozen in position, as if they have been cursed by a wicked fairy.

"What did she just say about my mum?" murmurs Luke, his mouth the only part of him that moves.

His words seem to break the spell and the others leap into action.

"Let's go, mate," says Ameet, putting his hand on Luke's shoulder. "She's not worth it."

"We're going to be late for registration!" Lucy grabs hold of Ayesha's hand and pulls her away. "We'll see you at break-time, Layla!"

"We should go too," Jasmine tells Layla, but when Layla doesn't move she shakes her head and joins the throng of kids making their way to class, Ameet beside her.

"It's OK," Layla says softly and for a moment, Tally relaxes, until she sees that Layla's eyes are not on her. "I told you. She can't help it. You just have to ignore her and not mind too much if she says hurtful things."

"I'm standing right in front of you!" calls Tally, wiggling her hands. "You shouldn't talk about me as if I'm not here."

"Tell her that I'll ignore her and she can ignore me." Luke closes his eyes and when he opens them again, the fire has been put out. "And tell her that if she ever speaks about my mum again, then she'll be sorry."

And then he spins round and disappears into the crowd.

"Where are we meeting at break-time?" asks Tally, shifting her weight from foot to foot. "It looks like it's going to rain again so we should find somewhere under cover because I do *not* want to get wet!"

Layla frowns. "Were you not listening to any of what just happened?" she asks. "It was bad enough that you got Luke in trouble before half term, Tally. What you just said about his mum was completely unforgiveable."

"What did I say?" Tally looks puzzled. "I didn't say anything that he didn't say."

"What?" Now it's Layla's turn to look confused. "You said that thing about them having to put up with him as a son. Don't you remember?"

Tally resists the urge to stamp her foot. "Of course I remember, Layla. And I also remember that he said the exact same thing to me! So it's fine!"

Layla groans. "No. It's not fine. And it's not the same thing. He didn't hurt your feelings when he said it, and it's a little bit true anyway – your mum and dad *do* have to put up with you."

"He did hurt my feelings, actually," snaps Tally, feeling scared. Layla has never spoken to her like this before and if even she thinks that Tally is a pain, then maybe it's really true. "But I bet I'm easier to put up with than he is. I only told the truth – I would totally run away if he was in my family."

"You have got to stop saying that," hisses Layla, her cheeks flushing red. "I'm serious, Tally. You've gone too far this time."

"Why?" Tally hisses back. "Why can he say it and I can't? That's not fair!"

"You know why." Layla looks around at the emptying corridor. "You were there at school last year, just like the rest of us. And I know that nobody ever talked about what happened to Luke, but we all knew. Don't act like you've forgotten. Luke's mum ran off and left him with his dad. That's why what you said was so awful."

And then she's gone and Tally is left alone with the too-late remembered memory of Luke crying in the year six cloakroom and the sinking sensation that everything has gone very, very wrong.

CHAPTER 21

The bell is ringing as Tally and Nell walk through the gates. Nell dashes off immediately without saying a word, but Tally walks slowly, her eyes scanning the yard. There is no sign of Layla or Lucy or Ayesha – wherever they are, they aren't here. Nobody is waiting to walk with her into school. Her heart starts to speed up as she contemplates the idea of having to spend the entire day alone. But then again, it's hard to know which is worse. Being alone or tagging along behind them, being ignored all the time.

The first lesson is drama. Mrs Jarman is waiting when the class enters the studio, a big smile on her face.

"We're going to make a start acting out our new script today," she tells them. "Put your bags down by the wall and take a seat."

In the middle of the room is a circle of chairs, and sitting together on the far side is Lucy and Ayesha. Tally walks slowly to join them, picking at the skin around her fingers as she goes.

"Hi," she says quietly, sitting down in the seat next to Ayesha. "I didn't see you by the gate this morning."

Lucy murmurs something to Ayesha, who makes a sniggering sound.

"Where were you all, anyway?" asks Tally.

She won't give up and she's been doing her research. She borrowed Nell's magazine last night (well, Nell said she stole it but she had every intention of giving it back and it would never have got ripped if Nell hadn't tried to wrench it out of her hands) and there was an article about how to make friends. It was actually called "How to be the Life and Soul of the Party". Tally hates parties because they're too noisy and the music is usually not Taylor Swift, but she read it anyway. And the article said that she should find interesting things to talk about and ask questions so that other person feels listened to and important.

She leans forward and looks right at the girls.

"I wanted to tell you about my dog because I know that you like dogs. Isn't your dog called Rosie, Ayesha? I bet she's really cute. My dog is cute too!"

Ayesha turns her head away. "You haven't got a dog," she says, and there is something about the tone of her voice that makes Tally feel chilly. "It's just another one of your stories."

Tally stares at her in disbelief.

"I have got a dog. His name is Rupert and he's a greyhound. He used to win lots of races but now he's only got three legs so he can't compete any more."

"Maybe he could win a three-legged race then," sniggers Lucy. "If he was actually a real dog, that is."

She leans closer to Ayesha and starts whispering. Tally's head starts to buzz as she thinks about what Lucy has just said. She wants to stand up and scream, but if she does that then nobody will ever like her because normal people deal with their emotions in a calm, controlled manner.

"That's not very kind," she says quietly. "And he *is* real. I'm not a liar."

Lucy glances up. "Yeah, right. And do you mind?" she says, her voice sweet like a cupcake. "Only we're having a private conversation here."

"It's not about you, honest," adds Ayesha and then they huddle their heads together while giggles waft upwards like smoke signals that Tally cannot interpret.

And she wonders why, if they aren't talking about her, it hurts so very much.

"Are we all here?" asks Mrs Jarman, sitting down and looking around, frowning when she sees one empty chair. "No – there's someone missing."

"It's Luke, Miss," says Aleksandra, looking worried. "I saw him first thing this morning in Mr Kennedy's office."

A ripple of interest flows around the circle of year seven pupils.

"I heard that he had a fight with one of the year ten kids," says one of the boys.

"I heard that Luke just jumped him for no reason," adds another. "There was blood everywhere, apparently."

"Someone in my tutor group told me that Luke is getting excluded," says Ayesha, finally pulling away from Lucy. "Like, permanently."

"That's quite enough idle speculation," says Mrs Jarman, her face looking serious. "Let's make a start on the lesson, if you can all stop the gossiping for one minute. Now, this play is set in—"

But before she can continue, the door opens and Mr Kennedy walks into the drama studio. Luke trails behind him, his shirt covered in mud stains and one sleeve ripped at the shoulder.

"I'd like a quick word," he tells Mrs Jarman, before turning to look at Luke. "You can go and sit down. And remember what I said. This is your final warning, young man."

The teachers leave the room, although Tally is relieved to see that they keep the door open. Luke throws his bag on to the floor and storms across to where they're all sitting.

"You OK, mate?" asks Ameet. "What's going on?"

Luke kicks the empty chair so that it spins into the middle of the circle and then stands in its place.

"Nothing," he says, shrugging his shoulders. "Nothing good, anyway."

"Did you really beat up a year ten kid?" asks Lucy, her eyes wide. "Is it true that he's had to go to hospital?"

Luke snorts. "You shouldn't believe everything you hear, you know."

"Bring that chair over here," Ameet tells him, glancing anxiously at the door. "She'll be back in a second and you don't want to get in any more trouble."

"Apparently, *Trouble* is my middle name, according to Mr Kennedy," mutters Luke, but he does as Ameet asks and pulls the chair back to where it's supposed to be, sinking down on to it like he's run a marathon. "And that's just one of the seriously irritating things that I've had to listen to him say this morning."

Tally has been sitting quietly but she sits up straighter when she hears this.

"So what *is* your middle name?" she asks, directing her question towards Luke. "Because people say that to me too and I hate it. My middle name is Olivia."

Luke stares at her, a surprised expression on his face. For a second, it seems as if he's about to reply but then he slumps deeper into his seat.

"Who even cares," he mutters. "We all know that your middle name is Weirdo."

"You shouldn't call her that," murmurs Aleksandra, but her voice is so quiet that nobody except Tally even hears her.

The door closes and Mrs Jarman walks towards them. "OK, year seven. Let's get going with these scripts, shall we?"

She picks up a pile of books from the floor and starts to walk around, handing one to each person.

"I'd like you to turn to page two and take a look at the list of characters," she tells them. "They're written in order of importance so if you think you'd like to read a longer part, you need to be considering one of the names in the first part of the list."

Tally opens her script and scans the words. Before today she had every intention of asking if she could have a main part. She loves acting and she's good at it, she knows that. And reading from a script is the best because you don't have to figure out how you're supposed to be behaving or what you're supposed to be thinking or feeling – it's all written out for you, right there on the page.

"So, put your hand up if you're interested in trying out for a longer part," says Mrs Jarman.

A couple of kids raise their arms.

"Is that it?" Mrs Jarman looks disappointed. "Is nobody else prepared to take on a challenge?"

She casts her eyes around the class, lingering on Tally for a moment. Tally looks quickly at the floor. The way that Lucy and Ayesha are behaving has changed everything and there's no way that she can take a main part when she feels so unsure of her friends and school and what she's done wrong.

When she feels so unsure about herself.

"How about you, Luke?" The teacher turns to look

at him. "You've always got a lot to say. How about channeling some of that energy into some drama?"

"No way." Luke doesn't look up and Tally feels a brief, momentary pang of sympathy for him. "I think I've got quite enough drama going on right now." His fists clench and then he sits upright in his chair and grins at Ameet. "And I'm talking about real, genuine drama – not some stupid play written by a dead dude about fifty thousand years ago."

He turns and stares at Mrs Jarman and Tally stops feeling sorry for him. "I don't even know why we all have to take this subject. It's not exactly teaching us anything, is it?"

There is a rush of air as the class collectively inhales and then silence as they all hold their breath. Luke and Mrs Jarman stare at each other and Tally is reminded of the old Western films that Dad likes watching on Saturday nights, the ones with cowboys and duels and stand-offs.

Mrs Jarman is the first to break. She nods her head and stands up, before walking across to her desk. Tally breathes out and suppresses a groan as everyone starts murmuring quietly. This is very, very bad. There is a new sheriff in town and his name is Luke.

Mrs Jarman returns to her seat, holding a piece of paper in her hand.

"Change of plan, people," she says, her voice very calm, considering that a year seven pupil has just outstared her. "Put your scripts on the floor under your chairs. We're going to do something slightly different for a moment."

She waits until everyone is silent and then unfolds the piece of paper. Tally recognizes it instantly.

Top Tip #3: When everything is going wrong, go small.

"What do you think that means?" asks Mrs Jarman, looking around at each of them. "When everything is going wrong, go small."

Tally freezes. This wasn't supposed to happen. Her Top Tips aren't for anyone else to hear. They're just for Mrs Jarman, because she understands. The rest of them won't get it. She shrinks into her chair and twists her fingers together, trying to push the feelings of panic away.

"It doesn't make sense," says Ameet loudly, earning himself a grin from Luke.

"Are you sure about that?" asks Mrs Jarman. Her voice

is still calm but her eyes are glinting like the hardest of diamonds. "Maybe think about it for a second."

A girl on the other side of the room hesitantly raises her hand.

"Does it mean that we should curl up and make ourselves small?" she asks. "Like, if we're in danger or something."

"Oh, yeah – it could be a survival thing," chimes in Aleksandra. "Like, from caveman times. If there was a lion about to eat you up, then you'd curl up in a ball. Like basic animal instinct."

"*You're* basic," snorts Luke. "Good luck with surviving if a lion is after you and your only action is to curl up on the floor."

Everyone laughs and the tension that has been floating in the air dissolves. Tally relaxes her fingers and raises her head slightly.

"I think it means that you should be quiet," offers Lucy. "If everything is going wrong then just say nothing and maybe it'll all go away."

Mrs Jarman looks at her and smiles. "And would you say that's an effective tactic?" she asks. "Does saying nothing or opting out of the situation make it any better?"

Lucy shakes her head. "I guess not. Unless the thing that's gone wrong is that our car has broken down yet again and my mum is trying to fix it. If that's happening then it's definitely better to stay quiet!"

"I think it's a stupid thing to say," calls Ameet, still clearly attempting to win himself some points with Luke. "Go big or go home, that's what my dad tells me. If something is going wrong then you should just try harder until you make it work."

Tally opens her mouth and then promptly closes it again. There's no point in trying to tell them what it really means because they don't think like she does. She could spend all day explaining and they still won't get it and she'll just end up looking stupid. She doesn't know why Mrs Jarman has done this but she does know one thing. She is never going to put another suggestion in the Top Tips box ever again.

"I want you all to think about something that has gone wrong recently," Mrs Jarman tells them. "Choose a time where things weren't working out the way you wanted them to."

"How many things can we choose?" asks Luke, elbowing Ameet in the ribs. "'Cos, you know, some of us might have quite a long list!"

Mrs Jarman looks at him and smiles. "Nobody needs to be scared about doing this activity," she says. "I'm not going to make anyone share anything that they would rather stays private."

"I'm not scared," scoffs Luke. "There's nothing frightening about *thinking*, is there?"

"Some people would disagree with you there," says Mrs Jarman. "Sometimes, thinking about ourselves and who we really are is the most terrifying thing of all."

The room goes quiet and nobody is looking at anybody else. Tally can feel her hands starting to tingle and so she shoves them under her legs and traps them. Flapping is not a thing that can happen at school, no matter how strange a day this is becoming.

"Now I want you to ask yourself a question," continues the teacher. "Would going small have helped in this situation? If you had broken it all down into tiny steps and addressed one issue at a time, would that have made things more manageable?"

There's a pause and then a few people start to nod.

"Would anyone like to share their thoughts?" asks Mrs Jarman.

Aleksandra raises her hand. "I had a really bad day last week," she says slowly. "I argued with my mum and then I dropped my phone and my dad got really mad at me, and then when I got to school I thought that all my friends were ignoring me. By the time I went to bed I felt like everyone hated me and my life was rubbish."

Mrs Jarman nods sympathetically. "I think we've all had days like that," she says. "So how might going small have helped?"

"Well…" Aleksandra's eyes flicker around the room. "I think that if I'd stopped to think about it, the only reason that everything went so wrong is because I'd had lots of late nights and that made me feel tired and kind of bad about myself. So the things that went wrong were caused by that and not because nobody likes me."

Tally stares at the other girl. She always assumed that Aleksandra spent every day laughing and smiling and feeling brilliant, but it doesn't sound like that's true. She's never, not once, given any sign that she isn't having the best time.

Which means that she's hiding how she really feels.

"I think we can all understand what Aleksandra told us," says Mrs Jarman. "It can be really difficult to work out why things are going wrong if we don't go *small*. Big feelings tend to hide themselves in very small events – that's why we might cope with how we're feeling for a long time and then a tiny thing can push us too far and we automatically think that this is the thing we're upset about."

"I got hurt on my bike at the weekend," says one of the boys. "I was out with my mates and they kept going on at me to try a jump. So I did, even though I didn't want to and I came off my bike. Look."

He tugs at the bottom of one of his trouser legs and reveals a painful-looking bruise.

"So would going small have helped in this situation?" asks Mrs Jarman.

"Doing a smaller jump would have definitely helped him, Miss," quips Luke and even Mrs Jarman laughs at this.

"I guess I only did the jump because I was scared of looking like a wuss," says the boy, once the laughter has died down. "But it didn't really matter. The worst thing that would have happened if I'd said no is that my mates would have laughed at me. Instead, I got hurt."

"I bet they laughed at you anyway," adds Ameet and the boy nods, his mouth pulled into a comedy sad-face.

"I was in a bad mood before I even got to school this morning," says Luke suddenly, his focus on the wall behind Mrs Jarman's head. "And everything just got worse and worse, one thing after another."

Mrs Jarman is quiet for a moment and then she reaches down and picks up her script.

"I think you should all be aware that we have a safe space in school," she tells them. "It's a new idea, suggested by a pupil this year. It's the room next door to the staffroom and it's a quiet place where you can go anytime, whenever you feel that things are getting a bit much and you could do with a break."

Tally stares at her. That was her second Top Tip. *She* is the pupil who suggested a quiet space and now Mrs Jarman is telling everyone that they're allowed to go there? She's telling *Luke* that he can go there, as if he would ever need to have time away from everything.

Mrs Jarman flashes Tally a quick smile and then looks back at the script.

"So, another time, some of you might want to take yourself to the safe space *before* things go wrong. But for now we'll do something else. We'll start again and reset the day by achieving something positive, even if it's a really small thing. We're going to start reading through the first scene. Aleksandra, would you like to read the part of Sylvia?"

Aleksandra beams and nods as everyone picks up

their books and turns to the correct page.

"Luke, you will be Thomas." It isn't a question and Tally looks up as Luke stares at their teacher, who starts to read from her script.

"*Act One, Scene One,*" says Mrs Jarman, her voice clear. "*The scene takes place in an abandoned house. Sylvia is sitting on the floor. Thomas enters the stage and looks around.*"

Tally holds her breath. After everything that has already happened, how on earth can Mrs Jarman even consider asking him to do this? She's playing right into his hands. She's giving him all the power and now he can disrupt the rest of the lesson by refusing to join in. It doesn't matter that she's told him about going small – Luke won't understand. It isn't the same for people like him – he doesn't need to break things down into tiny steps, just to figure things out or to feel like he's actually achieved something. He's the kind of person who swoops through his days without a single thought. He's never going to—

"*This'll do nicely.*" His voice rings out into the room. "*Nobody will see us in here. It's the perfect hiding place to stash the body – good job, Sylvia.*"

Tally sits quietly for the rest of the lesson, her mind

whirring with thoughts. She is not the only person who has bad days. It's not just her who finds that things can get a bit much. She's never really thought about it before, but what if there are other kids in year seven who are different too and nobody has ever told her?

What if she isn't the only one?

CHAPTER 22

"Does she have to wear that thing at the table?" asks Nell.

Tally ignores her and focuses instead on manoeuvering a spoonful of soup through the mouth of the mask. It isn't as easy as it sounds and she has to keep her hand steady to avoid splashing tomato soup down her chin.

"Is everything OK, Tally?" Mum sits down opposite her and gives her a smile. "How was school today?"

Tally doesn't answer because she has no idea what she's supposed to say. School is horrible and sad and frightening. Nobody will talk to her and she spends each day on her own. Lunchtime is the worst because there's no way that she can go into the canteen without Layla, so she always ends up wandering the corridors. Sometimes she goes to the quiet room that Mrs Jarman set up, but none of her friends are there. It feels safe but it's lonely too. But if she tells Mum all of that then she'll want to know why nobody will be her friend and Tally doesn't have an answer for that question because she just doesn't know.

So it's easier to say nothing.

If it wasn't for Rupert, Tally doesn't think that she would have anyone. Every night, when Mum and Dad go into the living room to watch television and Nell disappears upstairs, Tally always heads straight to where Rupert is always waiting for her.

Mum gives a sigh and starts talking to Dad about his day. Tally zones out their voices and eats as fast as possible before pretending that she's going to her room. But as soon as everybody has left the kitchen, she creeps back downstairs and towards the utility room.

"Hello, boy," she whispers, checking that nobody is around before sinking down on the hallway floor, next to the stair-gate. "It's only me."

After days of visits, Rupert is growing in confidence. He still seems scared but every evening he creeps a tiny bit closer to where Tally is sitting on the other side of the gate. And Tally is discovering that while he doesn't say a lot, he is an excellent listener. She's told him all about Layla, Lucy and Ayesha and the way that they look through her as if she isn't there. She's wondered aloud about the things that were said in the last drama lesson and whether there are other kids in year seven who find things hard too. She's told him that she never means to behave badly but that sometimes she can't stop everything from going wrong. And the look he gives her, his big eyes fixed on hers, makes the swirling, churning sensation in her head go away, just for a few minutes.

She never has to pretend to look at the space between Rupert's eyes. It's easy to make eye contact with him.

"I heard Dad talking to Mum earlier," she says now, stretching out her hand and pushing it through the bars, a short distance away from Rupert's nose. He doesn't flinch and inside, Tally smiles. She hasn't tried to touch him yet because not everybody likes to be touched. She's going to let him come to her when he's ready – her job is to let him know that she's here, waiting for him.

"He said that he's been in contact with a dog shelter but that they haven't got room for you until next week. He told Mum that you were wild yesterday, pulling on your lead and leaping up when he stepped out of the garden gate."

Moving her hand back, Tally reaches into her pocket

and takes out her second-favourite squishy. "It's good news that the shelter won't take you yet," she says, squeezing it in her hand. "But you've got to work harder, because we're running out of time to show them that you're not dangerous. Mum and Dad have had enough. Mum says that you've got to go, and then who will I have to talk to, hey? Stop being so selfish and start following the rules. If you can't be like an ordinary dog then you're just going to have to pretend, OK?"

Rupert thumps his tail on the tiles and Tally laughs.

"Good! Right — let's go over the rules for being normal. You're a very clever dog so I'm sure that you can learn them quickly. Then everyone will love you and nobody will send you away."

She leans against the gate and starts to tick off each rule on her fingers.

"Rule number one: don't do anything unexpected. Normal people like it if you're quiet and calm, which means no jumping about or making weird noises or flapping or bouncing your legs up and down when you're trying to think of an answer, even if these things make you feel better. They're all a big no-no, OK?"

Rupert flicks his ear with his front paw and Tally nods.

"Rule number two: pretend to be someone else. Someone who isn't different. They can't see inside your brain, so you can still be you in there, but on the outside you have to make them believe that you are just like them. So that means pretending to be interested in the stuff that they're interested in and copying what they do."

Rupert yawns loudly and Tally shoots him a fierce look. "I'm only saying all of this to help you. It's very rude to yawn when someone is speaking – Mum says that it makes you look like you're bored, which I think is silly because I can't help it if my mouth wants to yawn when she's going on about homework, but that's exactly the kind of thing I'm talking about. You have to pretend. Even if it is boring."

The dog shifts his position so that his nose is pressed to the floor. He gazes up at Tally as if he has never heard anything so fascinating in all his years. Tally gives him an approving smile.

"That's much better. And finally, rule number three: make sure that you show your feelings the right way. If you're sad then they like it if you say 'I am sad', and maybe even cry. They don't like it if you shout and stamp or bark or jump up because that makes them think that you're angry and *not OK*."

Rupert whines and Tally rolls her eyes. "I know! It's ridiculous! But it's a big thing for them and it'll help you to fit in if you do what they do. SO, if you're happy you have to say 'I am happy' and have a very big smile. You do not sing a song very loudly and rub your hands together very fast, because then they'll think that you're worried and that means that everyone will get all upset and bothered about you not being OK when actually you're fine."

The sound of the living-room door opening makes Tally jump up.

"I've got to go," she whispers. "But think about what I said and try really hard, Rupert. Otherwise you'll be left all on your own and I can tell you right now, that isn't a very nice place to be."

Tally doesn't wake up until Mum comes into her room the next morning.

"Rise and shine, sleepyhead," sings Mum. "What would you like for breakfast today?"

"Nothing." Tally burrows back down under the duvet, squeezing her eyes shut against the intrusion. Billy is snuggled up next to her and she has absolutely no intention of moving, particularly if Mum is going to start interrogating her about breakfast the second that she opens her eyes.

"You can choose toast or cereal," says Mum, as if Tally hasn't spoken. "Dad isn't feeling good so he isn't going to work today. You can sit with him while you eat."

"I don't want to."

The words are a habit. If Tally stops and thinks about it, she would actually love to eat breakfast with Dad. He's been working really long hours recently and she's hardly seen him. If she eats breakfast with him then maybe she can talk to him about Rupert and ask him to persuade Mum to let them keep him until Mrs Jessop gets home.

"It's stopped raining for a change," says Mum, glancing out of the window. "The forecast is predicting snow now, but I don't know, it still seems a bit early to me."

"Mum!" Nell comes barging into Tally's bedroom, not even pausing to knock. Tally sits bolt upright and points her finger at her sister.

"Get out!" she screeches. "There is a rule about coming into my room and you just broke it. I'm warning you – you'll be sorry if you do that again."

"I need some money for the trip today." Nell pays no attention to Tally's threat. "We have to buy our lunch at the museum. Can I get some change from your purse?"

Mum stands up and shakes her head. "The last time I let you loose with my purse you took enough to feed the whole class. I'll come downstairs with you and get you some cash myself."

"Get out!" screams Tally, her face turning red as she flings back the covers.

"Like I'd want to stay in here." Nell doesn't even look in her direction before spinning around and flouncing out of the room.

Mum follows her, pausing when she reaches the door. "Toast or cereal?" she asks again. "As you're up."

"Toast," mumbles Tally, narrowing her eyes. She knows what Mum is doing but she is actually hungry so she's prepared to go along with the game for now.

"Lovely," says Mum. "Put your clothes on and it'll be waiting for you in the kitchen."

Tally gets dressed as slowly as she possibly can, sitting down and reading a comic in between putting on each sock in order to make herself as late as possible. But when she finally creeps downstairs, the clock in the hallway shows that there is still plenty of time until they need to leave for school. Tally scowls. Mum must have woken her up extra-early on purpose. That means that she's going to have to take even longer to leave the house this morning, just to show Mum that she hasn't won.

In the kitchen, Dad is sipping a cup of tea. He's still in his dressing gown, and Tally stares, unused to him being here when she gets up.

"Morning, sweetheart," he says, giving her a small smile. "You're all ready to take on the world, I see."

"How are you feeling, Dad?" asks Nell, pushing past Tally and into the room. "Mum said that you're unwell."

"I'm sure it's nothing," Dad tells her. "I probably just need a bit of rest."

He wraps his arm across his stomach and wrinkle lines appear on his forehead.

"Is it still hurting?" asks Mum, noticing him wince.

Dad nods and Tally steps back, grateful for the tiger mask that will stop any of Dad's germs from getting to her.

"Go back to bed," Mum tells him. "I'll phone work and let them know that you're going to be off for a couple of days."

"I'm sure that—" starts Dad.

"No arguing, Kevin." Mum's voice is stern. "You're

going to make yourself really sick if you don't start looking after yourself."

Dad nods gratefully and eases himself up from the chair. "Have a good day, girls," he tells them before walking slowly out of the room.

"Right, we need to get going," says Mum, putting a plate of toast on the table. "I need the pair of you to get yourselves ready on time and off to school without too much fuss and noise. I have to ring Dad's work and figure out what we're going to do with that awful dog, now that Mrs Jessop isn't coming home."

"What?" Both girls stand still, looking at Mum with shocked faces.

"What's happened to Mrs Jessop?" asks Nell.

"What are you going to do to Rupert?" asks Tally at the same time.

Mum turns on the tap and fills the kettle up with water.

"Mrs Jessop isn't well enough to come back to her own house," she explains. "She's being sent to live in a care home, where she can be looked after properly, but she can't take the dog with her."

"That's so sad," says Nell, and Tally nods in total agreement.

"Poor Rupert. He should be allowed to go to the care home too."

"What are you on about?" Nell stares at Tally. "I don't mean that it's sad for the stupid dog. It's sad that an old lady has to leave her home."

"Oh." Tally shrugs and picks up a piece of toast. She doesn't really know Mrs Jessop, but she does know Rupert and it's him that she feels sorry for.

"Can I trust you girls to sort yourselves out without any issues?" asks Mum, glancing at her phone. "I've got so much to do and if I don't make a start now then the rest of the day is going to be horrendous."

Nell scowls. "As long as she doesn't think that I'm going to school with her in that ridiculous mask then everything will be fine."

Mum looks at Tally. "You know that you can't wear it to school, don't you? Not even if it is Halloween."

Tally nods, but inside she is hatching a plan. Life would be so much easier if she could go to school as Tiger Girl instead of Tally. She knows that she can't really walk in through the gates wearing her mask but there's nothing stopping her from taking it with her in her rucksack. And maybe, having the tiger mask close to her will help, just a tiny bit.

Date: Friday 31st October

Situation: Being abandoned by my so-called friends at school and Mum sending Rupert away

Anxiety Rating: 12/10. As if the sleepover wasn't bad enough, now I've got even more to deal with.

Dear Diary,

I can't shake off the really bad feeling tonight. I want to stop going over and over the day, but I just can't – my mind keeps jumping to different things. When I'm like this my mum tells me to try "changing the channel" and think positive things. Sometimes that works, but tonight whatever channel I change to they all end up turning bad. And now it feels like I have so many channels running at the same time that my brain is not behaving in the way I want it to. My mum's friend says it's like my brain is a phone with too many apps open and they are causing it to freeze and that's exactly true. It's one of the worst feelings.

Tally's autism facts: The good and bad feelings

Pro: Good feeling

The good feeling isn't just another way of saying

happiness or excitement but a whole new expression neurotypicals have yet to discover. You can even get the good feeling when you're unhappy! It's a soft, cosy, "protected in bubble wrap" feeling where no bad things can touch you.

I usually get the good feeling when I'm somewhere I love or in a situation that I love. I love it when it rains and I'm in a car – or even better a tent – especially at night. My number one good feeling is the thought of going on holiday on an aeroplane at night when it's raining (this is making me smile right now). Also, hotels are on my good-feeling spectrum. What else…? Being on a horse, by the sea, cuddled up with animals on my bed, when the suns shines with those rays breaking through the clouds and it looks like heaven is checking in on you. But this is more than happiness. It's like the biggest joy that takes over, and you never want it to end. In fact, I can start feeling so anxious about it ending that I can ruin the good feeling. My absolute number one good feeling would be meeting Taylor Swift. When I do I'm going to tell her how she has made my life better and I love how she keeps on being who she is and ignoring the haters. Like, if she could deal with what Kanye did to her, then I can deal with anything autism throws at me.

Con: Bad feeling

The bad feeling is really the same thing as the good but the absolute opposite. If I had to pin it down I would probably say random anxiety in random places. But there can be some predictability to it. It usually involves doing things I really don't want to do. I get the bad feeling in certain places, like Marks & Spencer (shops and the bad feeling go hand in hand) or doing things like taking down Christmas decorations or coming back from holiday. Bedtime is one of the absolute worst bad feelings there is.

CHAPTER 23

The days plod slowly by and nothing changes other than the bad things get worse. Every morning Tally goes in search of the girls and every morning it takes longer and longer for her to find them. And even when she does, they're always in the middle of a conversation that she doesn't understand, and if she tries to join in they have no interest in anything she has to say. Layla spends every lunchtime huddled over her phone with Jasmine, while Ayesha relays messages between Luke and Lucy, giggling and sniggering in a way that makes no sense because nobody ever says anything funny, as far as she can tell. It's possible that Lucy agrees with her because she's stopped laughing too, but there's no point in Tally asking her, not when she ignores everything Tally says.

She's tried to ask Layla if she's done something

wrong but Layla just sighs and says *"Oh, Tally,"* in an exasperated way. Tally isn't stupid. She knows they wish she'd just go away. The problem is that she has nowhere *to* go, so she just has to carry on loitering on the edges, always on the outside looking in. Her days are spent standing around awkwardly, pushing her hand inside her rucksack to feel the familiar comfort of her tiger mask whenever nobody is looking at her.

Which is most of the time.

Even Mum hasn't noticed that she's not OK because she's busy looking after Dad, who's still feeling unwell but refusing to go to the doctors because he's just a bit "under the weather". And it hasn't stopped raining for weeks, which is why today's PE lesson is taking place in the freezing cold hall.

"Right then, we're going to stop there!" shouts Miss Perkins. "You can all make your way over to the benches and sit down QUIETLY."

Tally breathes a sigh of relief and bends over, pulling deep gulps of air into her lungs. She hates PE lessons and she really, really hates fitness training. Miss Perkins has been making them do bleep tests, and despite running her fastest, Tally just can't reach the wall before the loud, piercing noise shrieks around the hall. She's spent most of today's lesson trying to dodge the rest of the class, who race ahead of her and always seem to be running in the opposite direction to the way that she is going.

"Some of you did reasonably well with that activity," says Miss Perkins, putting her hands on her hips. "But some of you are horribly out of shape. At your age you should be able to complete the first ten levels with ease. And one or two of you—" She pauses and looks directly at Tally. "One or two of you just can't seem to be bothered to make any effort whatsoever. And that is unacceptable."

Tally can feel her cheeks flushing red. She *was* making an effort, but every single time the awful bleeping sound happened it made her fists clench and her whole body stiffen and it's difficult to run quickly when your legs feel like they're made out of wood.

"You can all go and get changed." Miss Perkins tilts her head to one side. "Except for you, Tally. You've barely broken a sweat this lesson so you can go to the PE cupboard and tidy it up before you leave."

The rest of the class are sniggering and whispering to each other as they stand up and start to head out of the hall.

"Make sure you don't get lost in there," says one girl as she walks past Tally. "Remember what Mr Kennedy said on our first day!"

Tally closes her eyes for a second and when she opens them again, everyone has gone and Miss Perkins is waiting by the door.

"I want it to be completely tidy," she calls. "It's break-time now so if you're quick you shouldn't be late for your next lesson. And Tally? Maybe this will encourage you to have a better attitude in PE."

And then she sweeps out and Tally is left sitting alone on the middle of the bench, gazing at the PE cupboard, which is on the opposite side of the hall. She knows that she doesn't have a choice, but it doesn't make the decision to stand up and make her feet walk across the floor even a tiny bit easier.

The door to the cupboard is closed. Tally counts to ten inside her head and then flings it open and stares inside. The contents of the PE cupboard stare menacingly back at her. Basketballs are strewn across the floor and the netball vests are flung in a messy heap on two of the shelves. Beanbags and tennis balls and plastic cones compete for space in the wire baskets that line the edge of the cupboard and everywhere she looks there is chaos and confusion.

It is horrible and all that Tally wants to do is turn and run far away. She thinks about the tiger mask tucked safely inside her bag in the changing room and wishes that she could wear it now. Tiger Girl could do this task without wanting to scream or cry. Tiger Girl wouldn't curl up into a tiny ball and make high-pitched noises until someone came to rescue her.

But Tiger Girl isn't here and if she doesn't sort out the cupboard then Miss Perkins will only make the next punishment worse. And she hasn't got time to waste if she's going to make everything tidy *and* get to the drama studio in time. She doesn't want to make Mrs Jarman cross with her, not when she put another Top Tip into the suggestions box at the end of the last lesson.

The inside of the PE cupboard smells. Tally tries to hold her breath but it's a hopeless tactic. When she finally has to breathe in, the musty smell of dirt and sweat and grass and plastic hits her in the back of the throat and she thinks for a moment that she might be sick. Blinking back tears, she picks up a basketball and stares around the space, wondering how she's supposed to make any kind of order from something so disorganized.

A bell rings and then there's the sound of feet pounding down the corridor outside the hall. Break-time lasts for fifteen minutes, which means that she hasn't got time to think. Quickly, she scans the room and assesses the shelves that look the worst. She can do this. It's just like solving a puzzle and she's good at those when she's in the right mood.

Minutes tick by and Tally stacks and sorts and tidies. By the time she's finished, the netball vests are neatly folded and the wire baskets are filled with items that belong together. The plastic cones are slotted one on top of the other and the basketballs are crammed into a large bin that she found lurking at the very back of the cupboard.

"It hasn't looked like this for a while," says Miss Perkins, appearing in the doorway. "You've done an excellent job, Tally. I shall have to make you PE cupboard monitor for the rest of year seven!"

Tally spins round, her face falling. "Oh, please don't," she begs. "I'll try to run faster next lesson, I promise!"

Miss Perkins gives her a tight smile. "Excellent. Well, make sure that you do. And you can start right now because the bell is about to ring and you're going to be late if you don't hurry up."

Tally nods and races to the changing rooms, pulling off her scratchy PE kit and throwing herself into her uniform as quickly as possible. The bell rings while she's still lacing up her shoes and then it takes her a while to cram her kit back into her bag, so by the time she rushes through the school and up the stairs to the second floor, the corridors are empty.

She can hear laughing as she approaches the drama studio. Slowing down, she pushes the door open as quietly as possible, hoping that she can slip into the room unnoticed by Mrs Jarman.

Two things occur to her as the door swings closed behind her. The first is that Mrs Jarman is nowhere to be seen. The second is that something is going on in the middle of the room. The entire class is gathered in a group, pushing and shoving as they try to see whatever is causing all the interest. Tally walks forward slowly and as she edges closer, the crowd shifts, and suddenly she can see exactly what they are all looking at.

There is a tiger in the drama studio. It's on all fours, prowling and rearing up as if it's about to take a swipe at the year sevens, who are all pointing and laughing as if it's the funniest thing that they have ever seen.

"Grrrrrr!" roars the tiger.

Tally freezes, her heart pounding so hard that she thinks she might be about to die.

"Grrrrrrr! Look at me, Weirdo Adams in my scary tiger mask! You should all be terrified at the sight of me. Seriously – you should be quivering in your shoes right now!"

The tiger crouches on its haunches and then leaps into the air, making a few of the girls squeal. And then it sees Tally and it points one of its tiger claws in her direction, making everybody turn.

"Hi, Tally," the tiger says casually. "Hope you don't mind but I've borrowed your mask. I wanted to know what it felt like to play make-believe since, you know, most of us haven't done this stuff since we were five years old!"

Tally opens her mouth but no words come out. The tiger stands up.

"Haven't you got anything to say? That makes a nice change."

Give it back.

Inside Tally's head, the words are so loud that they make her flinch, but her voice still seems to be broken. She can feel the pressure building, growing stronger and stronger, and she knows that there's nothing that she can do to stop it.

"Do you want to know how I got hold of it?" asks Luke, pulling off the mask. "Because that's what I'd be wondering, if I was you." He laughs. "Not that I would ever want to be like you, obviously. I couldn't believe it when we saw you outside McDonalds, dressed up like a freaky little weirdo. We all laughed about that for ages!"

"Luke. Just stop it now." Across the room, Lucy is looking worried. "It was supposed to be a laugh but this isn't funny any more."

"That's right," says Luke, following Tally's gaze towards the girls who, until recently, she thought she could trust. "Lucy and Ayesha saw it in your bag when they were getting changed after PE. They took it out and showed everyone. And I do mean *everyone!*"

"Shut up, Luke!" shouts Lucy but Tally can't really hear anything properly, not when the sight of her mask in his hands is drowning out everything else. He has her mask. The mask that makes her Tiger Girl. He has taken her one *good thing* and ruined it for ever.

"Give. It. Back." Her voice is quiet, and only those who are standing close to her hear it, but they all instantly take a step backwards.

"Make me," taunts Luke, holding out his arm and

letting the mask dangle from his fingertips. "I'd love to see you try."

The laughter of the rest of the class pours into her ears and reverberates around her brain. She clamps her hands to her head and crouches on the floor, huddled into her knees in an attempt to make it all go away. But the noise keeps on coming and she can feel bodies pressing around her, squishing the air and making it impossible to breathe.

"La, la, la, la, la," she hums, pressing her fingers deeper into her ears and trying to remember the tune of her favourite song. But even Taylor Swift has deserted her and the sound that comes out of her mouth is discordant and scratchy and just makes everything worse.

"What's wrong with her?" calls a voice, sounding panicked.

"She's lost the plot!" adds another. "She's such a weirdo!"

"Is she pulling her own hair?" asks someone else. "Luke – you shouldn't have taken her mask. We're going to get in serious trouble if a teacher comes in and sees her like this."

"Everybody just needs to calm down!" shouts

someone else and some part of Tally's mind register's that it's Aleksandra. "Stop yelling! You're scaring her."

A door slams and the sudden breeze feels cool on Tally's hot forehead. It makes her pause for a second and when she opens her eyes, she sees that the class have all moved away and are staring at her from a distance, like she's a dangerous animal. She's seen that expression before, on the faces of Mum, Dad and Nell when they look at Rupert.

She can't stay here but she doesn't know if her body will work properly. Slowly, tentatively, she tests her arms, wiggling them up and down. She can move and she can breathe, and even though she just wants to sink into the floor and go back to being invisible, she needs to escape this place even more. Shakily, she pushes herself to her feet and picks up her bag, ignoring Aleksandra who is walking towards her with a worried expression on her face.

"Just take it, OK." Luke steps forward from the crowd, her mask still clutched in his fingers. For some reason it's quivering, as if his hands are shaking. "I don't even want it."

He throws the mask on to the ground but Tally has already gone.

CHAPTER 24

She runs with no idea about where she's going or what she's going to do when she gets there. All she knows is that she can't stay in the drama studio for another minute longer and that wherever she goes, it needs to be as far away as possible from what has just happened.

Hurtling down the corridor, Tally pushes open the door that leads to the stairs. The sound of everyone's laughter is still in her ears, making it hard to think about anything else, but the sight of Mrs Jarman standing in front of her is impossible to ignore.

"What on earth is going on?" asks the teacher, taking one look at Tally's face and putting her bag down on the floor. "Tally? What's happened?"

She can't tell her. She doesn't want to talk about it. It's all Mrs Jarman's fault in the first place because she should have been there and she wasn't and that means that she didn't even read the Top Tip that Tally added to the box a few days ago about keeping to the timetable and not changing things without giving a warning.

"Nothing, Miss," she mumbles. "I'm fine."

Mrs Jarman gives her a look, but it isn't *the look*, which is good because Tally knows that the fury is lurking just beneath her skin and she doesn't want to show Mrs Jarman just how upset she really is.

"You don't look very fine to me," she says. "Something has obviously happened so we're going to go to the drama studio and get this sorted out."

"No!" Tally clenches her fists. "I'm not going back in there and you can't make me."

The teacher raises her eyebrows. "I'm not going to make you do anything. But we *are* going to get to the bottom of this."

She picks up her bag and steps past Tally, walking through the door and away down the corridor. She is completely calm, as if Tally's entire world hasn't just screeched to a crashing halt.

Tally watches her go, telling herself that if Mrs Jarman looks back and demands that she does as she's told then she'll make a run for it. But the teacher just keeps walking, past the drama studio and up to the library. She doesn't check that Tally is following her, not even once and she doesn't shout at her to hurry up.

Mrs Jarman walks into the library and reappears a moment later, the librarian beside her.

"They can all get on with reading their scripts," she says. "Thank you so much for stepping in."

The librarian nods and pushes open the door to the drama studio. There is a brief second of noise and then the door closes and the corridor is silent once again. Mrs Jarman turns and heads into the library and Tally is left all alone.

It's the *not-looking* that swings it. Mrs Jarman is letting her decide and not telling her what to do. Slowly, Tally makes her way towards the library, picking up pace as she passes the drama studio. Her hand hesitates at the library door but when she pushes it open and peers inside, she can see that the room appears to be empty apart from the drama teacher.

"It would be nice if you could sit down," calls Mrs Jarman, gesturing to the chair opposite. "Then we can talk about why you're so upset."

Tally stares at her. "I'm not upset," she says. "I was upset when my goldfish died and I was upset when Nell borrowed my book and ripped one of the pages but I'm not upset now. I am so much more than upset."

Upset doesn't make your skin so cold that it is difficult to move. Upset doesn't make your ears fill with a rushing, pounding noise that is impossible to ignore. Upset doesn't make a person want to curl up in a ball and close her eyes and disappear.

"So what are you?" asks Mrs Jarman, leaning forward. "Because you look quite upset to me. Are you feeling unwell? Or have you had a falling-out with your friends, is that it?"

Tally closes her eyes. Mrs Jarman doesn't understand any more than the rest of them. It was a mistake to think that she might.

"I'm fine," she whispers. "I just want to go home. Please."

"Well, I can't send you home if I don't know what the problem is," says Mrs Jarman. "And you must have heard the saying – a problem shared is a problem halved? Maybe if you talk to me we might be able to find a solution?"

Tally opens her eyes and blinks rapidly.

"I don't think that talking about it is going to help." Her voice is quiet. "And I'm fine, Miss. Really."

Mrs Jarman sighs and stands up. "Well, I can't force you to tell me," she says. "But neither can I send you home if there isn't anything wrong with you. And I need to get back into class, which is also where you should be."

Tally takes a step back. "No! I'm not going in there again. I hate them and if you try to make me then I'm going to get really, really angry."

Mrs Jarman's face creases into a frown. "So tell me what has happened!" she says, throwing out her hands. "What can the rest of the class have possibly done to make you feel like this? For goodness' sake, let me help."

"You can't help me!" shouts Tally, her arms starting to flap. "They stole my stuff and they all think I'm weird and a snitch even though all I did was tell the truth."

She starts to pace up and down, letting it all come out in one, wild burst.

"I don't like Luke and so maybe I did want him to get in trouble, but I don't see why that means that nobody will talk to me because they do that kind of thing all the time. And it doesn't matter what I do to pretend to be like them, they hate me anyway. So I have to try harder and harder to be normal, but I don't even know what normal is supposed to look like and every time I think that I've worked it out, it all changes."

Tally pauses and drags in a big gulp of air. "And I am tired and crumpled and broken and I keep trying to uncrumple myself and get fixed but I don't know how to do it!" Then she whirls around and stares at Mrs Jarman, her eyes wide. "I don't know what I'm supposed to be doing and I don't know the words that I'm supposed to say to make me like everyone else!"

There is a moment of silence. Tally's voice hangs heavily in the air between them and she forces herself to be still as the drama teacher gazes at her before casting her eyes around the room.

"There are a great many words in this library," she says, which is not what Tally is expecting at all. "And lots of them are written by people who, perhaps, think differently to others. Maybe that's why they write books – to explore their feelings in a way that makes sense to them."

She takes a step forward, but keeps some space between her and Tally. "I think this is a fabulous place to remind ourselves that if we were all the same, the world would be very dull indeed."

Tally shakes her head, feeling suddenly exhausted. "But that's what they all want," she murmurs. "That's why people think being autistic is a *bad thing*. Because it stops me from being the same as everyone else. It stops me fitting in."

Mrs Jarman smiles. "The only *bad thing* is that you've wasted so much time trying to be someone different, when the someone different that you already are is so amazing. Maybe you should spend less time trying to fit in and more time being yourself. There's only one of you, Tally – just like there's only one of me and one of Lucy and one of Luke."

"Thank goodness for that," Tally mutters, staring at the floor.

Mrs Jarman makes a snorting sound. "Well, exactly," she says. "And as there is only one of you, don't you think that you should really say and do the things that make you Tally, and not try acting like you're somebody else?"

"That's a rubbish idea." Her head snaps up. "They'll all hate me even more if I act like *me*."

"Hmmm." Mrs Jarman doesn't look convinced. "I really don't think that's true. But you said earlier that someone has stolen something of yours? Tell me what's been taken because that is a problem I can definitely solve."

"It doesn't matter any more." Tally rams her hands into the pockets of her coat. "Just forget about it."

The image of Luke dangling her tiger mask from his fingers flashes through her brain. He said he didn't want it. Well, neither does she. Not now. She'll never be able to wear it again, not since he ruined it.

"—to get back to the lesson," Mrs Jarman is saying when she zones back in. "You can stay here until you're feeling a bit better."

Tally nods and walks across to the chairs, letting her bag fall off her shoulder as she slumps down on to the soft cushions.

"And Tally?" Mrs Jarman pauses with hand on the door handle. "It's OK *not* to be OK, you know?"

Then she is gone and Tally is left with a feeling of emptiness that is even worse than the anger that burned so brightly only a short time before.

CHAPTER 25

Tally doesn't move from the library until the end of lunchtime and nobody comes anywhere near her apart from once, when Mrs Jarman dashes through the door with an overflowing folder of paper in one hand and the tiger mask in the other.

"I think this is yours," she says, putting it on the table. "And don't worry. I've had a big chat with the class and nobody is going to be taking things from your bag again."

Tally wants to leave the mask where it is, but the look on Mrs Jarman's face suggests that she expects her to be pleased to see it, so she picks it up and rams it into her coat pocket. She doesn't know what she's going to do but she isn't keeping it, that's for sure.

The afternoon passes slowly. Tally puts her head on the desk in every lesson and despite repeated attempts by each teacher to get her to sit up, refuses to look at anyone or anything. Layla tries to whisper something to her during English, but when Tally doesn't respond, she gives up, just like the teachers have done.

Just like everybody always does.

The instant that the bell rings for the end of the day, Tally is out of the door. She storms down the corridor and out into the cold November day. She doesn't stop to button up her coat and she doesn't stop to wait for Nell at the gates. Instead, she marches fast, putting as much distance between her and the school and everybody in it as she possibly can.

It starts to rain. Furious drops of water that fling themselves out of the sky, relentless in their desire to flood the ground. Tally is drenched in seconds. She pulls up her hood and rams her hands into her pockets to keep warm. And then she feels the rubbery mask beneath her fingers.

She doesn't hesitate, not even for one second. Pulling it out, she flings it into a puddle and then stamps right over the top, pushing the tiger face into the murky water. Mrs Jarman was right. There is nobody like her, so she might as well give up on pretending. Everybody hates her and she hates them twice as much.

Tiger Girl isn't real, and after today, she knows that being Tiger Girl isn't going to help.

There is only her.

By the time she reaches the front door, Tally isn't cold any more. She's a burning, hot whirlwind. She's a volcano, ready to erupt, and she doesn't care who knows it because Mrs Jarman told her that she should stop trying to fit in, so that's what she's going to do. She feels like a jigsaw piece that is in the wrong puzzle box. It doesn't matter how hard she tries, she's never going to be like the others. They won't let her.

She pushes open the door. The house is warm inside and all the lights are on. It's too bright and too hot and too much.

"Is that you, girls?" Dad's voice calls from the living room. "I'm in here. Mum's just popped out to the shop. Come and say hello."

Tally doesn't want to say hello to Dad. She wants Mum. Mum will understand. She'll take one look at Tally's face and she'll know what to do. She'll find Tally's heavy blanket and she'll fetch Billy from Tally's bed so that she has someone to snuggle. She won't ask her any questions and she won't make her angry.

"Girls? Is everything OK?"

Tally leans against the wall and lets herself slither down until she's on the ground. Her wet coat leaves a damp mark against the wall and her muddy shoes have made dirty footprints all across the carpet.

"Tally?" Dad clutches on to the doorframe and gazes at her, his face pale and unwell-looking. "What are you doing? Where's Nell?"

Tally shrugs and picks a piece of mud from her shoe. It squishes between her fingers and she shudders, flinging it away so that it lands on the floor next to Dad.

"Hey!" he protests. "Pack that in! And take your shoes off – you're making a complete mess of the carpet!"

Tally narrows her eyes, squinting up at Dad until he turns into a blur.

"Where's Nell?" he repeats. "Is she OK?"

Tally ignores him. She'll give him one more chance to get it right.

"For goodness' sake, Tally," snaps Dad. "Answer the question. Where is your sister? Did something happen on the way home from school?"

He shouldn't shout at her. Mum is always saying that to him so it's not as if he doesn't understand. Getting angry and cross is the worst way to deal with her when she's stressed, that's what the doctor told them when she first got her diagnosis, but Dad just will not listen. And there is no excuse for breaking the rules.

He's still talking but he isn't making any sense. All she can hear is a buzzing sound, as if it isn't words that are coming out of his mouth but a swarm of angry wasps. His face is turning red and he's looking anxiously at the front door and she realizes that he's far more worried about where Nell might be than about what her day has been like.

He doesn't even care. He probably wishes that he just had one, perfect daughter who isn't difficult or broken or hard work. He probably loves Nell far more than he could ever love Tally. He probably wishes that she'd never been born.

The buzzing turns into a roaring sound, louder than a whole ambush of tigers. Words float past Tally's ears but she ignores them as adrenalin rushes to her hands and her feet and her body prepares to take over.

And then she moves. Faster than a lion, more powerful than an eagle. She is anger and humiliation and fury and hurt. She is Tally and she is not Tally.

She isn't thinking about Mum or Dad or Nell.

She isn't thinking about Luke or Lucy or Ayesha.

She isn't thinking about her tiger mask and the fact

that she has been let down and abandoned by everyone who is supposed to be there for her.

She isn't thinking about anything at all as she flings her bag to the ground and pounces.

The crash of a chair hitting the wall echoes around the kitchen and Tally can feel her fingers flexing as anger flows out from the ends of her hands. Dad tries to grab her arm and Nell suddenly appears from somewhere, yelling something that Tally doesn't understand. She wrenches herself out of Dad's grip and reaches for the nearest thing that she can find, which from the sound it makes when it hits the wall, is possibly some of Mum's favourite china.

"Calm down!" screams Dad and a tiny part of Tally wants to tell him he sounds anything but calm, and yelling at her isn't going to help. But she hasn't got any words right now. Only actions. She pummels his chest, pushing him as hard as she can, trying to give herself some space so that she can just *stop*.

And then the front door slams open and Mum is there, her face shocked and her breath coming in short gasps as if she's been running.

"I got your text," she tells Nell. "I came as fast as I

could."

Tally blinks and looks around the kitchen. The room is completely trashed. Chairs are tipped over and there is a pile of broken crockery on the floor. It looks awful and unfamiliar and not like home at all.

"You look really tired and cold," says Mum, walking slowly towards Tally and ignoring the snort of derision that comes from Nell. "I'm sorry about that, Tally. We all are. What can I do to help you feel a little bit better?"

Tally hesitates, but she's ready for it all to be over, and Mum just handed her a way out.

"Hot chocolate," she mutters, closing her eyes so that she doesn't have to see the messy kitchen. "Maybe with marshmallows."

"You go and get your pyjamas on," Mum tells her. "I'll just do a quick tidy-up in here and then I'll sort you out a drink."

"Are you serious?" Dad sounds stunned. "Have you seen this room? It's like a one-girl warzone in here, Jennifer. And you're going to reward her with marshmallows, for god's sake?"

"Let's just sort this out one step at a time," murmurs Mum, guiding Tally out of the room. "Something has obviously happened to cause this." She turns to Nell.

"Put the kettle on, love, there's a good girl."

Tally lets Mum help her upstairs and into her bedroom. She stands still as Mum unzips her coat and gently pulls her school jumper over her head. She doesn't say a single word because there is nothing to say. There are no words that are going to make this better

Date: Tuesday 11th November

Situation: The very worst day of my life.

Anxiety Rating: 50 out of 10

Dear Diary,

I am completely and utterly exhausted.

I don't really want to write about what happened at school today. It's too awful. I'll just tell you that I was like a bottle of Coke that was shaken round all day – I really wanted to take the top off so I could explode everywhere and let all the pressure out, but knew I couldn't. I *had* to keep a lid on it. And that means that I imploded instead, which is even worse than an explosion because *not* letting the feelings out means that they just get bigger and bigger until I think they're going to drown me. And everyone saw.

So as soon as I got home, all it took was one comment from Dad for me to let out all the frustrations of the day. Have you ever seen a bottle of Coke exploding and the destruction it causes as everything around it gets covered? Well, that has nothing on me once I get going.

Tally's autism facts: Masking

Sometimes other people don't like the way that autistic people think or feel or behave. So when I'm at school or in new situations, I have to work really hard to squash myself into a new shape. A shape that everyone else thinks looks normal. Sometimes I do this by copying what everyone else is doing or saying. Sometimes I work really hard to make everyone laugh – I spend a lot of time listening to my friends when they're chatting and trying to figure out what I should be saying in a conversation. It's a lot of work. Other times I might be feeling really sad or scared but I know that people won't like it if I let my head and body do what it needs to do, like stim or shout or run off. So I push those feelings deep, deep down and act like everything is fine. The only problem with that is that you can't hide how you're feeling for ever. I know that better than most.

Pro: Sometimes hiding how I'm feeling is a good thing because it makes other people happy instead of thinking I'm weird. It helps me make friends and it helps me to not cry when teachers speak harshly to me. Basically, it makes me seem *not autistic*. Sometimes it's like I'm

Cinderella at the ball – I hide myself until the clock strikes and then the real me is revealed … because I'm always the same person underneath.

Con: Sometimes when I don't act like myself, I feel like I've lost who I really am. When I'm at school or at a friend's house I'm always working hard to be who other people think I should be, but when I get home I feel so exhausted that the feelings underneath come out uncontrollably. And when I say uncontrollably, I mean *uncontrollably*.

CHAPTER 26

"I'm not going to school. I'm busy."

Tally doesn't bother to shout. She hasn't got the energy to do anything, not even kick off as Mum tries over and over again to encourage her to put on her school uniform. She just sits cross-legged on her bed and continues to organize her soft toys. The squishiest ones go in a neat row on the left. The ones with a harder middle go on the right. In order to make her selections she has to pick each toy up and squeeze it, hugging it into her body so that she can really figure out how it rates on the cuddly scale.

"We've talked about this before," says Mum. She isn't giving up. "If you don't go to school then Dad and I could get into a lot of trouble."

Tally shrugs. The trouble that they might experience is nothing compared to what's going on with her. Are they going to be ignored and teased and made to feel stupid? Does everyone hate them? No – so it doesn't matter what Mum says. She isn't going to school and nobody can make her.

"If you'd only tell me the problem then I'm sure we can sort it out." Mum sits down next to Tally and picks up Billy from his place in the squishy row.

"What did you do that for?" yells Tally, yanking him out of Mum's hands. "Now I'm going to have to start all over again. So don't blame me if you get told off for me not being in school because it's all your fault."

Then she swipes all the toys back into the middle of the bed and starts humming under her breath, ignoring Mum until she finally gets the message and goes away.

It takes ages to finish sorting the animals. Halfway through the task, Tally starts to wish that she could just give up but that's not an option. Not if she wants to calm down her noisy head. Eventually they are all arranged in order, and Tally slides carefully off her bed and plods slowly downstairs, her tummy rumbling and ready for food.

As she approaches the kitchen door she can hear Mum and Dad talking on the other side.

"Well, I've phoned the school and explained that she won't be in," Mum is saying. "I spoke to Mr Kennedy, the head of year seven. I've asked him to find out if anything happened yesterday but I'm not holding my breath – I don't think he had a clue who Tally even is."

"Maybe I should have a word with her," says Dad. His voice sounds tired. "If we start letting her stay at home then where is it going to end? We don't want her refusing to ever go back, do we? And she needs to be in school."

"You can try," Mum tells him. "I don't know, maybe you'll have better luck than me. I couldn't get a word out of her about what's made her so upset. But I think we should leave it for now – she's not in any kind of mood to listen to us at the moment."

Tally hears the sound of a chair scraping across the floor and then Dad's footsteps.

"In that case, I think I'll take the dog for one last walk before we have to take him to the shelter later this afternoon. I doubt that the poor old thing is going to get a lot of exercise when he's there. And you never know, the fresh air might help me to shake this illness. I've had enough of sitting around, I really have."

Tally pushes open the door and barges into the kitchen.

"What shelter?" she demands, glaring at Dad. "What are you on about?"

Dad glances at Mum and pulls a strange face.

"We had a phone call yesterday evening—" starts Mum.

"You can't send Rupert away!" shouts Tally. "It's animal cruelty!"

Dad shakes his head. "It's not cruel, Tally. He'll be looked after at the shelter."

"It's the best place for him," adds Mum. "He'll be warm and fed and safe."

"But nobody will know him!" Tally wails. "They'll all be like you and think that he's a bad dog when he isn't! He's just frightened – but nobody is going to bother working that out, are they?"

"He has to go, Tally," Mum says, quietly. "I'm sorry, but he isn't a safe dog to have around children and we can't keep him shut up in the utility room for ever. It isn't fair on him."

Dad walks across to the wall and takes his jacket from the coat hooks.

"I'm taking him for a walk and then I'm going to drive him straight to the shelter," he tells Mum. "I think it's best if we get this over and done with as quickly as possible."

They can't just take Rupert away. They can't. He's all that she's got and without him, she'll be left completely on her own. Tally can feel the fear spreading through her body, making her legs shake and her fingers squeeze themselves into tight fists. Home is supposed to be a safe place. It's supposed to be a place where she feels understood and cared about – not abandoned and ignored.

"I hate you!" screams Tally, stamping her feet. "I hate both of you and I wish you weren't my mum and dad because you're terrible parents and you only care about yourselves."

Then she runs out of the kitchen and into the living room, where she turns on the television and watches episodes of *Peppa Pig* until her heart stops pounding and her head isn't fizzing with fury. If she can watch one entire hour of Peppa then maybe, just maybe, she can calm herself down.

It takes a long time. She keeps watching when the front door slams and Dad goes off to take Rupert for his walk, and she keeps watching when, twenty minutes later, it slams again as Nell returns from school. She doesn't let her brain think about anything except Peppa and George and the familiar, comforting scenes on the screen in front of her.

She is partway through the episode about Daddy Pig losing his glasses when the phone rings. Mum's raised voice floats through from the hallway and then Tally hears her calling for Nell before she pushes open the door and dashes into the living room.

"Tally! You have to turn that off and put your shoes on. Do it now – and be as fast as you can."

Tally doesn't look away from the television and she doesn't move. She's just starting to feel a little bit calmer. The hour isn't up yet and if she stops watching now then everything is just going to go wrong all over again.

Nell walks in and Mum spins round to face her.

"We've got to go out. I've just had a call – Dad's been in some kind of accident and he's been taken to the hospital. We have to get there *now*!"

Tally leans closer to the screen.

"Can you talk outside, please? I can't hear my programme."

She reaches for the remote control and turns up the

volume, her heart pounding like a big bass drum. Just focus on Peppa and George. Don't listen to the terrifying words that are coming out of Mum's mouth. Take deep breaths and count to ten. It's all going to be OK. It's definitely all going to be OK.

"I need you and Tally to get into the car," Mum says to Nell, ignoring Tally's request. "I just have to find my bag and then I'll be right with you."

Her voice is high and hurried and it makes Tally's bones screech.

"What happened?" It sounds like Nell is crying but Tally can't look away from the screen because if she looks then she'll have to listen and if she listens then she'll have to know and she doesn't want to know. She can't hear that something bad has happened to Dad – she just can't.

"All I know is that he was walking the dog and then he collapsed in the street," says Mum in a gulping, gasping kind of way. "Someone saw him and called an ambulance. I'm sure it will all be fine but let's just get to the hospital as quickly as possible."

She races out of the room and Nell gives a big sniff before stepping closer to Tally.

"Come on," she says. "You heard what Mum said. We

have to go to the hospital."

Tally shakes her head. Her stomach is hurting and her skin is prickling and sweaty, like there are tiny ants crawling across her body. "I can't. My programmes haven't finished yet. I've still got ten minutes to go."

There is a beat of silence and then Nell erupts.

"Are you serious? Dad might be really ill, Tally – and you're more interested in a stupid pig?"

Tally snaps her head round and glares at Nell.

"Don't say that my programme is stupid," she snarls. "*You're* stupid. And I can't put my shoes on until it's over."

Nell takes two strides across the carpet and flicks the switch on the television. The screen sinks into darkness.

"There. It's over. Now stop being so selfish and put your shoes on unless you want me to drag you to the car in bare feet, 'cos I'll do it if I have to."

Tally pushes herself further into the sofa and narrows her eyes. Nell's face is fierce and her voice has a hardness that Tally hasn't heard before. She's fairly sure that Nell means every word that she is saying. Unfortunately for Nell, Tally means her words more. She can't go to the hospital, even if Dad is in there. Her body is empty, like a car without any fuel and her head is filled with a swirling, cloudy terror. She's got nothing left.

"Don't even try to touch me," she warns Nell. "I'm not going to the hospital and nobody can make me."

The two sisters stare at each other in silence. Nell's eyes are glistening and her face is pale as if she's very cold, but Tally feels hotter than fire, hotter than lava, hotter than the sun.

Mum runs back into the room and takes in the scene.

"Right. If Tally won't come then you're going to have to stay here with her," she says frantically, looking at Nell. "I'll ring you as soon as I know anything, I promise."

"No!" protests Nell, reaching out and grabbing Mum's arm. "That's not fair! I want to see Dad."

Mum pulls her in for a hug. "It's probably best that you both stay here," she tells her. "Let me find out what's happening and then we can go from there. Neither of you are allowed to open the front door until I'm back, OK?" And then Mum makes a moaning sound. "Oh, I don't know what to do. Maybe I should take you with me? Or I could try to find someone to come and sit with you?"

She pulls her phone out of her pocket and tries to unlock it but her hands are shaking so much that it falls to the floor.

"We'll be fine," Nell tells her, retrieving the phone and handing it back to Mum. "Just go. And ring us as soon as you can."

Mum doesn't look convinced but Nell gives her a little push towards the door. "Go! And drive slowly."

"You are a wonderful girl," Mum says, giving Nell another quick hug. Then she walks quickly across to Tally and bends down to drop a kiss on top of her head. "It'll all be OK," she whispers. "I promise, Tally. Daddy will be fine."

"I don't want you to go," mutters Tally, but Mum has already gone. Nell sinks down on to the sofa next to Tally, leaving a wide space between them and they both listen as the car pulls away. Then they sit in silence and Tally does her very best not to think, not to think, not to think.

But it's impossible not to think when that's all you can think about doing. Because there's a lot to think about and none of it is good. Dad collapsing in the street. Dad being rushed to hospital in an ambulance, its blue lights flashing and the siren making everyone get out of the way. Tally hates ambulances and police cars and fire engines, partly because they're so noisy but also because they always mean something bad has happened. And now that *bad thing* has happened to Dad and all that she can think about are the last words that she said to him. Mum always says that you should be careful what you wish for, but she didn't mean it. She still wants him to be her dad, but now he might not be and he'll never know that she was just in a bad mood.

She knows that Mum promised that he would be fine, but Mum isn't a doctor and she isn't psychic. She can't possibly know that everything is going to be OK. And if Mum doesn't know then nobody can know.

And that is the scariest thought of all.

CHAPTER 27

By the time the phone rings, Tally is already sure about what Mum is going to say. She has scripted it out in her head and tried to make herself feel brave so that she doesn't completely lose it when Mum tells them that everything has gone wrong. She clenches her fists as Nell listens to Mum's voice, craning to hear the words that she is dreading.

"Are you sure?" says Nell, gripping Tally's hand so tightly that it makes her squeal. "OK! We'll see you soon!"

Then she turns to Tally, a huge beam on her face. "He's going to be all right! It's all OK!"

Tally blinks and stares at Nell in confusion. The whole time that they've been sitting here she's been imagining the worst. Neither girl has moved since Mum left, and as the room has got darker and darker, so have

Tally's thoughts. It takes her a moment to jolt her mind out of the scary place that it's been living in for the last hour and back to something more normal.

"Apparently it's something to do with his appendix," says Nell, her words flying out at one hundred miles an hour. "That's why he's been feeling unwell for a while and it could have been really bad but they've sorted it now and he's going to be fine!"

Tears are pouring down Nell's face and Tally pulls away from her, not sure if she's misunderstood.

"I'm happy-crying!" splutters Nell. "It's OK, Tally. Really, it's all going to be fine."

Mum didn't lie.

Tally flings her arm around Nell and now the space between them is non-existent. They sit, cuddled up on the sofa, until they hear Mum's key in the door and then Nell leaps up and turns on the light before dashing out into the hall to greet her.

Tally follows more slowly but then she sees Mum standing in the doorway, her face blotchy and tired but her eyes smiling.

"Do you want a hug?" she asks, holding out her arms. And Tally doesn't hesitate, racing across the floor and flinging herself at Mum.

It's an hour or so later when Mum tells them that she has to head back to the hospital.

"I need to take a few things in for Dad," she explains. "He's going to be in hospital for a little while, just so that they can keep an eye on him. Why don't you both help me to pack him a bag?"

So Nell and Tally follow her into Mum and Dad's bedroom and Tally sits on the bed while Mum pulls down an overnight bag from the top of their wardrobe.

"He'll need some pyjamas," she says. "And a toothbrush."

"What about something to read?" asks Nell. "It might be a bit boring for him, having to lie in bed all day."

Mum nods. "That's an excellent idea. Can you fetch his book from the bedside table?"

Between them, Mum and Nell fill the bag with things that Dad might need. They put in deodorant and socks and a hairbrush, which Tally thinks is a bit pointless as he's hardly got any hair. She sits and watches and tries to think about what she can add to the bag, but she's never had to stay in hospital before so it's impossible to figure out what should go in.

"Are you sure that you'll be OK while I pop back?"

Mum asks Nell for the millionth time. "I'm sure that I could find somebody to come and stay with you while I'm gone."

Nell shakes her head. "We'll be fine. I've been babysitting for other people for a while now, remember? I'm pretty sure that I can look after Tally for an hour or so."

Tally scowls. She is not a baby and she doesn't appreciate Nell suggesting that she is. She's about to start complaining, but then she sees the anxious look on Mum's face and clamps her mouth shut again. Dad is in hospital and Mum is worried. She can ignore Nell's stupid comment, just this one time.

"I won't be long." Mum zips up the bag. "I'll make sure that he's settled for the night and then I'll come straight home. Don't try to cook the supper – I'll sort something out for us all when I'm back."

"Don't forget to wear your seatbelt," Tally reminds her, trying to be useful. "That's a non-negotiable, remember?"

Mum laughs – a sudden, shocking bark of a sound that reminds Tally of something important. "Maybe you can both watch television together while I'm out?"

Nell nods. "Don't worry. I won't leave Tally on her

own. We're just going to sit in the living room and chill out, aren't we?"

Tally nods, distracted.

"I need to put something in the bag," she says, clambering off the bed and rushing out of the room. "Don't go yet."

She dashes across the landing and into her own bedroom. Then she races downstairs to where Mum is putting on her coat.

"You can take Billy," she pants, thrusting him into Mum's hands. "But tell Dad that he's just to borrow, not to keep."

Mum leans forward and gives Tally a big hug. "That's a lovely thought," she says. "Billy can keep Dad company in the hospital and stop him from getting too lonely."

She opens the front door and looks at Nell.

"Stay together," she reminds her. "I won't be long. And don't open the front door."

Nell and Tally watch Mum leave. As she opens the car door, Tally suddenly has second thoughts about letting her beloved Billy go somewhere as horrible and frightening as a hospital where there are germs and diseases. She opens her mouth as wide as she can and shouts loudly to get Mum's attention.

"Mum!"

Mum pauses and looks back at the house.

"Yes, love?"

"It's Billy!" yells Tally. "I need—"

And then she pauses. If the hospital really is frightening and awful, then Dad is going to need something to make him feel strong and brave. Billy can always go in the washing machine when he comes home – that should get rid of any germs.

"I need you to make sure that Dad knows that he can't keep him!" she shouts. "It's just a borrow, OK?"

Mum gives her the thumbs-up sign and then climbs into the car. Nell closes the front door and gives a big sigh before looking down at Tally.

"Do you want a biscuit?" she asks. "I think we deserve one. And you can watch *Peppa Pig* – I don't mind."

But Tally is not interested in biscuits or television because she remembered something when they were upstairs in Mum and Dad's room. Something very important that everybody else seems to have completely forgotten.

"We have to go and find Rupert," she tells Nell. "Dad was taking him for a walk when he got poorly, but Mum didn't say anything about him being at the hospital so I don't think he went in the ambulance with Dad."

Nell stares at her. "Of course he didn't. Dogs can't go in ambulances and they certainly can't go inside a hospital, unless they're guide dogs or therapy dogs or something. And Rupert is the opposite of a therapy dog – he's a nightmare."

Tally grits her teeth. "He isn't a nightmare and right now, he's out in the dark all on his own, and none of you even care enough to wonder where he might be."

Nell leans against the wall, looking upset. "It's not that we don't care," she says. "It's just that what happened to Dad was awful and scary and he's more important than a dog."

Tally walks across to the cupboard and pulls out her trainers. "But Dad is fine now, that's what Mum said. So it's up to us to find Rupert." She sits down on the floor and looks up at Nell, her eyes wide. "He must be so frightened, Nell. He hasn't got Mrs Jessop and now he hasn't got us. And he's only got three legs so if any nasty bully dogs find him then he won't stand a chance."

She starts to fasten her laces. "I have to find him and if you won't come with me then I'll go on my own."

"It's not that I *won't*," says Nell. "It's that I *can't*. And neither can you."

Tally pauses. She knows what it's like when people confuse *can't* for *won't* and for a moment she feels sorry for Nell.

But she feels sorrier for Rupert.

"I'm going and you can't stop me," she tells her, getting to her feet.

Nell steps forward, panic on her face.

"No! You heard what Mum said. We have to stay together, Tally, and I promised her that I wouldn't open the front door!"

Tally reaches for her coat and glances out of the window. It's pitch-black outside and she shudders, imagining herself walking the streets by herself. There could be all kinds of danger out there, but it's warm and cosy in the house and Mum will be back before too long. She could just snuggle up under her blanket and keep watching *Peppa Pig* and nobody would blame her.

Only she can't, because the only thing that Rupert has done wrong is to be different. And she knows exactly how it feels to have nobody understand you. She knows how much it hurts to be left outside in the dark, all on your own. And she could never do that to someone else, especially not Rupert.

"You don't have to come," she repeats, reaching for

the door handle. "I won't tell Mum and I'll be back before she gets home."

"Why do you have to be so difficult?" howls Nell, her face scrunching up like she's trying not to cry. "Hasn't today been hard enough already?"

Tally shrugs and opens the door. "Sorry," she says. "I don't know how to make it better. I just know that I have to find Rupert. And I didn't promise not to open the front door so I'm not breaking any rules."

And then she steps out into the night, zipping her coat up as high as it will go and burying her hands in her pockets as she walks down the garden path and out on to the street.

There is a streetlamp further down the road and she walks quickly, keen to step into the puddle of light that spills around its base. But when she does, it doesn't provide the comfort that she had imagined it would. Instead, she feels lit up and exposed and it is a relief to step out of the light and back into the shadows where nobody can see her.

Hidden in the darkness, Tally prowls down the road, listening for any sound that might give her a clue about where Rupert could be. Mum told them earlier that Dad had collapsed by the gate to the park and so she heads in that direction, imagining herself as a tiger stalking her prey – but in a nice way because she is going to rescue Rupert, not eat him for supper.

And the further that she walks, the braver that she starts to feel. The shadows wrap themselves around her like a mask, and if her hands are flapping and her legs are jiggling then it doesn't matter because nobody can see her, out here in the black of night.

She reaches the end of the street and turns the corner towards the park, tensing as footsteps suddenly start pounding behind her. All her senses are tingling but she resists the urge to turn around and instead picks up her speed until she is almost running.

"Tally!" The voice is familiar and she slows down as Nell runs up to join her. "Wait for me!"

"I thought you weren't going to come," Tally tells her. "You told Mum that you wouldn't open the front door."

"Yeah, well – I also told Mum that I wouldn't leave you on your own, didn't I?" answers Nell, resting her hands on her knees and gasping for breath. "And I think *that* promise is probably the most important one."

Tally smiles. "I'm glad that you're here," she says. "I think that Rupert is going to be very glad to see us."

Together, the two girls keep walking. Nell's head

swivels from side to side as they head down the street and she jumps at every tiny sound, making muttering noises under her breath. Tally tries to ignore her and focus on listening for any sounds of a dog in distress, but eventually, the sounds of a sister in distress become too distracting.

"What's wrong?" she asks, as they cross the road towards the park. "Are you scared?"

"Aren't you?" retorts Nell, jerking as an owl screeches loudly from a branch overhead. "It's horrible out here. I can barely see a thing."

Tally shakes her head.

"I'm not scared," she says. "At least, I don't think I am. I'm not really thinking about it. I'm only thinking about finding Rupert."

And then she reaches out and takes Nell's hand in her own, giving it a quick squeeze the way that Mum does to let her know that everything is OK. And it's not a lie, not really, because she's sure that Rupert will be waiting for them when they get to the park.

But when the large metal gates of the park loom out of the darkness, Rupert is nowhere to be seen.

"Rupert! Here, boy!" calls Tally and Nell joins in, their voices ringing out into the night.

"Maybe he got locked inside the park?" suggests Nell. "There's no way that I'm letting you climb over the gate, so don't even think about it."

"He isn't in the park," Tally tells her. "He's a very clever dog. If he isn't here then he'll have found somewhere sensible to go, I know it."

"We can't keep wandering the streets all night," says Nell, stamping her feet to keep warm. "Mum is going to be really worried if she gets home and we've just disappeared. I was in such a rush to catch up with you that I didn't even leave her a note. And I haven't got my phone either. Are you listening to me, Tally?"

Tally is not listening. Instead, she is closing her eyes and thinking as hard as she can. And the thing she is thinking about is the awful sleepover that she had at Layla's house, when there was only one place in the whole world that she wanted to be.

Her very own home.

"I know where he is!" she says, pulling Nell's hand. "Come on! He's gone home."

And then she's off, running as fast as she can, away from the park and back through the streets, heading back the same way that they have just come, Nell keeping pace beside her.

When they reach their own street, Tally slows down.

"Mum's car isn't back yet," says Nell as they walk along the road. "We might just get away with this after all. Come on – if we're quick we can make it look like we never even left the house."

But Tally doesn't turn in through the gate. Instead, she stops and looks carefully to either side before crossing the road.

"Where are you going?" hisses Nell, darting after her. "I thought you said that Rupert would have gone home?"

"I did," whispers Tally. "And don't be loud. I don't want to scare him."

She pushes open a gate and walks up the path. And there on the front doorstep of Mrs Jessop's house, drenched and shivering with cold, is Rupert.

"Don't go too close," murmurs Nell. "He's dangerous, remember?"

Tally does what Mum always tell her to do when somebody says something incredibly foolish and ignores Nell's warning.

"It's OK," she whispers, creeping closer to the shaking dog. "I'm here now. You're safe, Rupert."

Taking it slowly so as not to scare him, she walks up to the door and then sinks down on to the wet step, instantly feeling the bitter chill seep into her body.

"You must be so cold," she tells him. "I'm going to take you home in a moment and get you nice and warm."

"What are you doing?" asks Nell, her voice low.

"Telling him what's happening," Tally tells her, reaching out towards the dog. "Everything is far less scary if you know what to expect, isn't it, boy?" Her hands stroke his back gently and then her fingers get to work on the strap that goes around his head. "I'm taking off your muzzle," she whispers softly. "And then I'm going to stand up and you can choose if you're going to follow me home or stay out here on your own. It's up to you, OK?"

"Don't take it off!" yelps Nell but it's too late. The muzzle is on the floor and Tally is already standing up and walking down the path.

"Don't look back at him," she mutters to Nell, as she walks past her. "Just walk with me and don't make him think that we're expecting him to follow us. He has to choose."

Nell looks at Tally in disbelief but says nothing as she follows her out of the garden and up to the edge of the pavement. And then headlights swinging into the street puncture the darkness and the girls watch as Mum's car pulls up opposite them.

"Oh no," moans Nell. "Now we're for it."

But Tally is already marching across the road, as if she doesn't have a care in the world. Nell's jaw gapes open as her little sister saunters past Mum and into their own front garden, the three-legged dog limping closely behind her as if he would follow her wherever she chose to go.

"What on earth is going on?" shrieks Mum, staring at Tally and Rupert. "Why aren't you inside the house? Where has that dog come from? And why isn't he wearing his muzzle?"

So it is left to Nell to explain the night's events to Mum as they follow Tally up the path and into the house.

"You found him outside Mrs Jessop's house?" asks Mum, watching carefully as Tally dries Rupert with the towels that she has insisted on claiming from the bathroom. "I suppose he must be missing her very badly."

"He knew that you were going to send him away," Tally tells her. "Even though he's not dangerous. He was just sad and that is not the same thing."

"I can see that," says Mum, but she still doesn't take

her eyes off the dog. "He certainly seems to like you, Tally."

Tally nods. "He does like me. Because I like him and I don't make him feel like there's something wrong with him, just because he isn't exactly the same as all the other dogs. I let him be..." She pauses, one hand on Rupert's back and the other under his chin. "Well, I don't really know what I let him be, actually."

Mum sniffs loudly. "I think you just let him *be*," she tells Tally, which is confusing and makes absolutely no sense, but for once Tally doesn't really mind. "You are a very caring girl, and while I'm not happy that you both went out looking for Rupert tonight, I'm glad that you found him."

"So does that mean that you aren't going to send him away?" asks Tally. "Because he's my best friend and I haven't got any other friends, so that means that he's actually my only friend and if you send him to the dog shelter then I'll have nobody. But if we keep him then he can sleep in my room and I can play with him and read him stories and train him to run really fast on three legs."

Mum sniffs again and rubs her face with her hand. "There's a lot of things in that sentence that we need to talk about tomorrow," she tells Tally. "But for now, no – I'm not sending him away. However, he is definitely not sleeping in your bedroom, and we're going to have to book him into some dog training classes to teach him some better manners. You'll have to go too."

Nell sniggers. "Maybe it'll teach Tally some better manners," she says. "It might kill two birds with one stone."

Tally sticks her tongue out at Nell. "My manners are perfect, thank you very much."

And then she gets Rupert's bed from the utility room and puts it in front of the kitchen radiator so that he can stay warm and safe all through the night.

CHAPTER 28

When Tally climbs into bed, her head is whirring with so much information that she's sure she'll never be able to get to sleep. So it comes as something of a surprise when Mum suddenly appears in her room.

"Good morning, sweetheart," she says, sitting down on the bed. "Did you sleep well? Yesterday was quite a day, wasn't it?"

Yesterday. Memories swirl through Tally's mind. Dad being taken to hospital. Rupert getting lost. Her and Nell going to rescue him.

Tally sits up and stares at Mum.

"Is Rupert still downstairs? You didn't send him away while I was asleep, did you?"

Mum puts her hand on Tally's arm. "Of course not. I told you that he could stay for a little bit longer and I won't break that promise. And now you need to get out of bed, because we're going to visit Dad after breakfast and I don't want to miss the start of visiting time."

Tally scowls and dives straight back under the covers.

"No. I'm staying in bed."

Mum stands up and walks to the door. "That's a shame. If you won't get up and help me take Rupert for a quick walk then he certainly can't stay here. Dogs need exercise, and as Dad isn't here to walk him, we're going to have to do it."

And with that she strides out of the room and down the stairs, where Tally can imagine her picking up the phone and telling the dog shelter that they can take him away.

She leaps out of bed and flings herself into the first clothes that she can find, which happens to be a very soft top covered in tiger stripes and a pair of purple zebra-print leggings that Mum bought her last Christmas. And then she hurries downstairs and into the kitchen where Mum is eating a piece of toast.

"Fine! I'll walk him with you," she says. "Even though this is blackmail, you know? But I'm going to be the one who holds his lead."

Mum nods. "Excellent! Just eat this piece of toast

that I've made for you while I give Rupert his breakfast and then you'll both be ready to go."

Tally folds her arms and glares at Mum.

"I don't want any toast."

Mum doesn't reply. Instead she walks out of the kitchen, returning a few moments later with a bowl filled with dog food, which she puts on the floor next to Rupert's bed.

"You can go for a walk once you've eaten your breakfast," she tells him. "And if you don't eat it, then I'll know that you don't really want to stay here."

She turns to Tally and gives her a smile. "Dogs have to tell us how they're feeling using their actions," she says. "And an unhappy dog won't want to eat. If Rupert doesn't eat his breakfast then I'm afraid he's telling us that he'd be better off living somewhere else."

And then she walks out of the kitchen and Tally hears her going into the living room and closing the door.

The kitchen is silent apart from the humming noise that the fridge always makes. Tally looks at Rupert. He is lying in his bed and gazing up at her. He isn't paying even a tiny bit of attention to his food.

"She does this to me all the time," she tells him. "She thinks that she's being clever."

She pauses for a second and stares at the closed kitchen door. "But I don't think we have a choice today, Rupert — so be a good dog and eat your breakfast because it's the only way that you're going to be able to stay here."

Rupert blinks but he doesn't move.

Tally frowns and puts her hands on her hips.

"Eat the food," she instructs him sternly. "You have to."

Rupert growls quietly, as if he doesn't like being told what to do.

Tally understands and tries again, "Look. You can choose whether you want to eat the food or not, OK? But if you do decide to eat it then Mum will let you stay and that sounds like a very good deal to me."

Rupert nudges her leg with his nose and Tally's tummy makes a swooshing feeling, like she's a candle that has started to melt.

"It's up to you," she tells the dog. "And I'm sorry if I sounded cross. I just want you to be happy, but you're making it really difficult for yourself. All you have to do is eat. Look — it's easy. Just do this!"

Reaching out, she grabs the piece of toast that Mum made her and then she sinks on to the kitchen floor, sitting cross-legged in front of Rupert and taking a big bite of toast.

"Mmmm, it's delicious," she says. "But I bet it isn't as yummy as your dog food! Why don't you have a taste and see?"

She takes another bite and nods encouragingly at Rupert. The old dog stares at her for a moment, and then he clambers to his feet and lowers his face to the bowl.

Inside, Tally feels like cheering, but she knows that this would be a very bad move. If she gives Rupert even the slightest idea that he's doing what she wants him to do, then he might get distracted and stop eating. Instead, she pretends to ignore him and continues to munch on her toast, making loud, appreciative noises with each bite and occasionally sneaking a peek at the dog out of the corner of her eye.

Only when his bowl is empty and her toast is finished does she give him any attention.

"Oh, you ate your breakfast," she says, trying to sound casual. "That's good. Not that I was bothered either way whether you ate it or not. It was totally your choice."

And then, because it's really very hard pretending that you don't care, she flings her arms around his neck and pushes her head close to his.

"Well done!" she whispers. "Now we can go on a walk and Mum will let you stay for a bit longer. Good boy, Rupert. Good boy!"

Mum doesn't seem all that interested when she returns to the kitchen and sees that both the dog food and the toast have been eaten and Tally is glad that she doesn't make a fuss about it.

"Let's take this dog for a walk," she says, pulling Tally's coat from the hook and handing it to her. "And then we'll go and visit Dad."

The walk is over too quickly. Tally tries everything she can think of to make it last longer, suggesting that Rupert needs to be taken all around the park and then play some stick-chasing games. But after twenty minutes, Mum says that it's time to head home.

"He's an old dog," she tells Tally. "And he had quite a fright yesterday. He'll be happiest having a sleep on his bed now, while we pop out for a while."

"Can't Nell and I stay here?" Tally asks, the second they're inside the house.

Mum shakes her head. "Not today. After yesterday's escapades I think that I want us all to stick together. And besides, Dad is looking forward to seeing you."

"I can't wait to see him," says Nell, and Tally wonders how she can be so brave about going to the hospital but so scared about something as silly as the dark.

Just like the dog walk, the drive to the hospital doesn't take long enough. Mum parks the car and they all get out. Tally stares at the building ahead. It is grey and gloomy and huge and she knows that if she were to get lost in there then she'd never find her way out.

"This way," says Mum, leading them towards the main entrance. They walk past a man sitting in a wheelchair and a woman with her arm in a sling, and Tally lowers her eyes so that the only thing she can see is Mum's feet in front of her. The ground changes from concrete to tiles and then Mum's feet stop and Tally has to look up There are people everywhere and the lights are so bright that it hurts her eyes.

"Dad is on the fifth floor," mum says. "So we need to take the lift."

Tally steps back, accidentally bumping into Nell.

"No way. I'm not going in a lift. In fact, I'm not going anywhere and you can't make me."

Mum spins round to look at her youngest daughter, her mouth pressed into a hard line.

"Not now," she says quietly, glancing around. "Please,

Tally. We're already late because you took so long to find your trainers, which had somehow managed to hide themselves under my bed. I haven't got time for this today. Dad is waiting to see us and I don't want to leave him on his own, not after everything that's happened."

She sounds like she's about to start yelling, and Tally looks round too, checking that nobody is close enough to hear Mum having a meltdown.

"You go up to the ward." Nell steps forward. "I'll stay with Tally and we'll come and find you when she's ready, OK?"

"It smells wrong," mutters Tally under her breath.

It's a cold, sharp smell and it makes Tally's throat feel tight, as if she's swallowed a marble and it's got stuck. She swallows loudly, trying to push down the sensation that she can't breathe.

"Please can we just go home?"

But Mum is too busy talking urgently to Nell to hear her.

"He's on the fifth floor, in Ward Four," Mum says. "You can always wait outside the ward entrance. And text me if you need me – I'll come straight out."

The lift doors open and Mum steps inside.

"Text me," she repeats and then she moves forward,

as if she's changed her mind. "Actually, forget this. I can—"

The doors swoosh shut before they can find out what she was going to say and the girls are left alone.

"Right. The stairs are over here," says Nell, taking charge. "We're going to walk up five flights and then we're going to stand outside the ward and see how you're doing. You can do that, can't you?"

Tally gives a tiny nod because she's too frightened to do anything else and Nell's hand on her arm is the only thing that is keeping her from sinking on to the floor and crying.

Nell leads the way and together they climb the stairs, all the way to the fifth floor. It takes ages and they're both panting for breath by the time they reach the top. Nell opens the door and waits for Tally to step out into the corridor.

It is as horrible as she had imagined it would be. The walls are white and seem to go on for ever, like a creepy maze. People stride past dressed in clothes that look like pyjamas, some of them in blue and some of them in green and all of them looking busy and stressed out. Everybody is rushing and there are beeping noises, which make Tally's pulse speed up. Nobody is smiling, which isn't surprising, because there isn't anything to smile about. It's terrifying and loud and hectic and nothing feels even a tiny bit safe.

Nell leans against the wall and pulls Tally next to her. "Are you OK?" she asks. "I know this is hard for you."

Tally feels her eyes start to prickle. "I am not OK," she whispers. "I'm not brave like you, Nell. I don't think I can do this."

Nell laughs. "Yes, you are. Think how brave you were last night when you went looking for Rupert. You were the brave one – it was me who was scared."

Tally frowns. "That was different. The dark made it easier because nobody could see me." She waves her hand around, gesturing towards the bright lights. "Everyone can see me here. And I can see all of this."

"What about if you *could* hide?" asks Nell, putting her hand in her bag. "Would that help?"

And then she pulls something out and holds it up. "Can you go and see Dad if you wear this?"

Tally stares in disbelief at the tiger mask dangling from Nell's hand.

"How did you…? Where did you…?"

Nell flushes. "I found it that day when you didn't wait for me after school," she says. "Floating in a puddle. I was going to give it to you, but when I got home you were having a proper meltdown and I was so cross with you that I kept hold of it. I'm sorry, Tally."

Tally reaches out her hand and takes hold of the mask. Other than a streak of dirt across the nose, it looks exactly the same as it used to, even though it can't possibly be the same. Not after Lucy stole it and gave it to Luke.

"Put it on," Nell tells her. "Put it on and let's go and see Dad."

Slowly, hesitantly, Tally pulls the mask over her head, adjusting the position so that she can see through the eyeholes. Nell presses a button next to the door and a buzzer sounds, before the door clicks open. There is no time to think about anything as Tally is guided through the door and on to the ward.

"Can I help you?" asks a nurse, sticking her head out of an office.

Nell steps forward. "We're looking for our dad," she explains. "His name is Kevin Adams."

The nurse nods and points down the hallway. "He's in a room on his own," she tells them. "Room eight — it's down there and on the right. Your mum is in there already."

One, two, three, four, five steps. Tally can feel Nell right behind her. She takes shallow breaths and tries to remind herself that she is Tiger Girl and Tiger Girls are not afraid of a few silly germs.

Six, seven, eight, nine, ten steps. Nell's hand is on her back. Tiger Girls don't run away when they're scared and they don't flap their hands or make weird noises that make everyone look at them.

Eleven, twelve, thirteen steps. Nell moves her hand from Tally's back and on to her arm.

"He's in here," she says and then before Tally can change her mind, the door has opened and Dad is right there in front of her, lying in bed looking very, very pale.

"Girls!" Mum pulls them both inside, her arm wrapping around Tally's shoulders. "Kevin – look. The girls are here!"

Nell dashes across the room and sits down in a chair, leaning close to Dad's face.

"Oh, Dad!" she says and then she starts to cry, which seems a bit of an odd thing to do when she was fine just a minute ago. "Are you OK? I was so scared when Mum told us what happened."

Dad opens his eyes and looks at Nell.

"I'm sorry that I scared you," he tells her. "And I'm

fine. I just need to rest for a few days and then I'll be as right as rain."

Over by the door, Tally tenses. Dad is not a doctor. He does not have a medical degree. He can't possibly know if he's going to be fine or not.

"And you've brought a tiger to visit me!" Dad is looking at her, a smile tugging at the edges of his mouth. "I hope none of the nurses saw you bringing a savage beast on to their ward!"

And suddenly she has had enough. Enough of hiding and enough of pretending. She is not Tiger Girl. She is Tally. She was brave enough to rescue Rupert in the dark and she was brave enough to walk all the way up five flights of stairs and into this hospital room on her very own feet.

Tiger Girl doesn't run away and Tiger Girl doesn't flap her hands when she's scared or excited. Tiger Girl doesn't hum songs to herself when everything feels too busy or noisy. Tiger Girl doesn't get angry or upset or hurt because Tiger Girl isn't real. But Tally does all of those things and she is real.

She is here.

And maybe, right now, she can be her.

Just for a few minutes.

Pulling off the mask, she walks slowly up to the bed and stares down at Dad.

"It's me," she tells him. "Tally."

And he looks back at her and the smile that he gives her starts in his eyes, before spreading right across his face.

"Yes, it is," he says. "And I am very, very glad to see you. Do you think that I can have a bear hug?"

Her arms start to flap and she lets them.

Tally's Dreams for the Future

My dreams:

- For someone one day to publish my diaries to help the world understand what autism is like from an autistic person's point of view.

- To open the Tally Adams Animal Sanctuary for Permanently Damaged Animals (The PDA sanctuary - get it?!).

- To meet Taylor Swift.

- To start my own squishy factory – ADAMS' SQUISHY COMPANY LTD.

- To help people like me become proud and open about being autistic and to stop people treating us differently.

CHAPTER 29

Tally is sitting on the sofa next to Dad, watching one of his old western films when the doorbell rings.

"It's fine, I'll get it!" yells Mum from the kitchen. "Don't anyone else move a muscle! All just stay exactly where you are while I run around doing all the jobs!"

Dad grins at Tally.

"I think your Mum is ready for me to get back on my feet. I asked her for a cup of tea earlier and she told me that she's keeping a count of the number of cups of tea that I have to make for her, once I'm up and about again!"

Tally picks up a cushion and rests it on her knees.

"I was scared when you were in hospital," she says, her eyes fixed on the screen. "I thought that you were going to die."

Next to her, Dad nods seriously. "I was scared too," he tells her. "It's frightening for everyone when something like that happens."

Tally thinks about this. "Mum wasn't frightened," she says. "She was super-bossy and cross but she wasn't frightened."

Dad shakes his head. "I can assure you, she was. She just didn't want you to know it because she thought that would make you even more worried. So she hid how she was feeling but it still came out as other things, like being bossy and cross." He chuckles and pulls the blanket over his knees. "Feelings have a habit of doing that. You can try to hide them away but they won't disappear."

Tally is about to ask Dad what he means when Mum calls her name.

"Tally! You've got some visitors!"

Still feeling confused, Tally pushes herself off the sofa and opens the living room door. And standing in the middle of the hallway are the last three people that she ever expected to see.

"I'll leave you girls to it, shall I?" asks Mum. "Why don't you go into the kitchen and have a chat? Tally – you can open a packet of biscuits for your friends."

Tally scowls and turns away, marching into the kitchen where she leans against the sink and waits for the others to creep shyly into the room. They are not her friends and she does not want to open a packet of biscuits, not while *they're* here anyway. She might open them once they've left though and eat them by herself.

"You haven't been at school all week," says Layla, breaking the awkward silence.

Tally shrugs. If they've come all the way over here to tell her that, then they're really wasting their time because she already knows how long it's been since she was last at school.

And she knows why.

"We've come to say that we're sorry," says Lucy. Her cheeks are bright red and she's shuffling from side to side, a bit like Tally does when she's feeling agitated. "We shouldn't have taken your mask and we definitely shouldn't have given it to Luke."

"But you did," Tally tells her. "I know that you shouldn't have done it but you still did. And unless you've got a time machine, you can't change that."

Lucy looks across at Layla and Tally waits to see *the look*.

But it doesn't come. Instead, Lucy seems as if she's

about to cry.

"We know that we can't change what we did," Layla says quietly. "We've not been good friends to you, Tally – we all know that."

"We're really sorry," adds Ayesha, speaking for the first time. "We shouldn't have forgotten our promise to look out for you."

Tally narrows her eyes. She might not be the amazing Tiger Girl, but she isn't a little kid and she doesn't need anyone to feel sorry for her. She doesn't need anyone to look out for her either.

"Fine. You've said sorry so now you can go," she snaps. "You don't have to feel bad about what happened and you don't have to look after me. I don't need looking after. I'm not a baby."

The three girls look at each other and then all start speaking at the same time.

"No! Tally – that's not—"

"I didn't mean that you need—"

"WE MISS YOU."

Layla's voice is the loudest and the other two go quiet.

"We miss you, Tally," she repeats. "School isn't the same without you. It's boring."

Tally shakes her head. "You don't miss me," she says. "You don't even know me. You think that I like the things that you all like but I don't! I hate makeovers and I don't want to watch scary films and I'm not interested in boys and I'm tired of pretending."

"I hate scary films too," says Ayesha quietly. "I had nightmares for a week after we watched that clown film at Layla's house."

"And I don't like Luke." Lucy's voice is so quiet that Tally has to strain to hear it. "I just pretended that I did."

Tally frowns. "But why didn't you tell the truth? That's just stupid."

Lucy's eyes flicker towards her and then back at the floor. "I just wanted to fit in when we went into year seven. I thought that's what everyone would be doing."

Tally pauses for a second. She supposes that it kind of makes sense and she knows all about trying to fit in.

Layla steps forward, looking nervous.

"We really do miss you, Tally. You're funny and brilliant and you say things that nobody else would ever say and you do things that nobody else would do, and school is a whole lot more interesting when you're around."

"So you're not here because you feel sorry for me?" asks Tally, still suspicious.

"No!" howls Layla. "We're here because we feel sorry for *us*. And we know that we've not been good friends, but we'd really like it if you would just come back to school and be *you*."

Tally breathes out, a long, deep sigh of a breath.

"What about Luke and Ameet and Jasmine?" she asks. "And all the others? They saw what happened in the drama studio. I bet they're all going to be calling me Weirdo Adams."

"They're not," says Lucy, her face still very red. "Everyone felt really bad after you'd gone."

"We do have something else to confess though," says Layla. "Or I do, anyway."

She glances at Ayesha, who gives her an encouraging nod.

"After you got so upset, everyone wanted to know why you were so bothered about a mask. And so I told them about you." She pauses and swallows loudly. "I told them about you being—"

She swallows loudly and looks at Tally, her face crumpled up like she's trying not to cry.

"You might as well say it," Tally tells her. "If you've told everybody else. It's not a rude word, you know."

"Mrs Jarman was there too," adds Ayesha. "She got us

354

all to talk about the ways that we think we're different and the things that we do to try and fit in."

"How are any of *you* different?" asks Tally, her voice incredulous. "That's the whole problem. You're all the same. It's me who's different. It's easy for you."

Layla shakes her head. "That's not true, Tally." She glances at Lucy and Ayesha. "Maybe we're the same in some ways, but that doesn't mean that it's easy. Sometimes I have things in my head that I can't tell anyone and the only thing I can do is pretend that I'm OK."

"Mrs Jarman gave everyone a piece of paper and we all had to write down the different ways we cope with feeling anxious or worried," says Lucy. "Then we put them in a box and she read them out, one at a time."

"What did everyone write?" asks Tally, feeling curious.

"We didn't have to put our names on the paper," Layla tells her. "But one person said that they put their headphones on and listen to music. Someone else said that they just want to be alone and not speak to anyone, and another person said that being worried always makes them feel angry and they end up picking a fight."

"Someone wrote that they bite their nails," adds Ayesha and they all turn to look at Lucy, who pulls her finger from her mouth and scowls.

"Everyone wrote something," says Layla. "And then we talked about the fact that we all do different things and that's OK."

"And I don't know if you're going to want this or not, but Luke asked me to give it to you, so here it is." Layla puts her hand in her pocket and then hands a piece of paper to Tally.

Tally unfolds it and then turns away, her eyes scanning the messy writing while her brain tries to make sense of the words.

Hi Tally.

Look, I'm sorry, OK? Nobody told me that you're autistic and I wouldn't have called you Weirdo Adams if I'd known. Mrs Jarman said that I should write this note and tell you how I cope when things go wrong. I don't really know what to say though. I guess I'm still working it out.

Anyway, I'm sorry and I feel kind of stupid about the whole mask thing. When you come back to school I'm not going to do anything like that again.

Luke

Tally reads the letter for a second time. Anyone can

say that they're sorry. She thinks she'll wait and see if Luke decides to *show* her that he's sorry. That's the only way that her opinion of him is ever going to change.

"So now everyone knows that I'm autistic?" Tally turns back to the girls and jiggles her feet up and down. "The whole class?"

There's a pause and the four girls look at each other. Then Layla speaks, her voice very quiet.

"Yes."

Tally gives her a long look. "It wasn't really up to you to tell them, you know? It's my information and I'm the one who gets to decide who I tell."

Layla's eyes swim with tears. "I know and I'm really sorry. But I only said it to help them understand what it's like for you."

"And did it help?" asks Tally, seriously. "Do they understand?"

All three girls nod frantically.

"I told them how it makes you feel if people are too loud or too bossy," says Layla.

"What about when people are too unkind?" says Tally, giving Lucy a hard look. "Did you tell them how it makes me feel when people are too unkind?"

"I think they saw that for themselves," whispers

Lucy. "We're sorry, Tally. Really, we are."

Tally turns around and stares out of the window. The sky is grey and heavy, but somewhere up there, beyond the clouds, is a glorious ceiling of blue, stretching as far as the eye can see. She knows that it's up there, even if nobody else does.

And that's enough.

"OK," she says, not turning around. "I believe you."

"So will we see you tomorrow?" asks Layla. "Can we go back to being normal again?"

Tally smiles at her reflection in the glass.

"I don't think I liked your normal," she tells them. "So, no. I think I might make my own normal now. But I'm glad that you said that you're sorry. It's quite a hard word to say sometimes, so thank you."

And then she waits until the front door closes behind them before opening the chocolate biscuits and helping herself.

Date: Sunday 16th November

Situation: I'm not really sure. But I think it's OK.

Anxiety Rating: 3. Which is pretty great when you think about everything that has happened.

Dear Diary,

Today was strange, but I feel really relieved that I don't have to hide any more. I kept quiet about my autism in front of most people because I was scared that I would be treated differently. People can be so strange about it. They think that just because you're autistic you should have certain behaviours. Then they think you can't be autistic because you don't fit their stereotype of it!

"You don't look autistic," someone said to me when I was first diagnosed. What does "autistic" even look like?! I just said, "Sorry about that," and did my funniest comedy walk away from them, hoping that might give them what they were looking for. And then there's the inevitable question: "What's it like being autistic?" What a stupid question! I just ask them, "Well, what's it like being you?" Because that's basically what they're asking, as though all autistic people feel and do the same thing! If I'm feeling patient (rare), I say that like snowflakes, every single autistic person is different. And just like anyone else, every autistic person has different needs, personality, passions and hates.

I don't speak for all autistic people. I can only share my own experiences.

And I am going to share my experiences much more now and try to be more open about how I'm feeling and who I really am. It's not going to be easy because I've been hiding parts of myself for a while now – it's hard to expose bits of yourself that you're made to feel uncomfortable with. But look out, world, this is me now, Tally Adams, maskless, autistic and proud!

CHAPTER 30

The storm broke in the middle of the night, and this morning, the air is fresh. Tally walks along next to Nell, stepping carefully over the cracks in the pavement.

"You know that Mum would have driven us in, don't you?" complains Nell, wrapping her scarf around her neck. "I don't know why you told her that you didn't want to go in the car."

Tally ignores her and keeps her eyes on the ground. She must have rescued at least five worms on this morning's very early dog walk with Dad, and she knows that there's bound to be some more on the walk to school.

"It's freezing out here," mutters Nell. "I can barely feel my feet."

But Tally isn't cold. The words that Mum spoke

to her this morning are huddled in her head, keeping her warm and cosy. The words that have wrapped themselves around her like a snuggly blanket, telling her that Mum and Dad have been talking and they've both agreed. Rupert can stay for good. As long as he and Tally both keep eating their breakfast and going for walks and doing their homework (which isn't as silly as it sounds because Rupert has tons of homework from his dog behaviour class – almost as much as Tally usually gets), then he can stay with them and be Tally's dog for ever and ever.

Mum also started saying something about how Tally had to understand that Rupert, at ten years old, is a very old dog, but Tally stopped listening and ran off to tell him the good news, because she didn't want her happy mood to be ruined by the thought of something awful. She knows that she'll have to think about it one day. Just not today.

The school gates appear in the distance.

"I don't know why you always have to get your own way," moans Nell. "Next time, I'm telling Mum that it's my turn to choose and I am definitely choosing a nice, warm car journey to school. You can walk on your own if you want to."

Tally blinks, surprised at the sudden tears that spring to her eyes. Things have been better with Nell since the night that they found Rupert, but she feels sure that Nell still doesn't like her and that even though Nell gave her back the tiger mask, she doesn't understand Tally any more. Not like she used to. Mum says that Nell is busy being a teenager and that it isn't anything to do with how she feels about Tally, but Tally isn't daft – she knows that Nell just thinks she's a massive, annoying pain.

As they get closer to the gates, Tally's heart starts to pound in her chest. Maybe it was a mistake to come back here. Perhaps she's being stupid to believe that anything can possibly change at school when her own sister can't stand to be around her. She thinks about the tiger mask, tucked safely into the bottom of her bag just in case she needs it, and tries to feel strong. She wants to be her but she's still not convinced that it's safe to show everyone what she's really like.

A group of year seven kids walk past them, pushing and shoving each other as they go. Tally makes herself small and looks down at the ground, hoping that they won't notice her.

The group is almost past her, deep in conversation

about some film that's coming out at the cinema next weekend. She breathes out, long and slow. The first hurdle is almost over.

"All right, Tally?"

Her head snaps up. There, right beside her, is Aleksandra from her drama class. The same Aleksandra who said that sometimes, things go wrong for her too. The same Aleksandra who told Luke that he shouldn't call her weird.

Aleksandra gives her a big, easy smile and then turns back to the conversation about the film.

"Hi," Tally whispers, staring at her retreating back.

She can't remember the last time that someone spoke to her like that. Someone who isn't Layla or Lucy or Ayesha. She didn't know that anyone else could even see her.

"I'm meeting Rosa by the shop," Nell tells Tally. "You'll be OK going inside."

It isn't a question, so Tally doesn't give an answer. She walks past Nell and up to the gates, her eyes fixed on the mass of people gathered in the yard.

But then something makes her turn around and watch as Nell crosses the road and walks down the pavement. She keeps looking as Nell stops and stares at something on the ground, her mouth moving quickly like she's giving herself a fierce telling-off or wrestling with a particularly bad thought. Then her shoulders slump, as if she's given up, and Tally cranes forward to see what she's doing.

Across the road, Nell bends down and picks something up, her face wrinkled in disgust. She scurries across the pavement and lowers her hand and Tally stares in disbelief as her big sister gently places a worm on to the safety of the grass verge.

Nell stands up, rubbing her hands vigorously on her coat. Then she looks straight across at Tally and shakes her head, her mouth pulling itself into a grin that matches the one on Tally's face.

"OK?" she mouths, across the road.

"OK," mouths back Tally.

And as she turns back towards school, and lets her arms flap instead of forcing herself to be still and hide away, she thinks that it actually just might be.

ACKNOWLEDGEMENTS

Libby would like to thank her mum (Kym), her dad (Steve) and sister (Rosie) for believing in her. Plus the staff at Valley Primary School and all her friends (especially Aurelie, Brooke, Ellie, Eniz, Erin, Lexie and Matilda) for being so supportive.

Rebecca would like to thank Adam, Zachary, Georgia and Reuben – four people who are not afraid to stand out.

We would both like to thank Libby Warren-Green (GrowingUpAutistic @LibbyAutism), Hope Whitmore, Anna Wolfenden, Freya Wall and Polly & Elsie Couldrick for their thoughts and contributions. Also, Julia Churchill and the team at Scholastic for bringing us together for this incredible experience.